A NTIS●C AL

Arun Krishnan is the author of *The Loudest Firecracker* (Tranquebar Press, 2009). Currently based in Seattle, he has worked for a number of ad agencies, technology companies and non-profit organizations like IBM, Stein IAS and Concern Worldwide. His writings and podcast archives can be found at cuttingchai.com.

ARUN
KRISHNAN

HARPER
BLACK

First published in India in 2015 by Harper Black
An imprint of HarperCollins *Publishers* India

Copyright © Arun Krishnan 2015

P-ISBN: 978-93-5177-596-6
E-ISBN: 978-93-5177-597-3

2 4 6 8 10 9 7 5 3 1

Arun Krishnan asserts the moral right
to be identified as the author of this work.

This is a work of fiction and all characters and incidents described
in this book are the product of the author's imagination. Any resemblance
to actual persons, living or dead, is entirely coincidental.

HarperCollins *Publishers*
A-75, Sector 57, Noida, Uttar Pradesh 201301, India
1 London Bridge Street, London SE1 9GF, United Kingdom
Hazelton Lanes, 55 Avenue Road, Suite 2900, Toronto, Ontario M5R 3L2
and 1995 Markham Road, Scarborough, Ontario M1B 5M8, Canada
25 Ryde Road, Pymble, Sydney, NSW 2073, Australia
10 East 53rd Street, New York NY 10022, USA

Typeset in 11/13 Arno Pro Regular at
Manipal Digital Systems, Manipal

Printed and bound at
Thomson Press (India) Ltd.

For my parents, Appa and Amma,
and my wife, Pamela

Oh, the shark, babe, has such teeth, dear
And it shows them pearly white
Just a jackknife has old MacHeath, babe?
And he keeps it out of sight

– *Mack the Knife (the Louis Armstrong version)*

A Bowl of Matzo Ball Soup

The *New York Daily News* said that over the last seven days I may have impacted the future of social networking and quite possibly damaged the American economy forever.

It was a remarkable week. And yet, it began simply enough, with a small notification that appeared over the social folder of my new iPhone 6 smartphone.

I was seated in a bar on the corner of 127th Street and Morningside Avenue. Two men cheered as a player on the overhead TV threw a ball into a basket. One of them was wearing a stylish Panama hat. He was a typical New Yorker, a person who appeared content when he was well dressed. His companion had on a more ordinary cap with a logo of the New York Yankees. He did not even say thank you when the bartender gave him a drink.

He was not a gentleman. I ignored him.

I have always believed that it is important to be a gentleman.

When Mr Clarkson had first visited my orphanage in India, a few days before my fourth birthday, he asked me what I wanted to be.

I thought of the only English book in the orphanage. It had a picture of a white man dressed in a grey suit. The man carried a cane in his right hand. He was getting into a mushroom-shaped foreign car. The director of the orphanage had taught me to read the title of the book. And so it came to pass that before I had learned to say 'apple', 'boy' or 'cat', I learned to say, 'How to be a gentleman.'

I told Mr Clarkson that I wanted to be a gentleman. He smiled. He adopted me.

I sipped on the Famous Grouse. As it always did, the whiskey was able to murmur a reassurance, give me a lingering pat on the back and inspire a warm and smoky hope, all without saying a single word.

'That's a nice T-shirt,' the bartender said. 'Are you a Buddhist or something?'

On the front of my T-shirt, one hundred and one Buddha faces revolved in serene orbits over a larger countenance of the Blessed One. They imbued me with a personality that was different from my own.

'Yes,' I said, pulling at a string underneath my T-shirt and raising it over my collar. 'See that? It's a sacred thread.'

I belonged to one of the low castes. But that was in India. America is an upwardly mobile society. In America, I could be a Brahmin. In America, I could wear a sacred thread.

'It's kind of heavy,' she said.

'Indian cotton,' I replied vaguely.

'Ah,' she said. 'Indian cotton.'

It could have been the cotton. In my humble opinion, the weightiness could also be attributed to the concealed leather sheath that was attached to the sacred thread. The sheath carried a global G-2 chef's knife made out of hard molybdenum stainless steel.

Anthony Bourdain had recommended the knife on a TV show. He had said that it was the only knife you would ever need. He was right. I had used it to cut onions. Cantaloupes. A noisy pigeon on my windowsill. It was the only knife that I had ever needed. It was the only knife I would ever need, should someone ever decide to do unto me what Mrs Clarkson had once done unto me.

'I like it,' the bartender said, as though I had just gifted the thread to her. 'Where are you from?'

'From a place called Gaya in India,' I said. 'It's a small town. But it's actually quite a famous place. It's where the Buddha gave his Fire Sermon.'

'The Fire Sermon?'

She leaned forward. She had a large silver ring on her right hand. She shone with an eager curiosity. Her T-shirt slid smoothly over the curves of her bottom. I turned my gaze to the red stripe that ran along the length of the stirrer. A gentleman does not stare.

'It's one of the Buddha's most famous sermons,' I said. 'In the Fire Sermon, the Buddha identifies bodily sensations that are always on fire…'

She smiled. She rested her elbow on the bar counter.

'Bodily sensations on fire, huh?' she said. Her forearm touched mine for an instant. She smiled.

'It's not just bodily sensations,' I corrected her. 'There are so many things that are on fire. According to the Buddha, we are on fire all the time. Our eyes are on fire, the impressions received by the eyes are on fire, our ears are on fire, sounds are on fire, the tongue is on fire, tastes are on fire, the mind is on fire, ideas are on fire, sensations are on fire…'

'I get it,' she said. She sounded testy.

But that was no reason to stop.

'With the fire of passion, with the fire of hatred, with the fire of infatuations, with the fire of birth, the fire of old age, the fire of sickness…'

She had begun to fidget. She twisted her hair anxiously into knots of the hangman's rope. I felt calm and equanimous. I enjoy watching the insides of people fill up with unease and anger, even as they are listening to the words of the Buddha. It is the most benevolent way by which one can cause pain to others.

I could go on and on. And so I did.

'With the fire of lust, with the fire of jealousy, with the fire of ambition, with the fire of desire, with the fire of…'

The phone rang. She darted towards it. She managed to squeeze her ample hips past the small counter and answer the phone.

I looked at my smartphone. I tapped on the MyFace app. This was the socially correct thing to do. Looking at the news feed of the world's leading social network was what normal people in American society did when they had a few moments to themselves. I had seen them do it outside elevators, at restaurant tables and on the escalator to a cinema hall.

It was then that the red notification appeared over the icon of my MyFace app. The notification was in the shape of a drop that was a muddy shade of reddish brown. I tapped on it and saw a new message on my MyFace news feed.

Emily Hayes has checked into The Red Room.

I tapped on *The Red Room*. It was a restaurant located on 123rd Street and Amsterdam Avenue. It was only four blocks away from my current location. The gods had conspired to place Emily Hayes 0.3 miles away from me. I stirred the Famous Grouse. The ice clinked against the glass. My thoughts shivered. The Buddha might have said that they trembled like a fish on dry ground.

I slapped a ten-dollar bill on to the bar. I pointed apologetically at the screen of my smartphone and walked out of the establishment. The bartender seemed relieved to see me leave. But she blew a kiss at me all the same, as though compelled by some force of habit.

I followed the blue dot on the map and walked towards Emily. I felt energized at the prospect of seeing her.

It was that hour of the evening, unique to summer, when the sun does not scorch everything and everyone, but is merely content to provide light. Of course, even if I were making this walk during the hot afternoon hours, it wouldn't have mattered. It was always spring around Emily. The season of rejuvenation had never left her side. When I stood next to her, I always felt refreshed and alive, as though I had just come in touch with cool mountain air.

I waited for the traffic light to turn on the corner of Morningside Avenue. A mother with a stroller pulled up beside me. She spoke to her friend, a Hispanic woman with oval eyes and distinctly Mayan features.

'Hopefully you and your husband can sort things out. That will be good for you. For him. And for the kids. Everyone can win.'

She spoke in Spanish. I was able to understand her.

I had learned Spanish within six months of coming to America.

As I have grown older, I find that I need to be able to speak a language that is different from the one used around me by everyday people. In America, the English language placed me neatly into certain categories. I was the FBI's brown-skinned terrorist. I was Tom Friedman's hard-working Indian immigrant. I was someone who rebooted your computer from a call centre. If I continued to think in English, I would begin to identify with these categories. And eventually, society would have access to my deepest thoughts. However, I could encrypt my thoughts in another language. I could guard against the invasions of society and maintain my individuality.

Of course, I knew Hindi. But I did not want to speak it. Hindi reminds me of India. India reminds me of Mrs Clarkson. And when I think of Mrs Clarkson, I feel like hitting someone repeatedly in their face. I feel like slamming a window. I feel anxious. The scar on my forearm begins to burn.

I saw Emily Hayes as soon as I reached Amsterdam Avenue. She was sitting at a table in the outdoor seating area of The Red Room. She was slightly plump, blonde and beautiful. She smiled and, like a bolt of lightning, her smile illuminated the pavement and the darkening sky. For a moment, I forgot we were in New York, a city that had eight rats for each one of its eight million inhabitants.

I stepped into the playground of a housing project. I hid behind a slide and continued to watch her.

She leaned forward and caressed the hands of another man. Several lights were put out within me at the same time. I felt suffocated. I found I had to look away before I was able to breathe again.

I woke up my smartphone from sleep. I clicked on Emily Hayes's name on the MyFace app. As I scrolled down the length of her profile, I thought what the Hispanic woman had told her friend on Morningside Avenue was wrong. We couldn't all win. Some of us had to lose.

I had just lost Emily to another man.

I knew most of what was listed on Emily's MyFace profile by heart. But I continued reading anyway. Emily had disappointed me. However, there was a chance that her profile could, in some way, lighten my dreadful burden.

Emily Hayes was twenty-four years old. She was born on 22 June. She was originally from Portland, Oregon. She currently worked at the BBDO ad agency in New York. She had no religious views. She was 'Very Liberal'. She was interested in making friends. She liked listening to the Ramones, The Cure, Wilco and Belle and Sebastian. She liked reading Jane Austen. Her favourite book was *Pride and Prejudice*. She had recently re-read *The Brothers Karamazov*. She liked it. She was a member of the New York Public Library group. She liked *The Daily Show* on Comedy Central and *Downton Abbey* on PBS. Most recently, she had laughed out loud at a photo of a cat curled up on a floor. The photo had a caption: 'Your kitten has shut down for updates.' She liked Sriracha hot sauce at Chelsea Thai, a place that she had checked into two-and-a-half weeks earlier.

I followed her hands and saw the hands of the person they encircled. They belonged to Raj Malik. Raj caressed a lock of hair on her forehead. In that instant, I performed in the real world an act that had only been depicted in *Star Trek* and thousands of science-fiction novels. I teleported myself on to Emily's plate. She sliced through me with a knife.

I had first told Emily that I liked her at the Orchard Lounge fourteen months ago. I remember her every reaction that followed. She laughed in a caricature of delight. Then, she clapped her hands and threw back her face. She said I was 'adorable'. When I repeated my assertion, she broke into an 'aaaaawwww,' an expression of emotion that was not even individual to her, but one she had learned from the laugh tracks of comedy sitcoms. She hugged me. She had continued talking to me with no change of volume, tone or huskiness in her voice.

It had hurt.

Emily was not just a beautiful woman. She was the only human being I had felt fond feelings for in the course of my entire life. When I spoke to her, I felt like I had felt when I had first listened to *Sgt. Pepper's Lonely Hearts Club Band*. I felt as though every moment was special, and every moment was made just for me.

Maybe it was how her eyes became even darker and brighter with happiness when she saw me. Maybe it was how just thinking of her made me believe that I could overcome almost anything. Or maybe it was how she had saved me from a public humiliation on my first day at the new office.

I had been hired for the position of media planner at CJ&R at a campus recruiting event. Jeff Garner, who was the vice president of account services at the ad agency, had offered me the job.

The interview had gone smoothly. We talked about advertising. I demonstrated my superior math skills. Later that evening, I had supplied him with cocaine.

On my first day at the job, Jeff had called me to his office. He thanked me for the cocaine. He asked me if I could procure any more powder for him on the following weekend. I had nodded. He became effusive. He opened the door and walked with me into the hallway.

He asked me to 'Take it easy'.

'Are you also a fan of the Eagles?' I had asked him.

That was the first time I had heard Raj Malik snigger. Jeff wasn't capable of anything approaching a subdued emotion. He laughed loudly. He began to tell other people about what I had just said.

Emily had come to my rescue. She told Jeff to 'put a lid on it'.

Wave upon wave of gratefulness had washed over me. I could have been at the beach. I thought that Emily was just like Florence Nightingale. The only difference was that unlike the nurse who healed the wounded soldiers of the Crimean War, Emily didn't walk around carrying a candle. And it was a good thing, too, for I would have snatched the candle from her hands and burned the entire agency down.

Following this incident, Raj Malik's inarticulate sniggers had evolved into more pronounced scoffs. He told me that with my thick accent, the clients had begun to think they were calling not an ad but rather a taxi agency. He asked me to stop taking client calls. I ignored him. After all, Emily had thought I was good enough to be a citizen of her country.

As I walked home from the Orchard Lounge that night, I fell back on that crutch immigrants use to support themselves during moments of failure. I told myself that if Emily and I were not a couple, it was because of our cultural differences. I was brown. Emily was white.

Shortly after that night at the Orchard Lounge, Emily started dating John from Ohio. John was an account executive at BBDO. I did not like John. He was not a gentleman. He talked about sex in public. He told me that he had once performed sex on a woman with a pickle. He fed the girl the same pickle later in the night.

However, I liked the idea of John. He was from Ohio. He was white. He validated my theory as to why Emily had rejected my request to date her. But Emily had broken up with John.

And if I were to believe what I was seeing, she was now dating Raj Malik.

I tapped on Raj's name in the MyFace app. I had to understand why Emily would choose another brown-skinned man over me. Was Raj a more likeable person than me?

Leave alone likeable, Raj Malik's MyFace profile was incomprehensible.

He had liked a link that said 'Reggie Watts likes Van Halen'. He had shared a video that featured fifteen minutes of someone called Orf being shot down by everybody on *The Next Generation*. He was embarrassed by a petition that asked the people of Brooklyn to Embrace Indie Music. (Why was he embarrassed?) He liked a music group called Lucero and another called The Horrible Crowes. I hadn't heard of either of them. He had listed Devil's Advocacy as one of his interests.

And so on and so forth. I felt that drowning feeling of incomprehension I had experienced while listening to news anchors on Univision a year ago. Raj's MyFace profile was nothing more than a long listing of inanities. I could not fathom what Emily saw in him. It was almost as if she had gone out of her way to smite me personally.

They had finished with their dinner. As he moved his hand over the roundness of her ass, baseball, a sport in which I have little interest, came to my mind. I knocked Raj's head off his neck. With my more than thorough follow through, I sent it soaring over the diamond, over the man with the outstretched glove, all the way into the backward recesses of the seating areas of the stadium.

Eventually, they separated their bodies from each other. Raj walked up the steep hill that led north. Emily began to walk westward on 123rd Street. I powered off my cell phone. Turning off your cell phone when you meet an old friend is the gentlemanly thing to do.

I stepped out from behind the slide of the playground and on to the street.

'Arjun!' Emily said with an undeniable eagerness in her voice.

She hugged me. My anger disappeared as quickly as a drop of water does upon coming in touch with a hot metal surface. I felt glad to see just how delighted she was to see me.

She hadn't changed. She was still every bit as exquisite as a sixteenth-century Sufi song. I saw what Bulleh Shah had meant when he said you could see the beauty of god in every soul. But why would anyone want to see something so illusory like the beauty of god, when you could cast your eyes on the green silk scarf that shimmered on that long neck and the earrings that shone even in the dark?

Emily said that she had not done a good job of staying in touch with people from the ad agency. She said she had emailed Brett only once. He hadn't replied.

'In fact, I just met…'

I cut her off before she said Raj Malik's name aloud. I did not want to sully the moment.

'We miss you at the agency,' I said. 'Stellar account management now seems to have taken place in a bygone era.'

'The words you use. The way you speak. You haven't changed a bit,' she said. 'Is that a new T-shirt?'

'Yes,' I said. 'It's from Uniqlo.' The Buddha was certainly getting noticed today. I felt dapper.

'It's really nice,' she said. 'Do you mind if I remove the tag?'

She reached over my neck and detached the sticker that said 'M'.

'You really haven't changed. You're still as forgetful as ever!'

'Ah, so you remember?'

'How can I forget? I still remember the waiter at Tabla following you outside the restaurant because you had the napkin attached to your shirt…'

She laughed. I felt as blissful as I imagine people do upon hearing a bird chirp on a relaxing picnic.

'But what are you doing here?' she asked.

'I had gone to Central Park to listen to the Dalai Lama speak.'

'That's right! You're a practising Buddhist. It must have been a big day for you.'

'Oh, huge, huge,' I said, using words that were popular in the lexicon of the American man.

'What are you doing in this neighbourhood?' I asked Emily.

I already knew from her MyFace profile that she lived at 265 123rd Street and we were only a few blocks from her apartment. However, I didn't confess to being in ownership of this piece of knowledge. In America, it was socially acceptable to learn about other people's personal details through Google, MyFace and the Internet. However, it wasn't considered polite to admit to having looked this information up, even when a person had put it out there for all to see.

'I live here,' she said.

'I'll walk you to your apartment and then head on to the subway,' I said.

As we walked, Emily recounted an incident from the past. We had designed twelve online banners for an advertising campaign for Ford. The campaign had failed. This wasn't particularly surprising. On an average, less than 0.04 per cent of people that are shown an online ad actually click on it. With this particular campaign, that number was even lower.

'But you,' Emily said, 'told the client to ignore the click-through rate. Instead, you convinced them that most people who saw their ad would not click on the banner. They would see the banner, search for the advertised offer later and visit their website after a few days. What was it you called it?'

'A view-through.' I smiled.

'Yes, that's right. A view-through!' She clapped her hands with great delight. Emily had a body that was a rarity in modern society. It was honest. It always expressed the emotions that it felt.

We stopped by a garden on the corner of Amsterdam Avenue. The breeze stopped blowing. A dog stopped barking. I felt grateful for the silence. For that one instant, the city around us disappeared. All that existed in the world was just Emily and me.

We had arrived at her block. I began to experience the conflicting emotions a couple on a first date experiences when nearing the residence of one of its participants: a curious cocktail of eagerness and anxiety, desire and guilt, an almost Buddhist willingness to plunge into the here-and-now and a more Victorian sense of fear for future repercussions. I experienced all of these feelings in sufficient quantity for two people. Emily had continued talking in an uncaring way, as though she were still in that conference room all those months ago.

In hindsight, I realize I should have said goodbye. I should have accepted Emily's hug and walked to the subway station on 125th Street and Lexington Avenue. If I had done just that, all of this would not have happened. The world would have gone on spinning.

However, at that very moment, a black bird with an orange chest hopped on to the porch of Emily's apartment building. The sun had set. The bird should have been asleep. Instead, it was awake and active. It tapped with its beak on the ground. Knock. Knock. Knock. What did they say about opportunity? The ghost of an aphorism drifted through my mind.

'These brownstones are so lovely,' I said.

'Aren't they?'

'Yes, I remember something that *The New York Times* published about J.D. Salinger after he died. J.D. had always wondered what it would be like to enter one of these brownstone buildings and have a bowl of matzo ball soup.'

In fact, Mr Salinger had wanted to go into the charming homes that belonged to the orthodox Jewish families in Brooklyn. He had wanted to sit down with the members of a traditional family and eat a bowl of matzo ball soup. In a world where people strived to own yellow Lamborghinis and flat-screen TVs, I had been struck by how unique and beautiful J.D. Salinger's desire was.

'Did he really say that?' Emily asked.

'Yes,' I said. 'Someday, I too hope to enter one of these buildings and see them for myself. It would be a big to-do accomplished for my life in America.'

'I don't have matzo ball soup,' Emily said.

'No...'

'But I do have an apartment.'

'Ah...'

'Let me show you.'

She tripped as she ascended the flight of stairs up to her brownstone.

'I think I might be drunk,' she said. She held on to my shoulder for support.

She looked surprised. I too hadn't realized that she had imbibed from the wine bottle in generous quantities earlier that evening. I had mistaken her constant chatter, words that merged and tumbled over one another like stones in a wheelbarrow, for her normal exuberance.

'Why do you do that?'

'Why do I do what?' I asked.

'Your body goes completely stiff when I touch you.'

'That's not true,' I said.

But she wasn't listening. She narrowed her eyes in concentration as she tried to place the key in the keyhole. She moved her tongue over her lips. The knob turned. We entered the building. The door closed behind us. We crossed the length of the corridor. The tiles were covered with patterns of maroon butterflies. In the dim light, they appeared like moths.

'Please,' I said, allowing Emily to set foot first on the staircase.

'Why, thank you, sir,' she said.

The lights went off in the corridor. I could no longer see Emily's earrings. I fumbled for the railing. It was cold to the touch. I found myself transported to that outdoor shed in Delhi. The shed that was outside Mr Clarkson's house. The shed where they had found a cobra. Mrs Clarkson, my so-called mother, had locked me in that shed. She called me a pervert. She had said that I was a sick, sick child. She had slapped me. I had been only five years old at the time.

The cobra marked the fifth year of my existence. The beating at Delhi's Connaught Place marked my sixth. Throughout my childhood, I had been defenceless against the incessant roar of Mrs Clarkson's angry actions. It was why I carried the knife, to protect myself against anyone who might want to harm me with a hot iron, a metal rod or for that matter the fork-shaped tongue of a king cobra.

'You're sweating,' Emily said.

I opened my eyes. She had opened the door of her apartment. The lights had come back on.

'I'm OK,' I said. The sweat that fell on to my wrist from my chin was cold. My voice shivered.

Emily powered on her Motorola Droid phone as she stood in the half-dark, half-light twilight area of her doorstep. She tapped on the email icon. There were no new emails. She tapped on the MyFace icon. As the app attempted to establish a connection with the server, she said, 'Please come in.'

She waved her hands across the expanse of the four-hundred-square-foot room.

'So this is how a brownstone looks from the inside,' I said for the sake of continuity with the excuse that I had conjured up on the pavement.

The apartment was uniquely Emily's. There was none of the sanitized sameness that has come to characterize modern-day furniture. Nowadays, a living room can look like a reading room that can look just like a waiting room at an airport. The effect is similar to watching two jazz pianists on TV with the volume turned all the way down. You cannot discern the individual touches that make each of them special.

But Emily had rebelled against this culture of conformity.

The green-and-white candlesticks were Emily; the armchair with the leopard skin patterns was Emily; the orchid on the mantelpiece was Emily; the stand of hanging vases was Emily; the black-and-white picture of an ice-cream parlour was Emily; the pressed tin frame in which it was contained was Emily and the picture of a square-jawed man and his curly-haired wife was also Emily. In fact, they were the smiling countenances of Emily's parents.

Everything in the room reminded me of her radiant personality. I was pleased to see that there wasn't a photo of Raj in her apartment. A sleek forty-two-inch flat-screen TV was the only modern object in the room. I recognized the model. I had the same TV in my apartment.

'Your apartment is very nice,' I said.

'Are you sure you're all right? You're sweating.'

I tried not to think of the cobra. It still had its hood raised, too lazy, or too intent to move.

'It's nothing at all,' I said. 'I just need to sit down for a bit.'

I plopped down on the couch. I corrected my posture instinctively. Emily's ex-boyfriend John had once told me that American women are not attracted to men who don't have an upright posture.

'Maybe,' Emily said, 'I should update my MyFace status. Something like, You'll never guess who I have in my apartment right now...'

She looked at the orchid on the mantelpiece over a fireplace that had not experienced a warm glow in a long time.

'Or,' she said, 'maybe not.'

'Could I,' I said, 'have a glass of water?'

'Oh, of course! Where are my manners?'

'I think I see them. They are here.' I pointed underneath the coffee table.

'Oh Arjun,' she gave one of her exuberant laughs, 'you are just too much. What have I been doing without you?'

She made me feel warm and accepted like no other human being had. I felt close to her in a completely unquestioning sort of way, as I imagine children must feel towards their parents, or patriotic people towards their native lands.

She handed me a glass of water. It was cold to the touch. A drop of water slid off the cool side of the glass and fell on to my trousers. I felt alert. I mentally compiled a list of the social niceties that were expected of me in the current situation.

'How's your new job?' I asked.

But she wasn't listening.

'What's a word that I can form here?'

She placed her smartphone in front of me. Yellow tiles with letters on their faces were arranged in zigzag patterns on a blue board. I guessed that this was the Words with Friends app that everyone was talking about.

'Toxic,' I said.

'Really?'

'Really.'

She looked at the smartphone. She tapped on it five times. It beeped.

'Oh Arjun!' she said. 'You're the best.' She hugged me. I pulled away slightly as I felt the curve of her breasts.

'There you go again,' she said. 'You become so tense.'

'It's really nothing,' I said.

'At any rate,' she said, brushing my arm, 'toxic. That's such a great word. Now I'll be able to beat…'

'So, Emily, how's your new job?'

I knew I was committing a serious social faux pas. However, I had little choice but to interrupt. I couldn't bear to hear Raj Malik's name in these hallowed surroundings.

'It's more of the same,' she said. 'You convince clients to run these ad campaigns on MyFace, on the web and on mobile devices. But the campaigns seldom work. You end up spending all of your time trying to put your best spin on the campaign performance reports.'

'I'm sorry to hear that,' I said.

'There's this new campaign we designed for the new Guinness Black Lager. Can you guess what the click-through rate on those banners was?'

'0.20 per cent?'

'0.04 per cent! Can you imagine? We spend soooo many hours making this ad. And one out of every...'

'250,000.'

She raised her eyebrows.

'And just one out of every 250,000 people who saw this ad actually clicked on it!'

'Tragic,' I said. 'Especially for a beer.'

'Oh Arjun! What are we doing with our lives?'

For the first time that evening, she looked sad. It was a becoming emotion. Her beauty assumed a timeless quality, now that her features were touched by solemnity. I wanted to hold her. I wanted to touch her. I moved my hand beside her arm and caressed a thin film of air over the sleeve of her shirt.

'And just yesterday, I went to a panel discussion at this trade show,' she said. 'There was this executive from Young & Rubicam on the panel. He went on and on about synergistic approaches that deliver 360-degree branding. He threw out a lot of jargon and nonsense to that effect. I completely tuned out, as you can imagine.'

'I can imagine,' I said. 'There are politicians. There are paedophiles. And then there are people who spout jargon on ad panels. They are the lowest form of being alive in modern society. No one should have to listen to them.'

'I tried not to. But after a while, I tuned back in. Do you know what he said?'

'No,' I replied honestly.

'He said, the emergence and collision of social, local and mobile media is today's aspirational marketing trifecta – and at the intersection of SoLoMo, the consumer stands alone.'

I laughed.

'Can you believe he actually said that?'

'Yes.'

'And don't you feel strongly about it? Don't you hate it?'

'I don't.'

'But surely you've got to have an opinion about these morons in the ad industry?'

'Emily,' I said, 'I try not to have strong opinions. Generally speaking, I find that they are bad for one's health. Just today in the *Daily News*, there was an article about a Pakistani man who had burned an American flag at a protest march. He died from inhaling the fumes.'

Her smartphone lit up with what was presumably the rejoinder to the word 'toxic'. Emily ignored it.

'I thought I would do more with my life,' she said.

I wanted to reassure her. I wanted to remind her that she was an up-and-coming account executive at one of the world's most reputed ad agencies. However, it is pointless to tell a person who works in the field of advertising that they have actually accomplished something with their life. We have flushed away its most precious moments faster than we have entire advertising budgets.

'You will do something more with your life,' I said. 'I know it.'

She looked into my eyes with the same degree of attention that she had until this point in time reserved for her Droid phone. For a moment, I thought she was going to kiss me. But she stepped away from the couch.

'You're a good person, Arjun,' she said. She played with the long stem of the orchid.

'Let's have drinks,' she said. She walked to the other side of the kitchen counter.

A glass clinked against the sink. There were two short pours of liquor. A bottle cap twisted and opened. There was a longer pour of something that bubbled and frothed.

'Rum and coke,' she said. 'It's all I have.'

'That sounds delicious,' I said.

I leaned back into the softness of the couch. I rubbed the scar on my forearm. It was where Mrs Clarkson had burned me with an iron. She had said that I was a 'sick, sick' child for playing with her black bra. I was five years old. All I had been doing was playing with the basket of laundry.

Emily picked up her smartphone. She connected it to a pair of Harman Kardon speakers that rested on her windowsill. She tapped on the screen. A piano key made a heavy sound. A saxophone wailed. A cymbal tapped. John Coltrane broke into 'A Love Supreme'.

'Arjun, tell me one thing,' Emily said.

'I'll tell you two.' An empty stomach. The whiskey. And now the rum. I was feeling incredibly confident.

'I was MyFacing my cousin today. You know the one who lives in Madison. She is leaving for Sierra Leone next week. To help, you know…'

'Africans?' I said. It was how white leaders on TV described the people of the continent.

'War victims. When she told me about her trip, the first thing I thought was just how meaningful her work was. And what am I doing here in New York? Working with people who don't know the first thing about life, leave alone advertising…'

'You're right,' I said. 'We work in an industry of fools. Did you know that last year, even as the circulation of magazines and newspapers dropped, the rate of advertising spent on print media actually increased?'

'Is that true?'

'Sure.'

'God,' she said. 'What's the point? What's the point of my life?'

'You're taking the dark view,' I said. 'When you think about it, what's the point of any life?'

'Do the Buddhists say anything about that?'

'Well, Emily,' I said, resorting to that soft-spoken tone of voice I deploy when speaking on behalf of the Buddha, 'the Buddhists certainly do. There was once this man. He came to the Buddha and asked him if there was life after death. He asked if the world was eternal, if there was some grand purpose to our lives. And he said that unless the Buddha answered his questions, he would think that the Buddha was a fake. He would think that Buddhism did not have the answers. And do you know what the Buddha told him?'

'What?' she said. She stopped pacing. She looked at me with great hope and expectation.

'The Buddha said, imagine you have been struck by an arrow. Would it really matter if the arrow has been sent forth from the bow of a man or a woman? Would you insist that before the arrow was removed, you know if the shooter belonged to a high caste or a low caste? Would you say that I will not have this arrow taken out till I find out if the person who shot me was black, brown or white? And would you say that I will not have this arrow taken out till I find out if this person was from so-and-so village town or city? Would...'

Emily sat down on the couch next to me. She played with a lock of hair on her forehead. She looked distressed. Normally, the part of the Buddhist discourse where the hapless victim begins to fidget is where I derive the most enjoyment.

But now, I felt that something was wrong. I felt that Emily did not deserve to be tortured by the words of the Buddha. Emily wasn't your typical self-involved, petty New Yorker. She was Emily. She lived for other people. She was the only person who had made me feel that I deserved to belong in human society, in New York and indeed, the United States of America.

I cut to the end of my story.

'The Buddha told the man that just as it doesn't matter where the arrow has come from, it doesn't matter if there is life after death. It doesn't matter if the world is eternal, or whether our lives have some grand meaning. All that matters is that the arrow be removed. We must recognize that we are miserable and we must understand the root cause of our misery.'

'Oh, Arjun,' she said. 'That's beautiful.'

She smiled. A tiny cleft appeared on her cheeks. Prior to today, I had never noticed how from this particular angle, and with those dimples, she looked so much like Mrs Clarkson. I sipped on the rum. I felt an old, familiar sickness lurching inside me.

To distract my mind, I tuned in to the plucking of the heavy bass strings on the speakers. Emily's Droid phone had progressed to the next song in her Pandora playlist. It was now playing the opening chords to Miles Davis's '*So What*'.

Emily sat down on the couch. She rested her head on my shoulders. It might have been Miles. Or it might have been the Grouse. But at that particular moment, I recalled the playful smile the bartender had given me earlier that evening. I felt confident. I kissed Emily.

My kiss wasn't practised and soft. I slobbered. I groped. Emily pushed me away.

'No!' she said.

Her hands flew in the air. They hit me on my face.

I moved to calm her down. She pushed at me again. I held her hands and threw her against the couch. A button on her shirt came open. She had on a black bra…it was just like the one from all those years ago! I wanted to destroy that image of the bra and send it to a place where it could never be seen again.

I pinned Emily down on the couch. She kicked out with her legs and one of her feet hit me on the chin.

'Stop!' I must have shouted, for I never raise my voice, and now it sounded foreign to me.

I don't want to get into the details of what happened. That would be a most ungentlemanly thing to do. So all I will say is that I was forced to reach for my sacred thread. The knife was sharp. She was soft. There were the sounds of the knife. There were brief moments of clarity, of soft flesh and red blood, when I realized I was stabbing a real person. But I was mostly hitting out at an image of Mrs Clarkson.

I hit out again and again. The world went silent for a few minutes.

Emily stopped moving. Now that there was the sound of only one person breathing, the apartment seemed like an entirely different place. Only a few minutes ago, it was throbbing with life and promise. Now, it had been transformed into a useless dwelling in a pointless world, a world without Emily.

Emily's eyes were open. They were filled with a horror that would never go away. I attempted to understand what had happened. How could I have killed the only person who had actually cared for me?

Just five minutes ago, I would have done absolutely anything to bring a smile to Emily's face. And now I had taken her life. I tried to decipher what had just happened, but my mind lurched from one shameful memory to another like a drunkard in a dark alley. The sickness had not gone away. And no matter how many therapists Mr Clarkson sent me to see, it would never leave me.

Pandora had moved on to the next track. McCoy Tyner riffed about his 'Night in Tunisia'.

I took out a handkerchief from the pocket of my trousers. I wiped Emily's wrists where I had held her. I wiped the glass of rum and coke carefully and placed it on the glass table.

I picked up the scarf from Emily's couch. Even as a tourist knows that a photograph can never fully succeed in capturing the beauty of a vista, I realized that this piece of clothing would never be able to capture the truth and the magnanimity that were present in such great measure in Emily's personality.

Handkerchief in hand, I opened the door of the apartment. The hallway was dark and silent. If I had dropped a coin on the floor, it would have echoed. I stepped on the staircase. It had been lying undisturbed. Now, it resented being woken up. It creaked and complained with a long, drawn-out sound. I planted my hand on the railing and jumped three stairs at a time in the dark.

There was a fresh breeze coursing through the street. It cooled the drops of sweat on my brow.

'Yo,' a deep voice said. My heart jumped out of my mouth. How could the NYPD have already caught up with me?

But the voice belonged to a singer, who was about to recite the opening sentence of a hip-hop song. A large man in a camouflage jacket raised the volume of the car speakers from inside the confines of a black SUV. He lowered the window, extended one arm outside and beckoned towards someone with his index finger.

I thought I was looking at Yama, the God of Death.

In that moment, I saw that the police would catch up with me soon. They would fry me in an electric chair. Or they would inject poison into my veins. That wouldn't entirely be a bad thing. I deserved to die for what I had done to Emily. I wanted to die for what I had done to Emily. But I felt myself under the momentum of a nameless force. It prodded me on the backs of my knees. It compelled me to take the next step forward.

I walked into the subway station for the 2 and 3 lines. A police officer was checking the bags of incoming passengers. He would be sure to randomly check me. After all, I was a brown-skinned person, who could so easily be mistaken for an angry person from the Middle East.

There is a saying in America, 'It's eleven o'clock. Do you know where your children are?' The New York Police Department and the FBI did not always know where all the children were. However, they always knew where all of the Indians, Pakistanis and Bangladeshis were. Policemen have to be suspicious; that is expected of them. However, after 9/11, there had developed a certain quality of menace to their suspicion.

I propelled my body forward to crash it against the subway turnstiles.

'Excuse me, sir,' the policeman said.

'Yes?'

'How are you doing?'

'Fine, thank you.'

'Are you from Australia?'

'Me?'

'I mean to say… are you, like, an aborigine?'

'No,' I said.

He smiled. He reminded me that I need to swipe my metro card before moving through the turnstile.

I have never cried in my adult life. However, it took a massive exercise of willpower for me not to weep tears of gratitude in front of this officer. I had thought that I was forever condemned to being mistaken for a person from the Middle East. But now, there was every hope that I could be mistaken for an aborigine. I could pass for a benign bow-and-arrow shooting kind of guy, who believed that it was best for all concerned if tall buildings and old bridges were left alone.

'You sure?'

'Yes.' I smiled.

I thought about the handkerchief with Emily's bloodstains in my pocket. This was not a moment for polite conversation. This was a moment for active flight. It was time to wipe that smile off my face, and that too, without the aid of a handkerchief.

I lowered my eyes and walked through the turnstiles. The policeman did not come after me, even when I ran down the stairs to the connecting passageway to the downtown line. I walked at a rapid clip to the other end of the platform. A fat, white man and a thin, black woman glared at me. They clearly wanted to report me to the policeman. However, they didn't move. They weren't sure if they would be able to alert the policeman before the train arrived.

I decided to get off at Bryant Park. With its green grass and relative lack of policemen, it is the best place in New York for contemplative thought. The sun had set over the park. The green grass of the summer had turned black. I sat down on a chair whose backrest had a slight and elegant curve. I contemplated my options.

'Don't you walk away from me,' an elderly lady said to her husband at an adjoining table. But he got up all the same. He walked away from her. This must be how people in long relationships don't kill each other. They walk away during critical moments that severely test the will.

The tall trees at either end of the park were curved at their trunks. They made slight arcs as they tried to reach towards each other from either end of the park. A young child ran past my chair. He was staring at his ice-cream cone with great joy. He ran towards the horses on the carousel on the southern end of the garden.

If this were India, the child wouldn't have a park. The only available public land in his city would have been converted into a mall. The child would have run towards a Dolce & Gabbana store. Or, if he belonged to a low caste, he would have run towards a security guard who would have stopped him from entering the Dolce & Gabbana store.

I thought of that Indian security guard's unkempt moustache. I thought of the wooden cane, which, he assumed, endowed him with the right to be arrogant without being educated. I thought of time ticking on in the mall's Dolce & Gabbana store. And I thought of how nothing would change. The child would become a man. The man would try and enter the mall. He would be stopped by the same security guard. Even the cane would be the same.

I could not, and would not, ever return to India. If the police came after me, I would slip away like a laser beam does from a determined cat. The exact details on how I would accomplish this were unclear and vague to me at that moment in Bryant Park. However, the overarching principle of why I must accomplish my mission to remain in America was crystal clear.

In America, everyone could aspire to the pursuit of happiness. Everyone had a park. Everyone could shop at Dolce & Gabbana.

I needed to be inspired. I powered on my smartphone. I went to YouTube. I typed in '2008 Obama' into the search bar. There was no figure more inspirational and relevant for me than the

forty-fourth President of America. The man's middle name was
Hussein. He had managed to stay on in the country. He had even
managed to become the President.

I clicked on a video that featured him speaking at a rally in
Virginia during his first presidential campaign.

Can we get this country back on the right track?

Yes, we can!

Can we put hard-working Americans back to work?

Yes, we can!

The President of the United States now asked me a simple
question.

Can we avoid being arrested by the NYPD?

I answered him.

Yes, we can!

I would do it. I would make it in America.

A light on the antenna of the Empire State Building winked at
me. A woman pulled down on her skirt. My feet left the park and
touched the concrete of the city. New York was waiting for me.

A Buddhist Negation

Brett Cohen founded CJ&R in 1990. The C stands for Cohen. Nobody is really sure what the J and the R stand for. I guess it really doesn't matter. What lives by the flesh must perish by the flesh, and initials are but the merest phantasms of the flesh.

The agency had quiet beginnings, and I imagine there was a time when you could hear the whirring of the printer over the sounds of the people in the office. Things picked up during the dot-com era. During the so-called dot-com boom, CJ&R had clients that were valued more highly than General Motors on the stock market.

FastTV delivered streaming news broadcasts and movies via the Internet. Blackboard.com made it possible for teachers to avoid having to see, or speak to, their students. Everyone was waiting for Sticky Networks to tell us what it was they exactly did.

And then the bubble burst. Actually, it would be wrong to call it a bubble. Bubbles burst silently. The dot-com economy exploded like a bomb.

When the first nuclear bomb was tested in the Jemez Mountains of New Mexico, the resulting explosion was so bright that nearby residents swore that the sun had come up twice in one day. When the dot-com economy exploded, the sun set twice on the same day.

It seemed as though CJ&R would never recover. Brett was forced to lay off fifty-seven of the agency's sixty-five employees. CJ&R navigated much of the first decade of the new millennium representing small businesses that made modest media buys in magazines, newspapers and yellow-page books.

However, Brett Cohen was tough. Where other men would have cringed and done nothing (my adoptive father Mr Clarkson comes to mind), Brett repositioned CJ&R for the mobile and social world.

'By 2016,' he began to tell our clients and prospects, 'there will be more mobile phones in the world than human beings. There are more people on MyFace than there are in America and western Europe combined. You need to partner with an agency that can help you navigate this new world of social users and smaller screens.'

Mortal entities weaken and become ghosts. The ghosts reincarnate in other bodies and fill out again. CJ&R prospered. They hired more employees. They even made enough money to be able to pay the two thousand dollars to the INS for processing my work visa.

I was grateful towards Brett.

When I first came to America, I used to feel grateful for all kinds of things.

Thank you for allowing me to sit on your country's bus seat while you continue to stand.

Thank you for building such a nice park in the middle of the city.

Thank you for the 24/7 hot and cold water.

Thank you for the freeways.

Thank you for allowing me to fly on your airplanes.

You can imagine how grateful I was towards Brett. I slept from 11:00 p.m. to 8:00 a.m. However, for the rest of the day, I worked hard to ensure that the agency grew their media billings. Within three months, I got myself promoted from assistant media planner to media supervisor.

I think I could have even been made director if I had been able to present my viewpoints more forcefully at client meetings. However, I found this difficult to do, with Raj Malik scoffing at my Indian accent. He also made fun of me for using words like 'prepone', 'bamboozle' and 'hill station'. When Raj Malik smirked, I did not speak. I stammered and sputtered like a water tap in New Delhi.

However, I would not let him make fun of me tomorrow. I would rehearse thoroughly for the GAP presentation. I opened up the Google Translate tool. I began to check the pronunciation of every word that I planned to use. I was listening to the correct pronunciation of the word 'demand', when Brett Cohen knocked on my office door.

Brett was in his mid-forties. He lived in Pelham, New York. He was married to Jeanine Clarke. They celebrated their wedding anniversary on 4 December. Other than that, there was no personal information on his MyFace page. His profile was a carefully curated collection of links that were expressly designed to drive agency business. He had liked the pages of American Express, M&Ms, GAP, SchoolNet, and seven other clients that entrusted the agency with their mobile and social advertising. He had also posted articles he had written for CMO.com.

Brett liked The Beatles. He hadn't put that on his MyFace profile. However, when the ad agency had been invited to pitch the College Music Journal account, he had composed a song for the pitch. The name of the song was '*I want to be your band*'. The younger people at the agency had sniggered at this choice of Brett's song. But I had approved. In our jaded society, I thought it was important that we do everything we can to encourage people who are not scared of displaying earnestness.

'Arjun, something's come up,' he said.

'I'm on it,' I said.

'On what?'

'On the GAP presentation. I'll have a really nice deck…'

'Arjun, I'm sure you'll have something nice.'

'Thanks.'

'That's not why I am here.'

'It's not?'

'No. I'm here because of Emily.'

'Emily?' I tried to appear nonchalant. However, I could not help feeling that I was in an airport security line being selected for a special screening.

'Emily Hayes,' he said. 'Account executive. Remember, she used to work here?'

'Yes, of course.'

'I just got a call from the police.'

'And…?'

'And she's been found murdered in her apartment.'

The coffee cup fell to the floor. I dropped it hard enough so that some of the coffee splattered on to Brett's trousers. I might have overdone my reaction. Maybe an open mouth would have been all that was required to convey surprise. However, those brown stains would serve Brett a reminder all day of my genuine astonishment upon hearing of the murder.

'I'm sorry…' I handed him a handkerchief. He ignored it and reached for the box of Kleenex tissues on my desk.

'Don't worry about it,' he said. He seemed uneasy. Brett was always uncomfortable when discussing any matter that did not pertain to business. His eyes fogged over like they were made of pebbled glass. He adjusted his collar as though he were self-conscious about a bow tie.

'I read the newspapers this morning,' I said. 'I didn't see anything about Emily.'

By newspapers, I meant that old bastion of reporting news that really mattered: the *Daily News*. Unlike over one million of my fellow New Yorkers, I didn't care much for *The New York Times*. According to me, the so-called 'greatest newspaper in the world' does nothing more than serve up an endless stream of irrelevant content. I have no interest in Hosni Mubarak's kidneys. I don't care that the CEO of Twitter is a master of improv theatre. I don't have a cat, and even if I did, I would not want to learn about how I could get it to go vegetarian.

And I particularly didn't care for the large number of people who did nothing other than give their opinions on the pages of the *Times*. They surrounded the news from all sides and squeezed it so tightly that it became difficult to see.

I especially disliked Tom Friedman. He seemed to think that Superman was an Indian immigrant. In his articles, he wrote most unreasonably about our abilities. Most recently, he had written an article saying how Indians worked for forty hours a day while the French found it difficult to work for forty hours a week. Brett had sent me that article, as I imagine thousands of CEOs across the country had done to their Indian employees. As if the Department of Homeland Security wasn't bad enough, Tom Friedman was making life even more difficult for the immigrants. On a near-weekly basis, he raised the expectations that American bosses had of their Indian employees.

'The police just found out. They called me.'

'Ah,' I said.

'They told me something quite interesting ...'

'Ah.'

'They told me that Emily was seeing Raj.'

'Raj?'

'Come on, Arjun. How many Rajs do you think I know?'

'Raj Malik?'

'Yes.'

'They were dating?'

'Yes. Who knew, right? Apparently, Emily met him last evening.'

'Ah.'

'They were spotted together at some restaurant in Harlem. The police took in Raj for questioning.'

'Ah,' I said. I controlled the urge to give Brett a high five.

'They didn't have anything to go on,' Brett said. 'So they let him go.'

'I'm so sorry to hear,' I said. 'That is to say, I'm sorry to hear about Emily.'

Brett stared at the screensaver on my computer screen. It showed the Buddha lying down in gentle repose with his eyes closed. I had selected this particular screensaver with great care.

In America, people don't judge you by your innate qualities. Instead, they make instant judgements about you based on the things you like and dislike. And that's why the things you can display, your screensaver, your ringtone and the posts on your MyFace profile are so important. If Gandhi were alive today, it wouldn't matter that he was an environmentalist, that he was non-violent and that he cared about Muslims. He would also have to like Hodgson's October IPA, Dave Eggers and The Magnetic Fields, and show the world in a very public way that he was fond of them.

'Raj told me something very strange.'

'What?'

'Raj told me that he was eating dinner in a restaurant. And he happened to glance across the street. He told me that he might have seen you.'

'That's impossible,' I said.

'Arjun, if I may ask, were you in that neighbourhood yesterday?'

'I was,' I said. 'I went to Central Park to see the Dalai Lama.'

'And did you see him?'

'Yes,' I said. 'How could I ever miss hearing His Holiness speak?'

Brett picked up a ballpoint pen from my desk. He held it perfectly still between his fingers. He did not twirl or move it.

'Arjun,' he said, 'what did you think of Emily?'

'Oh. I thought she was one of the best account executives that we had. You know how so often the media department is an afterthought…even though we bring in all the billing for the agency?'

One should not miss any chance to air a grievance in the workplace.

'But Emily wasn't like that. She understood the importance of the media department. You know, with Fly Mobile, Emily had me meet with the client before we even began work on the campaign. They wanted to run a video ad for their new coupon product. I told them that with consumers being charged for extra bandwidth by the telecom providers, they should not run a mobile video ad. People would feel resentful for having to pay for the extra bandwidth. Moving away from the video really forced us to think of other approaches – and that's how we came up with that whole Tap to Fly campaign concept…'

'You came up with that?'

'Yes,' I said.

He placed the pen back on the desk.

'But what I am really trying to say is that Emily was the best account executive that I have worked with.'

'If you don't mind my asking, did you like her?'

So Brett wanted to play a hard game with me. If that's how he wanted it, I was ready. I was always ready. I prepared to go Buddhist on his ass.

'Well, Brett,' I said, switching to my soft-spoken tone, 'how could I not like her? To hate Emily or for that matter any other person…would be to hate myself. Have you heard of Nagarjuna?'

He looked with great longing towards the door. But I held his eye and continued to talk. I liked Brett. But he needed to be taught a lesson. He needed to learn never to question me in the future.

'We are all human beings,' I said. 'And as such we like to have philosophies that try to explain our condition of life. Nagarjuna was of the theory that any argument that tried to express a particular viewpoint was not a tenable one. He used the process of reduction ad absurdum, and using rational arguments, negated all viewpoints that tried to prove or disprove the meaning of any ultimate reality...'

On the street below, an ice-cream truck played a seemingly never-ending jingle as it tried to make its way through the traffic on Park Avenue. Eventually, it crossed the intersection at 28th Street and Park Avenue. The jingle faded. I was still talking.

'...and so our tendency to view the world as separate objects takes us into this world of samsara, which is the root cause of all ignorance. So yes, to answer your question, I liked Emily. And I take solace in the view that she hasn't entirely left the world. As Nagarjuna said, "If separate elements do not exist, how is it possible for them to disappear?"'

Brett had that look of fatigued resignation you see on the faces of taxi drivers at 3.45 in the morning. All they want is peace and quiet. But all they get is a drunken passenger in a chatty mood.

'I see,' he said. He got up and made his way towards the door of my office.

'Brett?' I said. He started at the sound of my voice. 'Was there a reason you were asking me all these questions?'

'No, no. Not at all. You know, I was just trying to understand Emily as a person. And I was trying to see if you know, you had coincidentally been in the same neighbourhood yesterday. If you had by chance happened to run into her or even seen her. But that couldn't be. Because you were watching...'

He couldn't even bring himself to utter the name of His Holiness.

'I am really sorry to hear of Emily's passing away,' I said. 'I will go to the Mahayana Temple in Chinatown today and light a candle for her.'

'I will need you for the SchoolBoard.net meeting,' Brett said.

I sat forward in my chair. This was the Brett I admired. Practical Brett. Let's-take-care-of-business Brett.

'We are going to discuss the lift in awareness as a result of our branding campaign.'

'Branding' is the word people in advertising use to describe a campaign that has not produced results. When ad agency executives cannot prove that their ideas have driven sales, they say they have run a branding campaign.

'I trust the campaign has lifted awareness?' Brett asked.

'After I am done with their presentation,' I said, pointing to my computer monitor, 'you will certainly find that to be the case.'

'Good man,' he said.

He stepped back into the room.

'Arjun,' he said. 'I don't know quite how to say this, so I am going to come right out and say it.'

I sat up in my chair.

'You do excellent work, Arjun,' he said. 'You are the best media person we have ever had ...'

'But?'

'But what I am really looking for is for you to be a good presenter. You have to speak louder during meetings.'

'Speak louder,' I said.

'Arjun,' Brett said. 'Don't mind my asking. You do good work. Great work. Then why do you stammer ... and get nervous in the middle of presentations? Like you did last week?'

I had stammered last week because Raj Malik had sniggered when I tried to pronounce 'hors d'oeuvres'. The client had heard him. I had heard him. And I was sure that god had heard him. But god hadn't punished him.

'I'll do well,' I told Brett. 'I won't let you down. I promise.'

Brett nodded.

'I need to know I can trust you to talk to and upsell our clients,' he said.

He left the room.

I went up to the office window. I looked down at the street. A homeless man was advocating in a loud voice that people needed to wear government cotton and stop supporting corporate polyester. He was frothing at the mouth. He was clearly mad.

However, his accent was clean and American. I wished I could talk like him.

But I could never pronounce my Vs so that they sounded different from my Ws. I could never bring myself to say plant so that it rhymed with ant. That would be like pretending to be someone else. If I changed my accent and the words I used, I would devolve into one of those pitiable software engineers who came to America. Someone with a name like Sameer, but who went through life pretending to be Sam.

But I wouldn't be like them. I wasn't a hypocrite. I would evolve into a self-confident and self-aware person who would be comfortable with every facet of his personality.

I shut down my computer. I had to leave work early today. Today was Tuesday. And Tuesday was therapy day.

Mr Clarkson had insisted that I go to America and start seeing a therapist after I had killed my neighbour's Pomeranian in New Delhi. I had told Mr Clarkson that I wasn't being cruel or malicious to the animal. I had merely acted out of self-defence. But he hadn't listened. He insisted that I begin seeing the 'best therapist that money could buy'.

When I had first started seeing Dr Firstein, she had administered the Rorshach test. She had made me look at a grey card covered with inkblots.

'What do you see, Arjun?' she had asked.

I had done my research. I knew that by administering the Rorshach test, Dr Firstein was trying to get a measure of my ego-dystonic aggression. She was trying to see just how much control I had over my anger through my conscious manoeuvres and unconscious defences. She was looking to see if I would say, 'Oh, that's a lady in a ballroom with her head blown by a shotgun,' and clap my hands with laughter.

If I were an amateur, I would have played it completely safe. I would have said, 'Oh, that's two flowers kissing in a garden.' But I wasn't an amateur, and this wasn't *American Idol*.

I had learned from my readings that concealing signs of pleasure derived from sadistic and violent acts was one of the classic defense mechanisms employed by the very people susceptible to these impulses.

'That's a lady in a ballroom,' I had said. 'It looks like someone might have shot her in the head. But that's terrible. Why would anyone want to do such a thing?'

She was probably asking for it, that's why.

She was probably someone like Mrs Clarkson, who had hit me with a cricket bat nearly every day of my childhood. A lady who had burned my forearm with a hot iron. A lady who had told me when I was five that if I misbehaved, the Delhi Police would come to my room at night and cut off my genitals. I could see why someone would want to shoot such a lady in the head.

However, not every thought that comes to the mind in a therapy session needs to be vocalized.

Dr Firstein had nodded. She had gone on to ask me another question. Her approach was different from those of the therapists I had read about in an article in *The Atlantic Monthly*. Unlike the therapists quoted in the publication, Dr Firstein had refused to prescribe any medication. Instead, she had continued to engage me in conversations that lasted from a few minutes to exactly one hour.

We had talked about John Lennon. We had discussed Tocqueville's *Democracy in America*. And we talked about Sally. We spoke about how Sally asked me to accompany her to an art exhibit. How she had invited me to her home for Thanksgiving. How she had called out my name and given me credit for my work at a client meeting.

Sally was an alias for Emily.

'You haven't spoken about Sally in a while,' Dr Firstein said.

I wasn't about to start now.

'Well, since she left the office, we've hardly been in touch,' I said. 'You know how New York can get.'

I never found out if Dr Firstein knew how New York can get. She looked at the wall. The clock had struck sixty.

'Let's continue where we left off next time,' she said. She moved her hands over her short hair. She took off her glasses and smiled. 'You seem to be liking it here in America more and more, Arjun. I hope these sessions are helping.'

'Sure,' I said. But I was only being polite. I did not need therapy to succeed in America. I needed to take care of Raj Malik. To use an Americanism, I would have to kill in the SchoolBoard presentation.

The Only Living Indian
In New York

The sun had dimmed, but the streets were streaked with a hot orange. My undershirt clung to my chest. The heat radiated from the pavement through the soles of my shoes.

There was a policeman at the entrance of the 28th Street subway station. I didn't want to risk getting arrested because of him looking at the colour of my skin and thinking that I was a terrorist. Or, for that matter, a murderer. I walked into an electronics store. *The Jerry Springer Show* was running on a carefully arranged matrix of screens.

I had read about Jerry Springer on Wikipedia while researching American pop culture. Mr Springer had been elected the mayor of Cincinnati. He must have been a bright man. Watching his show would greatly further my knowledge of American society.

I found that I could follow the show easily even without the volume.

A bald man sat on a chair. Jerry walked among the members of the audience. The bald man began to talk. After he had finished speaking, Jerry Springer went up to him. He said something. The audience laughed. A fat woman came out on to the stage. Her hair was so pink that it rendered every one of her other features into obscurity. The audience booed. The pink woman attacked the man. The man pushed her away. Security guards that were as big as bouncers rushed on to the stage.

I felt frightened. These people were so different from me. They were so different from what I could ever become. Assimilation seemed like an impossible task. I understood why the INS did not refer to us as 'visitors' or 'foreigners'. They called us 'aliens'. It was the most appropriate word. Americans were alien to us. We were alien to them.

The policeman had gone away. I ran down the steps of the subway station. As I waited for the train, I asked the Indian man at the news-stand if they had an evening edition of the *Daily News*.

'What's that?' asked the newspaper man.

'You know, like they have in India?'

'No, I don't.'

Of course, he didn't. He clearly looked like an illiterate fellow, who hadn't learned to read or write before or since he had arrived in this country.

'You know, the evening edition, where they print two papers every day.'

'Brother, they barely have enough money to print one newspaper every day.'

I should have known that. I had personally been responsible for taking over ten million dollars from newspaper advertising and shifting the ad spend to digital media.

'I'll take one,' I said.

I had a copy of the *Daily News* waiting for me at home. But it had been a long day. I felt tired and lifeless. I needed to read something that would lighten the burden of my worries and make them fade away and disappear.

Mr Clarkson had once told me that the key to a happy life is to live in the here and now. I thought it was idiotic, especially if the problems you were facing were in the here and now. When I want to feel happy, I find it is far more effective to think about the here and now of other people. It is easier to be happy when you realize that your situation could be so much worse.

Of course, there's little point thinking about a young child in faraway Myanmar or Eritrea. This child is so different from you in every way that you might find it difficult to establish the empathetic connection you need to look down upon other people with real conviction.

I find it more helpful to turn to the local news. It really helps you experience the here and now of people who are suffering in your neighbourhood, city or area.

As it always did, the *Daily News* delivered.

The lead story was about a Bronx man in a wheelchair. He had been arrested by the police. The man had opened a bottle of household cleaner called El Diablo, which was 98 per cent sulfuric acid. He had thrown the acid on his daughter's face.

A neighbour narrated the sordid incident to the journalist. The name of the neighbour who had narrated the story was Shakespeare. Only the *Daily News* could have succeeded in capturing such a delightful coincidence. I chuckled. My worries receded a little, as worries do upon hearing the sound of laughter.

By the time the F train had deposited me on Jackson Heights, Roosevelt Avenue Station, by the time I had finished eating the three churros I purchased from the Colombian lady on the railway platform, and by the time I had walked home to my apartment on 73rd Street, I knew that Raj Malik would have to die.

I had to kill him in a way that suggested suicide, so that his death would appear like an act of repentance. He had killed Emily. He had felt guilty. And he had taken his life. Brett would stop suspecting me of having any involvement with the sordid matter. What's more, Raj's permanent absence from the world would help me make a more effective presentation during the SchoolBoard. net meeting – and all of the presentations that followed.

I unlocked my phone. A notification told me I had a new email. The red number over my inbox icon irritated me as though it were a mosquito bite. I clicked on the envelope to read my email and remove it.

Raj Malik had written to me. He had asked if we could meet tomorrow.

'Don't worry, Raj,' I thought. 'We will meet today.'

On the corner of 73rd Street and Roosevelt Avenue, a male dog was humping a female dog. A small group of Pakistani men stood outside the Kabab King diner. They cheered. The immigrants were watching dogs fucking each other on the street. The Americans were watching the Kardashians fucking each other on TV. Voltaire was right. Men must have corrupted nature a little, for they were not born wolves, and yet, they have become wolves.

As usual, the elevator was out of service in my building. I thought about lodging a complaint with the superintendent. But after a long day at work, I did not have the energy to go through with this task. He would be drunk. And I was too tired to learn Albanian.

I walked up the stairs. On the third floor, the teenager in the apartment directly below mine was playing reggaeton music at a very loud volume. I touched my sacred thread. I thought about how easy it would be to ring the doorbell and slit his throat. But I controlled the urge. It would be foolish to be linked so directly to two murders on two successive days.

I poured a shot of Famous Grouse into a glass. The whiskey warmed my chest. I relaxed, as the bitterness disappeared and left a pleasant aftertaste.

I opened my Lenovo laptop and started up the TOR client.

The TOR client had originally been designed by the US Navy to protect the anonymity of Chinese and Iranian dissidents on the Internet. I thought it was an extraordinarily useful tool to have even in America.

The TOR client made it impossible for your Internet surfing behaviour to be tracked.

Usually when you visited a website, you did so in a manner that was similar to the flying crow – you took the shortest path from Point A to Point B. This direct method of navigation was why someone could follow your online surfing patterns with relative ease.

The TOR client took a shotgun to the crow and blasted it into a thousand pieces. It scattered your online journey into a large number of scattered and unconnected paths. With the TOR client, a person who wanted to track you would find it impossible to do so, be it in Iran, China, or for that matter, the United States of America.

After I had established a connection through the TOR client, I logged on to MyFace.

I had a notification. Andrew Clarkson has indicated he is your father. Accept? I ignored the notification. Andrew Clarkson was not my father. He had merely adopted me from the orphanage. He had not fulfilled the responsibilities of a father. He had not provided support during moments of need. He had not protected me during moments of danger.

I am not an active MyFace user. I had written one post on MyFace this year. I had uploaded a photo of a lion from *National Geographic*. Underneath the photo, I had written, 'What an awesome lion!' That's all the data that I was prepared to share with MyFace.

I drew in my breath as I saw Emily's photo.

Emily was laughing at something. She had covered her smile with the palm of her hand. Her entire body was reacting to the camera all at once, so that she appeared full of life and vitality. Her face glowed like the earrings she had on that evening in Harlem.

The news had gone public. A long row of obituaries written in OMGs and exclamation marks filled Emily's profile page. I found I had to scroll for an entire thirty seconds till I came to the post that had started it all, the one about her having checked into The Red Room.

I went to Google News and searched for Emily's name. Three New York-based blogs and the online edition of the *Daily News* had written about her death.

The *Daily News* article said that Emily Hayes, age twenty-seven, had been found dead in her apartment in the SOHA neighbourhood. The journalist had stated that Emily worked for BBDO. A senior executive at the agency was quoted as saying that Emily 'was among the best in the business'. It was an understatement. If only the journalist had asked me about Emily! I would have given a eulogy that was worthy of her. My ode would sound like a poem, but it would be one that was based entirely on fact.

I clicked on Raj's profile. He had forgotten to change the settings for his contact information from 'Public' to 'Visible Only To Friends'. He wasn't alone. There were millions upon millions of people who didn't even know that just last month, MyFace had made both the postal and email addresses of their users public by default.

Raj lived close to the E subway station on 53rd Street.

I applied shaving cream to my cheeks. The skin underneath my eyes was dark and puffy. I hadn't slept well last night. But as I moved the razor down my cheeks with sharp flicks, I began to feel better. By the time I had towelled the water off my face, I felt dapper enough to do the foxtrot.

I decided to put on a white shirt and a pair of blue jeans.

I had last worn a white shirt along with blue jeans six months ago.

After a tiresome client meeting at CJ&R, I had stopped by a deli on 27th Street and Lexington Avenue to buy coffee. The storekeeper had scoffed at me from high up on his fortress made up of chewing gums and condoms.

'This white shirt and those blue jeans,' he had said. 'They make you look like a delivery boy. If educated people like you dress like this, what will they [he had moved his hands in a sweeping gesture to cover the people walking along the avenue] think of us Indians? That we are all delivery men?'

But today, I wanted to look like a delivery man. I wanted to immerse myself into the pool of sameness. I wanted to join the class of the people who are faceless and who exist just so they can bring you food, drive you to your destination and iron your clothes. I wanted to be invisible.

The white shirt wasn't ironed. I hoped I appeared sufficiently working class. The blue jeans didn't fit around my waist. I stretched the button towards the slit. But each of them seemed to be charged with positive ions and refused to come towards each other.

Had I put on that much weight in the last six months? I didn't think so. I had continued to run. I had continued to eat vegetarian food. But the jeans did not fit. I had to take them off. As I slid my left leg out, I hit upon a moment of illumination. I realized why the jeans weren't encircling the circumference of my waist.

I already had a pair of trousers on.

I took off the original pair and put the jeans back on. Now, they fit just fine. I cursed at myself. If I was going to go around the city participating in activities that were deemed illegal by the New York Police Department, I couldn't afford to be absent-minded.

Just last week, the *Daily News* had written an article about a robber who had accidentally handed his gun to the cashier instead of his swag bag. I didn't want to suffer the fate of that robber. People like him got arrested. They also became the object of ridicule on MyFace.

I touched the sacred thread on my chest. It felt heavy. I checked my pockets. I had my keys and my wallet. I also had my iPhone.

I cursed at myself again. I was a media supervisor at one of New York's most innovative mobile ad agencies. And yet, here I was behaving like a common person who thought the smartphone had been invented just so that people could talk to one another.

The smartphone had been invented so that we could be tracked. With the smartphone, our parents, our policemen, our governments and our brands could keep a record of our location for each and every second of the day. They could correct us if we did the wrong thing or purchased the wrong product.

Apple had recently acknowledged to Congress that a hidden feature within the iPhone kept an accurate log of all the places that the owner of the phone visited without the user's knowledge. Using this location data, the police had served more than thirty thousand warrants last year.

I took out the SIM card from the iPhone and flushed it down the toilet. Using a mortar that I normally used to grind peppercorn, I smashed the screen of my iPhone. A hipster died in Brooklyn. I threw the phone down the garbage chute. I disconnected my Lenovo laptop from the power source and packed it in my Manhattan Portage carrier bag. I also reached into the distant past. I pulled out a Motorola Razor flip phone and placed it in the bag.

Manhattan is just on the other side of the Queensboro Bridge. But the city's narrow streets and tall buildings are a complete contrast to Queens's more relaxed and expansive ways. When I emerged from the station on 53rd Street and Lexington Avenue, I couldn't help feel that I had set foot in a completely different country.

If the buildings in Manhattan were different, so were the people. Unlike the Colombians, the Bangladeshis and the Indians that called out to their fellow kind in Queens, the people on the street in Manhattan were indifferent to my presence. This was something that I did not mind.

I stood on the corner of 55th Street and Second Avenue. I could see Raj Malik's building. It was a small and compact structure that stood next to an Italian restaurant with outdoor seating. I sat on a park bench next to a homeless person. Like me, he was a dispossessed member of society. We were both struggling to get accepted into the mainstream. I smiled at him. He seemed surprised. He turned away, muttering something under his breath. He might have called me a fag. I didn't blame him for his reticence. He had displayed the incoherent reaction of a dead person who has just discovered that he is still breathing.

You might call me a killer. But you too have killed. You kill the homeless and the poor each and every day when you ignore them and treat them as though they were dead. It is only when you smell them in a subway car that you look at them with resentment, for they have reminded you that they are alive.

I opened the laptop and connected to a Starbucks Wi-Fi network, which, thankfully, in modern-day America was never too far away. I powered on the TOR client. I logged on to MyFace. I clicked my way to Raj Malik's profile. His status hadn't changed since Emily had checked him into The Red Room. I meditated for ten minutes, following which I refreshed Raj Malik's MyFace profile. People say that water does not boil while you look at it. However, Raj Malik's status refreshed with a new update before my very eyes. He had ordered braised fish fillets with Napa cabbage from the Land of Plenty via seamless.com four minutes ago.

There were no security cameras at the door to Raj's building. I pressed the button that buzzed Raj's apartment.

'Yes?' he inquired in his nasal voice.

'Delivery,' I said.

He buzzed me in.

An elevator looked invitingly at me with open doors. However, I couldn't risk being recorded by any security cameras that might be concealed inside its walls and mirrors. I took the stairs.

I felt thankful that I ran twenty miles a week. Each floor went by as smoothly as the scenery does through the window of a train. On the eighth floor, I pulled at my sacred thread. I took out the knife from the leather sheath.

I rang the doorbell, taking care to stay away from the keyhole. Raj opened the door. I pushed my way in.

'Arjun?' Raj Malik said.

Going by his tone, I thought he might have wanted to ask me a question. I would never hear it. I thought it quite ironic that taking my name would be the last thing he would ever do. I plunged the Global Chef's knife into the Zone One region of his neck.

The Zone One region contains the subclavian arteries and veins, the dome of the pleura, the esophagus, the great vessels of the neck, the recurrent nerve and the trachea. Each of these pathways carries a lot of blood, all of which spurted from Raj Malik's neck like water does from the back of a whale. He fell to the wooden floor with the dull thud of furniture.

I was not the first person to win a battle by exploiting the Zone One region. In the course of history, it had helped many a warrior overcome his stronger and more unjust foe. Achilles had won the battle for Thessaly by stabbing an opponent far more powerful than him in the Zone One area. It is ironic that I knew this historical tidbit, for I had started to read Greek history only after Raj had made fun of me for my lack of knowledge of Western civilization and philosophy.

Raj Malik's apartment was messy, even dirty. I could see no influence of Emily's civilizing, feminine touch. This pleased me. There was a poster of the Beastie Boys on the wall over the mounted flat-screen TV. An Xbox was connected to the plasma screen. The cables, like his veins, were sprawled carelessly on the ground.

I was surprised to see that there were statues of Lakshmi, Rama and Ganesha on the bookshelf. Raj Malik spent all his day denying that he was Indian. And yet, he came home every day to Indian gods and goddesses.

The intercom buzzed. Raj's delivery had arrived. I went up to the door and locked it shut, taking care that my handkerchief covered my hand. The intercom buzzed again. I hoped that the delivery man would go away. However, there was every chance that a resident of the building would let him in. It was essential that I remain absolutely silent.

I stood in the middle of the apartment and closed my eyes. I felt a stream of air hit the upper edge of my lip. I began to feel little pulses of air on the crown of my head, the surface of my forehead and the bridge of my nose. The Buddha had used vipassana meditation to guide millions of his followers on the path to nirvana. But it had other uses. Using vipassana, one could enter a state of rock-steady silence. In the past, I had used this ancient technique to become completely noiseless, so that my apartment would appear to be empty when children rang my doorbell for candy on Halloween.

I waited for fifteen minutes. I looked at Raj Malik's dead body. Knowing that he would never be able to twist his lips into a smirk again filled me with a simple joy, the kind you experience at the first sip of cold beer on a hot summer day.

Tomorrow, the *Daily News* would ask his neighbours and colleagues what kind of a person Raj Malik was. I hoped that someone would say he was a conscientious man. Killing himself after having taken the life of his girlfriend was just the sort of thing he would do.

I stepped over his body. There was a sticker on his couch. It was a piece of promotional material that MyFace used to promote the social network. The sticker was blue. The white letters printed on its face stood out in bright contrast to the dark background colour. I knew the sticker well. There were hundreds of them at our office.

The words on the sticker said, 'I found you on MyFace'.

The stream of air from the fan hit the sticker. It lifted off the couch and, like an autumn leaf, swayed gently and fell towards the ground.

Death had yet to sweep through Raj and take over his body. His fingers were still soft and pliable. I curled them over the handle of the knife. I closed the door softly and ran down the stairs. The delivery man had gone away.

'Hello,' a voice called out to me from a passageway adjacent to the lobby.

An old man with glasses and diamond patterns on his sweater shuffled towards me. He seemed like a harmless enough fellow. However, I saw him for what he was. He was a witness. He was a man with one hand on the switch that would make me shiver and shake on the electric chair. I would have to take care of him.

'How are you doing?'

Another man wearing a polo T-shirt and knee-length shorts came into view directly behind him.

His appearance complicated matters. I saw it would be difficult to get rid of two people in a public hallway. I now understood, at a sensual level, how a pack of hunting dogs could take down a lion.

'What are you doing here?' he asked.

I could not answer this question honestly.

'Just...' I said.

They stared at me with their dark, clever, witness eyes, awaiting an answer.

'You know...' I added by way of clarification.

'Getting into trouble, huh?'

They were only a few inches away from me. They were lined up neatly like two flowerpots on a windowsill. I felt for the comforting reassurance of the weight of my knife. But I realized that I had left it in Raj's apartment. I felt as though my feet were on quicksand. I was about to commit an impulsive action born out of panic. I had already convinced myself that my hands were stronger than steel, when the man with the diamond patterns on his sweater smiled.

'It's been a while since we saw you.'

'It has...' I said.

'What was your name again? Raj...right?'

For the first time in our interaction, I had reason to smile.

'Yes,' I said. 'Raj.'

We exchanged pleasantries. We bemoaned the eccentricities of the weather. Normally, I find small talk grating. But now, the easy stream of mindless conversation calmed my nerves. I felt comfortable and confident. I threw in a few facts about global warming. I might have even said the words El Niño.

'On your way out?'

'You know it,' I said.

'Don't you go getting into trouble,' he said.

'If you don't say anything,' I said, 'I won't.'

He laughed. I opened the door and stepped into the city, whose population had reduced by two and so nearly reduced by three.

The night sky was dark. But I could tell by looking at the haze at the top of the Citicorp building that it had become cloudy. Sweat rolled down my forehead, slid down the bridge of my nose and fell on to my lips. I licked at it.

There was a halal cart on the corner. I asked the Middle Eastern man for a plate of falafel and rice. I opened the Styrofoam lid of the box. I ate the rice with my fingers, just like I would in India. I felt confident that I could do so. For now, there was not one person in New York who would make fun of me for my Indian ways.

On Cantaloupe Island

I took the E train at the 53rd Street-Lexington Avenue station. Most people in Manhattan did not know that the E Train was an express train. After it left Manhattan, the E stopped only at 23rd Street and the Queens Plaza station. After this hop and skip, it jumped all the way to Jackson Heights.

An Indian girl got on the train at Queens Plaza. Her pupils were only slightly darker than her skin. She had slender arms and long legs. He breasts swelled in a perfect curve. She looked at me with that strange combination of pride and contemptuousness that Indian women bestow on Indian men. They are proud because they bask in the desire that we show in our eyes. It allows them to think of themselves as the most beautiful women in the world. They are angry because they think we are sexually deprived creatures who are never more than a few seconds away from molesting them.

She was returning from a party. She wore a low-cut dress. The black outfit that she had on would have accentuated her cleavage in a classy way, if she had also not made the unfortunate decision of wearing a bra. Her body was in New York. But her mind and breasts were still trapped in the conservatism of small-town India.

There were no policemen at Jackson Heights station.

I called the boy. He must inhabit a satellite that orbited my world in a steady path, a shiny, white ball that was never more than fifteen minutes away from my current location.

'I'll see you in fifteen minutes,' he said.

Every car on Roosevelt Avenue was big, red and loud. The biggest, loudest and reddest of these cars belonged to the boy. I climbed into the front seat which was a few feet off the ground. I was hit immediately with a blast of salsa meringue. The music was loud and ferocious enough to mangle the words of the song and strip them of all meaning.

The boy began to drive. On 34th Street, we exchanged greetings. I gave him eighty dollars. He gave me a bag of cocaine.

'Watch out,' I said.

A pigeon was waddling around in a shallow puddle of water. It seemed dazed, as though it had just come out of a deep sleep. Instead of flying away in a flurry of wings as the car approached, it hobbled aimlessly on the road. What was it doing on the street anyway? Weren't pigeons supposed to sleep in the night? I thought of the orange-chested bird outside Emily's apartment. It, too, had been awake after dark.

New York City never slept. The humans in New York never slept. Now, if the birds began to stay awake too, the city would get to be a very noisy place.

The boy braked sharply.

'You like pigeons?' he asked.

He really seemed to like these feathered rodents. I didn't want to hurt the feelings of my cocaine dealer. I smiled. I nodded.

The boy smiled underneath the hood of his cap. He curled his fingers into a tight ball and proffered it to me. I bumped fists with him. Till this point in time, the boy's interactions with me could be best described as transactional. But now, with this fist bump, I felt privileged and upgraded, as celebrities must feel when the Queen taps them on the shoulder with a sword.

'Arjun,' I said.

'Fernando.'

Who would have thought? My coke dealer was named after an ABBA song.

I was surprised to find that the apartment on the third floor was silent. Maybe my neighbour was asleep. Or maybe he had gone to a nightclub to fill his head with more mindless music. I didn't care either way. I listened to the silence intently. At every instant, I expected it to break and be replaced by the sound of bass beats. But it held on to its peaceful and undisturbed state.

I poured a shot of Famous Grouse into a tall glass. I closed my eyes. I wanted to play out the sequence of events that had unfolded at Raj's apartment in my mind. I wanted to reassure myself that I hadn't forgotten anything by the body or left any trace that could be discovered by the police.

But all I could think of was the Indian girl. The swell of her breasts. Her long, tanned legs. Her teeth biting on her curled upper lip. Other visions came to my mind. Skirts held down in the subway. Bare shoulder blades. A gorgeous outward bulge stretched against thin cotton.

I laid out a line of cocaine on the table. I placed the bag into a stainless steel vial. I slid the vial inside the sheath on my sacred thread. I rolled a twenty-dollar bill and inhaled the line smoothly. I felt at ease with the world. I felt as though I belonged. This is how citizens must feel all the time.

I called Michelle and asked her if she wanted to have a drink.

She could have chosen not to answer the phone. She could have yawned and asked with a hint of annoyance in her voice what time it was. She could have then pretended to contemplate her options. However, Michelle hadn't been in America long enough to learn the proper deceptions that needed to be deployed in different social situations.

'Yes,' she said simply.

I had met Michelle at a Spanish Language Meetup at the Texas Rodeo Bar and Grill on 28th Street and 3rd Avenue. She had told me on our third meeting in her then faltering Spanish that she liked me. I had invited her over for dinner. She had spent one night in my apartment. We had even gone together to Atlantic City and spent one night together in the same hotel room.

We had slept side by side. But we hadn't slept together. I had not been able to take the leap that one has to take to go from having absolutely nothing to having absolutely everything. I had felt nervous. I had feared that I would disappoint her. I had thought she would accuse me of being a pervert, like Mrs Clarkson once had. I feared she would get angry with me, maybe even hit me.

Now, even as Michelle made her way to my apartment from Flushing, I marvelled at the lack of anxiety within my being. I felt like a man. I was like the mountain the Buddhists aspire towards during meditation; the mountain that Emily Dickinson says has 'His observation omnifold, His inquest everywhere'.

Herbie Hancock had begun to play 'Cantaloupe Island' when the doorbell rang. Michelle was wearing a tight, white top. She had clearly applied make-up to her cheeks and eyelashes. She had a nervous smile that had been painted on to her face.

Normally, I would have asked Michelle how her day had been. I would have offered her a drink.

But today, I didn't behave like a gentleman. I didn't make polite conversation. Instead, I grasped her firmly as soon as she entered the apartment. I kissed her softly yet firmly on her lips. I carried her to the bedroom.

To describe what happened after would not be a gentlemanly thing to do. So I will not get into the details.

I will say that if I finished too soon, if I came at the moment of penetration, it was only because this was the first time I had ever been with a woman. But such was the power that coursed through my veins that night that I did not let this mishap deter me. There was no halt in activity. No possibility was left unexplored. I commenced and commenced again. It was a good thing I didn't have the knife attached to my sacred thread. It would have felt heavy. And Michelle might have quite possibly been freaked out. The absence of the instrument had created what MBA students and mid-level managers liked to call a 'win-win' situation. By the time we were done, the hallways had become quiet, as though made of a hard, ancient stone. The planes had stopped flying in their approach to LaGuardia Airport. I could hear the wind rustle the leaves on the trees.

'What had gotten into you tonight?' she asked.

'I don't know,' I said. I sniffled.

My stomach rumbled. I coughed to cover it up, this remnant sound of poverty.

'I am going to scramble some eggs,' I said. 'Do you want some?'

She walked with me to the kitchen.

I cut some green chilies with a standard kitchen knife. I coated the pan with olive oil and threw in some mustard seeds. They began to pop. I added sliced onions. We looked at each other, sharing a silence that was too new to be entirely comfortable. As the onions began to turn a deep brown, I added in some ginger garlic paste, a hint of turmeric and half a teaspoon of chili powder. The eggs sizzled as they came in touch with the spice and the heat. As they turned into an opaque white, I toasted two slices of bread. I proportioned the eggs and the toast neatly in two plates. Finally, I poured us each a glass of Famous Grouse with club soda.

'Do you cook a lot?' Michelle asked. I smiled. Her Asian features and her greatly improved Spanish accent imbued her with a highly unique charm.

'I try to cook once a day,' I said. 'But I don't always manage to do it.'

When I had first come to the country, I used to cook every morning before leaving for work. Brett often liked to entertain clients at restaurants like Les Halles and The Blue Smoke, and I had to accompany him, often on little or no notice. At the restaurant, when people praised their wines and their pasta for reasons that were incomprehensible to me, I would think of the dal rice I had waiting at home. I would smile at the dinner table.

However, over the last year, I had come to develop an appreciation of vegetarian food from other cultures. Mozzarella was a reliable companion. French lentils were charming in their own way. Basil had personality.

'Once a day! You should become a chef or something.'

I laughed. I walked to the CD player and put on Duke Ellington's *Brunswick Sessions*. The trumpets began to play '*Moon Over Dixie*'. Michelle smiled. Mr Ellington began to sing, '*It Don't Mean a Thing/If It Ain't Got That Swing*'. The Duke had succinctly expressed in one sentence what Nietzsche and Spinoza had spent their entire lifetimes trying to enunciate.

Michelle began to sing along with the Duke. She had a remarkable voice. She was so in tune with Mr Ellington that, for an instant, she appeared like an apparition, a ghost who had left the Duke's ensemble on the CD and come into my living room.

'*Just give me that rhythm/everything you've got.*'

She came up to me and circled my neck with both hands. I tensed up.

But she didn't hurt me, like Mrs Clarkson had.

I had been five years old. I had heard a flapping of wings in my room. I had become scared and had run to the Clarksons' bedroom. However, Mr Clarkson had gone to a party. Mrs Clarkson had woken up. She had shouted at me. She had accused me of being a sick child, a pervert. After she had finished shouting, she had … I rubbed the scar on my forearm.

Now, all Michelle did was kiss me. She continued to sing.

'*It makes no difference/If it's sweet or hot.*'

'Wow, that's …' And so taken I was by her voice, that I reached for the most obvious word. 'Amazing,' I said. 'Forget about me being a professional chef. You should become a professional singer.'

She stopped singing.

'I didn't mean to make you self-conscious.'

She touched my face.

'It's not that,' she said. 'You're not the first person who has told me I sing very well. In fact, when I was a teenager, I was part of a group that played school campus songs. I was a professional singer. I even performed at many concerts in Taiwan.'

'School campus...was that like a college band?'

She shook her head.

'No,' she said. 'School campus was a kind of music that was very popular in Taiwan. We were mainly singing protest songs in Chinese. I guess school campus songs were our way of highlighting our culture at a time when Western music was so popular. Strangely enough, all of the school campus songs took inspiration from American folk music.'

'And was your band famous?'

'Sure,' she said. 'We were well known at the time. We were called The Little Jasmines.'

'That's brilliant,' I said. 'And what happened to the group?'

She stabbed at a piece of egg.

'I really don't want to talk about it,' she said.

I must have looked hurt for she got up from her chair and kissed me on my cheek.

'It's just that I am so happy now,' she said. 'I don't want to talk about unhappy things.'

'So I should shelve my plan of talking about the war in Iraq?'

She laughed.

'Arjun,' she asked, 'can I ask you a question?'

'Sure,' I said.

'Are you seeing someone?'

'No,' I said.

She bit down on her lower lip. There was something on her mind. She was trying to remain silent. But I knew that her words were like stones rolling down the sides of a mountain. They would break through the barriers posed by tooth and lip and manifest themselves on the other side.

'Do you like me?' she asked.

I liked her enough. It was one in the morning. She was here. She was alive.

'Of course, I do,' I said.

'Because you know… remember how I said I used to sing when I was in Taiwan.'

I stabbed at a piece of egg.

'There was this man at the club. My mother never really liked him. And…'

'Remember how you said you don't want to talk about unpleasant things tonight?'

'Yes?'

'Let's keep it that way.'

Her body relaxed. She hugged me and drew my head to her chest.

We sat on the couch. The music started from down below, a monotonous procession of bass beats, made even more mindless as they passed through the wooden floor and came to our ears divorced of the accompanying vocals and melodies.

Most of the time, we get angry because that's just what we want. We want to feel angry. Today, I wanted to feel peaceful. I switched on the TV to counteract the noise made by the music.

Michelle told me about a development at her job teaching fifth graders at a private school on the Upper West Side.

'I used to teach only math,' she said. 'But the school asked me if I could help out with Mandarin.'

'Do you like it?'

'I love teaching children,' she said. 'Math and Mandarin. And you? Do you like advertising?'

'Advertising pays the bills,' I said, speaking to Michelle, but continuing my conversation with Emily from two nights ago. 'I went into media planning because I was good at math. It was easy for me to get a work visa at an ad agency. But if you want to know, I have always really wanted to become a diplomat in the foreign services.'

She laughed.

'A diplomat! Wow! But aren't those people super polished? Speak English in a posh accent and all? Are you serious?'

Raj Malik hadn't died.

'Of course, I was joking,' I said. 'You know me. Always playing the clown.'

She laughed. She said she wanted to sleep a little more. I told her I had to send out some emails for work and that I would join her in bed shortly. I sat on the couch. I opened up *Don Quixote* on my Kindle. I turned to the page with the bookmark. Michelle would have enjoyed reading it with me. However, I wanted to be away from her. It would be better for both of us.

'*No todas hermosuras enamoran, que algunas alegran la vista, y no rinden la voluntad.*'

It was true. All kinds of beauty do not inspire love. There were kinds of beauty that only pleased the sight, but did not captivate the affections.

It was a fitting sentiment. My legs fell over the armrest of the couch. I fell asleep.

The Sensitive Policeman

The sun streamed in through the curtains. I looked out of the window. Bright sunlight fell on a water tank, a chimney, the green leaves of a tree, and illuminated every inch of the landscape all the way up to the Chrysler Building. I couldn't see any shadows.

I decided to go for a run. I turned on the TOR client and downloaded an episode of the BBC's 'In Our Time With Melvyn Bragg' podcast from the iTunes store. The latest episode of the podcast dealt with the siege of Tenochtitlan. The episode description said that Tenochtitlan was the defining battle that allowed the Spaniards to make their mark on the continent of South America.

I decided to run along Northern Boulevard. There was every chance that I would survive the speeding cars. If I did, I would run over Queensboro Bridge. I would then cut into the city to go up the pathway by the FDR Drive for approximately a mile, at which point, I would turn back and return to my residence. The five-mile run would last for forty-five minutes, which, by a happy coincidence, was the length of the podcast.

The podcast was neatly divided into topical segments that heightened the drama of the story. When the pace threatened to lag, Melvyn interrupted the academic who was at fault and kept the story moving along.

In the fifteenth century, an army of Spanish soldiers had sailed upon Tenochtitlan, the city of the Aztecs. They had been impressed with what they saw. Melvyn started the podcast by reading aloud the words of one of the soldiers on the boat that had approached Tenochtitlan. 'The great towers, temples and buildings rising from the water all made of stone seem like an enchanted vision,' the man had written. 'We are not entirely sure that this is not a dream.'

By the time I had run over Queensboro Bridge, the Spaniards had gained an upper hand in the battle for Tenochtitlan. By the time I had returned home, the Spaniards had won the war. They had plundered gold, silver and sandalwood not only in Mexico, but across the entire continent of South America. Melvyn signed off. However, he had left me wanting to know more. I turned on the TOR client and performed a Google search for the siege of Tenochtitlan.

A photo of a woman came up on the first page. The image was that of an Aztec woman called Malinalli Tenépal. The Wikipedia blurb said she was known as Doña Marina to the Spanish. After Cortés had won the war, she slept with him and mothered the first child of mixed race in the South American continent.

She had long hair that fell down the sides of her angular face. She had dark eyes. The bridge of her nose was sharp and elevated. Her lips were curved, yet distinct from one another. Each of the features on her face was severe.

I closed the lid of the laptop. I recalled a face that was not so very different from that of Doña Marina…

I was five years old. Mrs Clarkson had come to the kitchen. She stood by the granite countertop. A pair of red salt-and-pepper shakers rested against the white tiled wall.

'What are you doing?'

She had slapped me.

'Oh, you sick child…playing with my lingerie. My lingerie! I should have known. I had told Dick not to bring trash into the house…'

She had caught me by the arm and taken me to the laundry room. She plugged in the iron. I closed my eyes as it hissed with menace.

Drops of sweat fell from my forehead into my eyes. I began to shiver. I clutched the cushion tightly. Like Mohammed Ali's right hand hook to George Foreman in Kinshasa, the memory had come out of nowhere. It had socked me on the sides of my head.

I felt two arms encircle me.

'Good morning,' Michelle said.

'You startled me,' I said.

I unwound my fingers so that there was no longer a fist. Michelle kissed me.

I put on the coffee. I poured granola, blueberries and strawberries in two bowls, and smothered them with generous portions of Greek yogurt. I squeezed out some honey from the bottle. The breakfast looked as good as it would taste.

'You didn't come and lie down next to me last night,' Michelle said.

'I guess I fell asleep on the couch,' I said. 'I must have been tired. It's the heat.'

Michelle was dressed in a small T-shirt and panties. The serpent of temptation raised its hood within me. I wanted to take her to the bedroom again.

Then my eyes filled with the Zen-like mist that for a few seconds first thing every morning makes things appear just like they are. I remembered Michelle's comment from the previous day. I recalled how this seemingly gentle woman could be capable of a cool and pointed cruelty.

And so I put the bedroom idea on hold.

Besides, I was eager to collect the *Daily News* from the doorstep. I wanted to see if I had made it to the headlines.

However, I wanted to open the newspaper alone. I didn't want Michelle to observe the quickening of breath, the hushed wait for the pun in the headline, and the relentless rereading of the article.

'You really like Buddhism,' Michelle said. She was standing by my bookshelf.

'Yes,' I said. 'I am totally into, you know, the Buddha.'

She passed her eyes over the row of books on the middle shelf. Alan Watts. The Dhammapada. The Dalai Lama. Sogyal Rinpoche. The eight volumes of the Buddha by Osamu Tezuka. And eleven other books that, in their own way, tried to explain the Four Noble Truths.

She picked up a book from a lower shelf. It was a copy of *Charlie y la Fábrica De Chocolate*.

'I'm sorry,' I said.

Michelle's father had been killed in an incident in a chocolate factory in Taipei. He had been filling an eight-foot-deep tank with hot chocolate when he was hit by a mixing blade. The blow was fatal. I felt bad for Michelle. She couldn't even watch *Willy Wonka & the Chocolate Factory* without feeling as though she were watching *The Silence of the Lambs*.

'I am going to be late,' she said. 'I should be going now so that I can change in time to get to school.'

'Me too,' I said. 'I have a lot going on at work. In fact, I think I might be working late tonight.'

'How late?'

'I'll call you,' I said.

As I saw her off at the doorstep, I picked up the *Daily News*. I hoped that she hadn't observed how my hands had trembled.

I had done it. My actions had made the front page of the *Daily News*.

'Dead Wrong for Each Other' the headlines screamed in that large red font only otherwise used to display phone numbers during infomercials.

Unlike the headline, the article itself was devoid of opinion. It was written in a clear and articulate manner and covered all the basic facts.

A twenty-year-old ad agency executive Emily Hayes has been found stabbed to death in her apartment on Saturday. She had been stabbed over and over. Less than twenty-four hours later, her boyfriend Raj Malik was found also dead in his Midtown East apartment.

The superintendent of Emily's building discovered her body when she opened the door for a scheduled visit from the exterminator.

'I knocked on the door repeatedly,' she said, 'and there was no answer. I tried the door open and what I saw was terrible. You can't explain it. Emily was the nicest girl. Who would want to do this to her?'

'I don't want to comment on an ongoing investigation,' said Officer Crisafi of the NYPD. However, sources have confirmed that a sticker displaying the logo of the popular social network MyFace was found next to Raj's body. It is still unclear if this particular finding carries any significance.

I turned the page. There was an article about a fifteen-year-old girl who had committed suicide. She had thrown herself in front of an oncoming train at the Huguenot station in Staten Island. She had been bullied by her classmates on MyFace after having sex with two football players. She had ended her life by stepping backwards off the railway platform in front of a shocked classmate. Her last words were, 'Finally, it's over.'

The world is divided into three kinds of people. There are those who are able to suffer in silence. Like the fifteen-year-old girl in Staten Island, there are those who are not able to suffer in silence. And there are those who fight back. Che Guevara had fought back. Gandhi had fought back. I would fight back.

I placed a pot of water to boil on the stove. I cut a few slices of ginger and threw them into the pot. When the water began to boil, I added sugar, milk and tea leaves. I poured the tea through a strainer into my tea cup that had an image of Homer Simpson embossed on its side.

I took my tea along with the newspaper into the bathroom. I sipped deeply. The hot liquid stirred my bowels. I rustled the paper and turned the page. There was a majesty involved in the ceremony of reading the news from a printed newspaper in the bathroom. It was one that could never be derived from the more utilitarian laptop or iPad.

I didn't need to see the weather page to find out if there would be policemen in my forecast today. With Emily and Raj dying in two days, the chance of policemen was 100 per cent. It was important that I wear the right T-shirt to the office.

In America, your T-shirt, like your ringtone, screensaver or MyFace cover image, had become an important medium that you could use to express who you were as a person.

I thought of wearing the T-shirt that had an image of the Buddha. But what would happen if the policeman was Super Irish or Super Italian? What if he was the kind of person who placed Buddhism in a fuzzy and nebulous category of 'world religions' that also included Islam? Today, the Buddha presented a risk that was simply too enormous to take.

I decided to wear a T-shirt that said, 'I bowl. What's your superpower?' It had an image of a bowling ball and a glass of beer. This T-shirt conveyed the message that I was a fun-loving American who didn't stab people in his spare time. The T-shirt also accentuated the differences between Osama and myself. That bearded assassin might have watched porn. But he would never pursue other all-American activities like bowling and having a beer.

There were no policemen at the Jackson Heights station or for that matter at the subway on 28th Street and Park Avenue. I stopped by the coffee stall on the pavement. It was run by a Greek man who spent his weekends playing a guitar at Greek weddings.

Normally, he had a wry remark to make about the weather. If it was sunny, he would say, 'I brought the sun out for you.' If it was raining, he would point to a blade of grass on the side of the pavement and say, 'My flowers need the water.'

However, today, he was upset that the Germans had defeated the Greeks in the Euro Cup. He had hoped for a result that was the direct opposite. He had hoped that the Greek football team would be able to exact revenge for the austerity measures that Angela Merkel had imposed on his country.

'That bastard referee,' he said. 'He gave two yellow cards. If I could go to Poland right now, I would kill him.'

He made a punching motion and followed it up with a stabbing action. I smiled. I reflected on how even the most genial of us can be moved to murderous acts.

I had guessed correctly. There was a policeman in the office. He wasn't dressed in uniform. He did not carry a heavy assortment of keys, flashlights and guns. All he wore was a dark-grey suit with a striped tie.

'Arjun,' Brett said. 'This is Detective Crisafi.'

I shook the detective's hand. In America, shaking hands firmly is one of the ways you can show people that you are a real man. Other ways include riding a Harley-Davidson, shouting 'huge' at sports bars and never confessing to loving the poetry of Emily Dickinson in public.

'He's here to ask questions about Emily.'

'Terrible,' I said. 'Terrible. I read the *Daily News*. I just can't believe what has happened.'

'But before you talk to the detective, I was wondering if you know...'

Brett had the shamed look of a man who is conscious of a breach in etiquette.

'I was wondering if you could speak to the folks from M&Ms? They are here to talk about the performance of their MyFace campaign. Detective, I am sorry if I sound callous in the face of such tragedy...but they are our biggest client. Would it put you out too much if you could talk to the other employees in the office in the meantime?'

'Of course, of course,' the detective said. He was an American policeman. He would not want to come in the way of the workings of the free market.

'Go right ahead,' he said.

I followed Brett into the conference room. I carried my notebook into the meeting. I was a compulsive note-taker in the workplace. I could not let my absent-mindedness trespass into my professional life. If I missed a deadline at work, my forgetfulness could quite possibly result in ridicule, a firing, or worse, the loss of a work visa and immediate deportation.

Normally, my mouth goes dry as I walk into a client meeting. Phantasms of worst-case scenarios not concrete enough to be specific, but strong enough to invoke terror, course through my mind. I open my mouth, but find that someone has scraped at my throat with sandpaper. I cannot speak.

But today, I walked in like that paragon of American confidence, Clint Eastwood. I spoke in a clipped staccato. I answered questions from the corner of my mouth. I might have even narrowed my eyes. I was invincible. The marketing personnel from M&Ms were visibly impressed.

'I told you about the Oriental in the media department,' Brett said. 'He will save you a lot of money.'

I raised my hand. 'Guilty as charged,' I said.

Brett and I had rehearsed this interaction on many occasions. We always succeeded in inducing the desired reaction. The uneasy chuckling at Brett's politically incorrect remark, followed by bellows of laughter at my easy acceptance.

'I like this guy,' the starched blue shirt said.

In America, if you give a signal that it is all right to be politically incorrect, white businessmen feel more relaxed. They chuckle. They even chortle. They like you more. And this is important. To succeed in the workplace, it is critical that you gain the approval of white businessmen.

The critics might say that I did well because Raj Malik wasn't there in the room. However, the truth was that even if there were a thousand Raj Maliks smirking at me from their chairs, I would have conquered. This was a moment in time manufactured by god just so that I could shine. I passed through the slides masterfully. The red laser pointer danced like a whirling dervish as I examined different points from all possible angles. When I was done, I flicked at an imaginary speck of dust on my sleeve.

'Thanks so much. That was really good,' said another blue shirt. 'Can you email us the presentation?'

I said that I could.

'So, in your opinion, MyFace is a strong medium that actually works?'

I thought about Emily and Raj.

'Yes, it does,' I said.

The detective had just finished talking to our creative director, Annabelle. She should have seemed scared. After all, two of her colleagues had just been stabbed to death. But her eyes were bright, as though they were auditioning for the role of a lighthouse.

We are always more excited than alarmed when we listen to tales of people killing each other. This is not a sickness that has come over us in recent years. It has always been that way. In the olden days, the Romans paid money to watch gladiators kill each other. Today, *Gladiator* is among the top 100 highest-grossing movies of all time. We don't merely put up with the killers in our society. We need them.

The detective entered my office. He reminded me of a reflection in a funhouse mirror. Everything about him tended to thinness. He had a long, stretched-out face. His eyebrows were sparse. His moustache was slender.

He sat down with an easy grace. The chair didn't even swivel on its wheels. He took out a pack of cigarettes from the inside pocket of his jacket. He sighed and looked at me without saying a word.

'I don't smoke,' I said.

I had smoked twenty cigarettes a day while I was in India. But I had given up the habit within a few days of setting foot in America.

Before I had arrived in America, I had thought that smokers in the country spent their spare time delivering clever lines to blondes over martinis. However, I soon discovered that Hollywood movies were not doing a good job of depicting American society accurately. Leave alone standing next to a drink, smokers in America were made to stand outside bars. They were made to huddle with their kind in small chambers at airports.

I hadn't wanted to be a part of this low-caste and ostracized segment of American society. I had wanted to belong to the mainstream. And like any god-fearing American citizen, I had started to do cocaine.

'However, if you want to have a cigarette, I could place that T-shirt at the bottom of the door. You know, so the smoke doesn't go out…'

'Well,' he said. 'Thank you for your offer. But that would mean breaking the law.'

'It would?' I said. My accent became even more Indian as I pretended to be completely ignorant. 'Oh, I didn't know. You see, in India…'

'Is that where you're from? India?'

I nodded.

'I've always loved *The Guide*.'

I was surprised. He hadn't said he liked the Taj Mahal. Or chicken vindaloo. He had named a work of art that fairly grasped at the essence of the Indian soul. I was impressed. But I wasn't impressed enough to confess.

'So when did you get here, Mr…'

'Please.' I said. 'Call me Arjun. Two years ago.'

'And you like it here? America treating you all right?'

Before 9/11, I would have given a more nuanced answer to this question. I would have said, 'I really like it in America. It is the only country in the world where a man can move in and find an apartment, a job and, if he so desires, friends, in a matter of a few weeks.

'However,' I would have added, 'there are times, when I wake up in the morning and watch the political commentators shouting inanities at each other on cable news shows. I look at all the fuss that's made about some idiot winning a lottery ticket. At such moments, I can't help wonder as to what kind of a country we are going to become.' I would have paused for breath and continued, 'Why, just this morning, I was walking on Lexington Avenue. I saw a woman with a cane. She was blind. After I had walked by her, I saw a man. He was also using a cane, but that was only because he was so fat that he couldn't walk without support. At times like these, I can't help but feel that all might not be well with the state of the union.'

I would have said all this.

But after 9/11, the entire country had become like a mother-in-law. Now, even the slightest criticism was unacceptable.

So all I said was, 'I like it here. America is the only country in the world where a man can move in and find an apartment, friends and someone to date in a matter of a few weeks.' And I added, 'This is my home. If America ever played India in a football match at the Olympics, I would want America to win.'

'I see,' he said, draping his long fingers over his knees. 'And you came to America ...'

'Let's see,' I said. 'I came here two years ago. It was when the Yankees had won the World Series.'

Having a ready stock of sporting references was important to achieving success in America.

I loved tennis. This was fortunate, for it meant I was already well prepared to converse in the higher echelons of American society. I did not follow baseball or football. One was boring. The other's obsession with territorial conquest reminded me of war. However, I had a rudimentary knowledge of these everyday sports. They were useful even as I climbed the lower rungs of American society.

My words had the desired impact. He relaxed. He smiled.

'But,' I said, now building on this minor triumph, 'you could say that I was always American.'

'You could?'

'Yes, well, you see, my father is American.'

'Ah …'

I didn't want him to think of a disillusioned man in downtown Karachi plotting an attack on the Statue of Liberty.

So I added, 'My father is from Iowa. His parents had immigrated to America many years ago from Poland.'

'Really?'

'He used to work for the Voice of America radio channel. He came to India in the eighties for an assignment. He never left.'

'And he met your mother while in India?'

'No, he was already married while in America. He moved to India with his wife.'

Mrs Clarkson had stayed on with her husband in India, even though, if one were to judge by her constant refrains, she had never really come to like the country.

'So you're an American citizen.'

'Well,' I said. 'Not really. I was adopted. Mr Clarkson adopted me when I was four. He was paying a visit to my orphanage. We formed an instant connection.'

I had been adopted by a person who didn't have the good sense to process my adoption paperwork properly. If only Mr Clarkson had been savvy enough to bribe the proper government officials, I would be an American citizen today. I wouldn't be a common immigrant on an H1 B work visa.

'How did the whole being adopted thing make you feel?'

'I don't really remember. I was so young. I guess I felt happy I was moving to Delhi, which is such a big city. But what really mattered was that Mr Clarkson gave me the love of a thousand fathers…'

'And his wife?'

'Mrs Clarkson?'

'Yes. Mrs Clarkson.'

The detective perched his fingers on the bridge between his nose and his lips. He seemed genuinely interested. Other than Emily, I have never had a single person take such a profound interest in my life. I was touched. Who would have thought that this jaded New York detective would have such a compassionate side to his personality?

'Mrs Clarkson… she was very nice too.'

I looked away from his eyes. I played with a stapler.

'Why did you come to America?'

I could have spoken about the neighbour's Pomeranian. That was one answer I could have given the detective.

But I gave him the other answer.

'Well,' I said. 'India has a paucity of career choices for young people. If you perform well in your examinations, you're kind of forced to become either a doctor or an engineer. I didn't want to be either. So I applied to a number of communication courses in America. I was lucky enough to get accepted at the New School.'

'A fine institution.'

'Yes,' I said, 'Did you know that it was the most left-leaning media institution in all of America?'

He didn't know. Or seem to care. This spark of knowledge didn't light him up.

'And as soon as I graduated, I joined CJ&R …'

'That seems to have worked out well for you. Brett tells me you are one of his best employees.'

'He is a generous man,' I said.

Detective Crisafi sat back in his chair.

'Now, Mr…'

'Arjun.'

'Arjun. I am sure you are aware of what happened to Emily and Raj…'

I wasn't about to lie to this man, who had taken a keen interest in my personal life.

'Yes,' I said. 'I had a lot of respect for Emily. She was one of the best account executives that I have ever worked with.'

'And Raj?'

'I didn't know him that well.'

'Did you know that they were going out?'

'Not till Brett told me. I was surprised.'

'Yes,' said the detective. 'Many people I spoke to seem to have had the same reaction. It appears that even their MyFace profiles had not been updated to reflect their relationship status.'

'Ah,' I said.

He took out a small notebook and clicked on a ballpoint pen.

'Arjun, do you remember what you were doing on Sunday night?'

'Sunday night? I was at home…you know watching *The Simpsons*.'

'Were you with someone?'

'Not that I can remember,' I said. 'No.'

'And how about Monday?'

'I went home from work directly,' I said.

'And you were alone.'

I cleared my throat. It was the gentlemanly thing to do.

'I was with someone,' I said. 'Name of Michelle … my girlfriend.'

I hoped that he would see that I was a normal person and not the lonely, brooding killer-type of personality. I was a normal American, someone who actually had a girlfriend. I made a mental note to use the words 'Michelle' and 'girlfriend' together in the same sentence as often as possible.

'Would you mind if I contacted Michelle if necessary?'

He was not only compassionate, he was also polite. I gave him the number.

'And what time did Michelle come over to your residence?'

'Around eleven…'

'And you were alone before that?'

'I was.'

'At home? Watching television?'

I didn't want to come across like a lazy American who watched six hours of television a day.

'I was reading,' I said. '*Don Quixote.*'

I thought he would appreciate the reference. After all, he was a man who had read *The Guide*. I expected him to start a discussion about intertextuality and meta-theatre. But all he did was close his notebook.

'If I have any further questions,' he said, 'I'll be in touch with you.'

I saw him off to the elevator. He shook my hands. He had distantly cooled off since the start of the conversation. He didn't even say take care. This worried me. Getting a 'take care' at the end of a conversation was a basic constitutional right endowed to every person living in America.

Even Judge Edward Cowart of Florida had said 'take care' to Ted Bundy. He said it right after he said, 'You are sentenced to die by an electric current passing through your body.'

'Are you OK?' the Welsh receptionist said. Her name was Hannah. And she spoke with a Welsh accent. The combination was like that of sunlight on a cool spring day. One was content just to bask in her vicinity.

'Yes,' I said.

'You seem worried.'

'I'm not,' I said.

I was lying. She was right. I was worried.

Blotting Out My Transgressions

I decided to get the L28 peanut noodles from L'Annam for lunch. The dish satisfied two of my most important criteria for food. It was deep-fried. And it contained peanuts.

On the street, a woman was wearing a low-cut dress. It was all cut and no dress. I thought that had to be illegal in at least forty-seven of the fifty states. A delivery man stopped his bicycle so that he could hoot in appreciation. He used words that were short. His sighs ran into many syllables.

Austin, the Nigerian doorman, shook his head.

'If your hand or foot causes you to sin, cut it off and throw it away.'

'Who says that, Austin?'

'The good Lord Jesus Christ said that, sir.'

'Ah,' I said.

'Tell me, sir,' Austin said. He pulled on the lapels on his immaculate jacket. As always, he stood tall so that his body was at a perfect right-angle to the ground. He fixed his glare upon me.

'Tell me, sir, do you love the Lord Jesus Christ?'

'I do, Austin. After all, I went to a Catholic school for ten years. Let me tell you, those Jesuit priests are the best in the business.'

'I am glad to hear that, sir,' he said, as though he worked for the recruiting company that had been responsible for placing Jesuit priests in my hometown. 'But tell me one thing. Do you accept Jesus Christ as a god, sir?'

'Sure, I do,' I said.

We already have thirty-three million gods in India. I had no issues in having to worship one more. And besides, you would have to be a highly unimaginative person to not be able to see why people adored Jesus Christ. He healed the sick. Fought against the establishment. Converted water into wine. He was a gentleman of the highest order.

'Do you accept him as your only god?'

'No,' I said. 'But he's up there. I can say that for sure. After all, Austin, he died for our sins.'

'Is Jesus in your top three gods?'

Jesus Christ was not a participant on *American Idol*. However, Austin looked every bit as expectant as a singer waiting for a verdict from a judge. I could not disappoint him, for it would only serve to prolong the conversation.

'Sure, he's in my top three.'

Austin smiled just enough so that it did not appear like gloating.

'Tell me, Austin, if someone commits a really bad sin...like a drug deal, a robbery or a murder? Does Jesus forgive him?'

'If his repentance is genuine, his sins are blotted out. Didn't David say to the Lord, "According unto the multitude of thy tender mercies, blot out my transgressions"?'

'And were David's transgressions blotted out?'

'Yes, they were.'

Jesus went up a notch in my countdown list. After all, if he could help blot out my transgressions, the detective wouldn't be able to find them.

The L28 peanut noodles lunch special satiated my appetite. Now that I was content, I decided to make a two-million-dollar mobile media plan for M&M. It was important that we get their sign off and spend their money while they were still feeling happy and positive.

I logged into my email. There were three messages from Michelle. The first one said, 'Good morning, Sunshine'. The second one said, 'Thinking of you'. I didn't read the third email. I wondered if I should reply saying, 'Thanks for the sexual intercourse last night'. Or perhaps, this was an occasion that called for a more informal communication: 'Thanks for the sex'. Would that be the gentlemanly thing to do? I hadn't read anything or overheard any conversation that would help cast some light on this matter. I decided not to reply. Discretion was the better part of silence.

I opened Microsoft Excel. On a horizontal row, I plotted out the weeks that remained in the year. In a vertical column, I outlined the different media outlets for M&M's media plan. Now I had to decide just when I would run the ads for every media venue and just how much I would spend on each of them. Even as I was designing the plan, I knew that M&M's ad dollars would go to waste. Most mobile advertising companies charged advertisers for clicks. And because smartphones are so small, most people click on ads more often by mistake than they do on purpose. This meant that most of M&M's ad budget would be spent on people who hadn't intended to click on their ad. I wasn't confident that the marketing plan would work. However, I was completely confident that we could show M&M's that their marketing plan had worked.

I stepped into the elevator. I should have felt a sense of mild accomplishment, the kind a man feels when he has managed to spend two million dollars. But all I felt was fear. Even as I had made the plan, I could not stop thinking about the detective. How quickly had his demeanour changed! He had begun by asking sensitive questions, as though I were on a therapist's couch. However, towards the end, he had spoken to me in a cold manner, as he would to a person sitting in an electric chair.

I needed to go to a quiet place. I needed to think.

With my teenage neighbour playing loud music, I could not go back to my apartment. I would have gladly ridden the elevator up and down the height of the building, if it had continued to offer me solitude. However, a man got into the elevator on the seventh floor. He began to eat an apple. He bit into it with a loud crunch. He went on to tell me that this summer was hot. I did not reply. Till recently, the elevator had been the last bastion of silence in society. But it too had been defeated by the onslaught of senseless thought and mindless conversation.

I crossed Park Avenue and went to Desmond's Tavern. It wasn't as quiet as, say, Antarctica or Google Plus. However, it was definitely one of the quietest places in the world.

Desmond's Tavern was damp. It was dark. Not one person said a word. The pool tables lay untouched and barren. They could have been in North Dakota. A man with thick glasses made me a Famous Grouse with club soda. He might or might not have been Desmond. I didn't ask. I wasn't sure if polite or unnecessary conversation was permitted at Desmond's. A woman with thick glasses peered at a tear in the wallpaper. Woody Guthrie sang a song.

I sipped on the Famous Grouse. The thoughts began to flow.

The detective suspected me of one or both of the murders. He was not making polite conversation when he had asked me what I thought about Emily and Raj. He was suspicious. And I hadn't done anything to allay his doubts. I had no alibis. I had spent all of my time watching TV at home. My fictional alibi was so boring that it was unbelievable. I had done little else than live the life of the average American, watching TV for six hours a day.

I got up to use the restroom. I found that I had to grasp slightly at the table to balance myself. In my agitated state, I had sipped deeply upon the drink. I had finished it in only a few minutes. Having another drink would in no way contribute to the clarity of my thought process. I left a ten-dollar bill on the counter and stepped back onto Park Avenue.

A dirty beam of light from a street lamp splattered and sprayed on the ground. A homeless person gnawed on a piece of fried chicken. He tore into the leg with a vicious bestiality. He, too, was a murderer. If one were to judge by the way he was gnawing at the meat, he was a killer of a Neanderthal disposition. But there was no detective following him.

I am a vegetarian. In my opinion, in the hierarchy of life, a man is on the same level as that of a chicken, pig, fish or cow. You can kill a man, just as you can kill an animal. And because you wouldn't eat a man, there is no reason for you to have to eat an animal.

Austin had once told me that it was wrong to equate non-vegetarianism with cannibalism. He said that the Bible placed human beings at the apex of all creation. He wasn't stating anything new. The ancient Hindu text of creation, the Manusmriti, also said human beings could kill animals without compunction because they had a more advanced intellect.

A fat man jostled against me. He was accompanied by his also-fat friend. They walked into a restaurant. A young man wearing a white shirt with blue stripes came out of the door. His hand was already pinching his girlfriend's buttock. A woman wearing New Balance sneakers stumbled and tripped on the sidewalk. She was trying to walk while sipping her coffee. Like a dog, zebra or lion, these people too were wholly occupied in the pursuit of instant gratification. No matter what Austin or Manu said, I could not see how they were different from animals.

I had started off the evening wanting to think about the problem posed by the deaths of Emily and Raj. I was no closer to a solution. And yet, here I was thinking about irrelevant matters like the hierarchy of man in the animal world. This indiscipline in thought was not on account of any failing in my mental training. It could entirely be explained by external circumstances.

I was hungry. Mine was a deep and profound hunger. It could not just be satisfied by something that merely gave calories. It could only be satisfied by a food that delivered a wholesome experience. I needed to inhale the fragrance of cinnamon, taste the sharp bite of galangal and be satiated by the sweetness of coconut milk. I needed Malaysian food. More specifically, I needed roti canai from the Sanur restaurant in Chinatown.

There were no policemen at the Canal Street station. Canal Street was not crowded. With the setting of the sun, the desires of people wanting to buy cheap Gucci knockoffs and Ray-Ban sunglasses had also dimmed. The persimmons on the street stalls lit up the carts with their orange colour. I gulped down my saliva. I began to walk faster towards the restaurant.

I stopped in front of 401 Broadway. I noted with approval that the building was made of solid brownstone. I wanted it to stand forever and ever. After all, it was the building where my green card was being processed. My legal team was made up of a kindly Jewish man and a maternal Indian woman. I thought of their alert and intelligent eyes. I felt reassured.

My lawyers were on the fifth floor. A memory spoke to me from seven months ago. The memory told me that there was another floor in this building. I pressed on the button that said Suite 711. The door buzzed. I stepped inside.

A lady with a pink skirt greeted me with a bow on the seventh floor. I handed her forty dollars. She escorted me to a locker room. A tall Asian man sipped on green tea. As I took off my clothes, a Chinese woman sang to the plucking of a stringed instrument on the radio. She sang in a high-pitched voice. She was quite possibly very happy about something. Or she was very sad. I couldn't tell.

An attractive woman in her thirties asked me to enter a room. I lay down on a granite slab. She turned on a hot shower. She scrubbed me gently with a soft sponge. She asked me about my day. I told her that work was tough. I added that life was tough. She gave me her complete attention. Even my therapist was never this tuned in to what I had to say. This attentive lady said she would do her best to make me happy. I believed her. Unlike all the other women I had known, she would never rebuke, hurt or abandon me.

The lady dried me off. She asked me to enter another room. My head did not spin when I lay my head against the pillow. I had sobered down. She kneaded the muscles on my upper back. There was a shifting of tectonic plates. I took comfort in the relief that followed.

My thoughts began to settle like flakes in a snow globe. I began to assemble them in the proper order.

Emily had died. As had Raj. And if one were to go by the sudden change in manner of the sensitive detective, I was what the novels and TV shows called 'a prime suspect' in both the murders. I had no alibi for Emily's murder. As for Raj, Michelle had come to my apartment two hours too late.

The masseuse had begun to hum a song. I asked her what it was. She told me that it was an old Buddhist song that was to this day sung in parts of Osaka.

'The Buddha had achieved nirvana in India,' she said. 'But how come there are no Buddhists in the country?'

It was a good question.

'I don't think that Buddhism disappeared from India,' I said. 'It has merely been co-opted into Hinduism.'

'Co-opted?' Her fingers dove into the slope of my back.

'One can fight another value system that is alien to one's own in an attempt to make it disappear. Like, for example, the people of Afghanistan are fighting Americans with machine guns and suicide bombers.'

'Bad,' she said. 'Very bad.'

'Not only bad,' I said, 'it's also pointless. It's far more effective to co-opt the beliefs of another value system and make them a part of one's own.'

'So the Hindus simply accepted everything that the Buddhists had to say?'

'Precisely,' I said. 'And Buddhism disappeared.'

The lady asked me to turn around. She massaged my stomach, my neck and the sides of my cheek. However, as I lay on my back, it was impossible for both of us not to see through this farce of a massage. And soon enough, she came to the point and placed her hand suggestively on what the towel had covered only a few seconds ago.

Stop me if I have told you this before, but I firmly believe in what I had told Mr Clarkson all those years ago. I had told him that I want to be a gentleman. So I will not describe what followed in minute detail. As she moved her hands, she made little moaning noises. I felt my mind being carried away from the concerns of this material world. At first, my head was full of senseless thoughts. Then, it became blank. At the moment I came, I saw her lips, the diamond-shaped earring on her ear and the white towel that was neatly folded near my feet. My first contact with the real world was one of illumination. I recalled how the *Daily News* article had ended.

However, sources have confirmed that a sticker displaying the logo of the popular social network MyFace was found next to Raj's body. It is still unclear if this particular finding carries any significance.

However, this particular finding could be made to carry significance. The solution was simple. And because it was simple, it was beautiful. I could make the police believe that Emily and Raj were but the first victims of a serial killer who used the MyFace social network to identify and kill his victims. Their deaths were not personal acts of revenge. They were as de-personalized as a phone call one made to the customer-service department of a corporation. The murderer had pressed one for Emily. And two for Raj.

I got up from the bed. I placed sixty dollars in the hands of the woman.

'Wait.' She laughed. 'Let me use towel.'

'I have a towel at home,' I said.

On Broadway, a man stuck out his tongue. He inspected it closely in a rear-view mirror on the handlebar of his bicycle. A girl punched a boy in his stomach. She seemed delighted at having been teased. People ordered chicken rice from the halal carts. They stepped away from the cart as soon as the vendor acknowledged their order. There was no reason to spend one second more than necessary next to a grill that was only slightly hotter than the ambient temperature.

I wondered as to who should be the next victim of the MyFace killer. I paid great attention to the individual details of the people around me. I noticed in vivid detail the black mole under the eyes of an old man, the bangs on the forehead of a blonde woman, the already lifeless eyes of a subway commuter. I felt a bond develop between myself and each of these people. It must have been this feeling of interconnectedness that the Buddha had spoken about in the Fire Sermon.

However, I felt that my next victim could not be selected in a random manner. He or she had to deserve the punishment. At the same time, she or he needed to be disassociated from my life, so that the weathervane of suspicion would blow away from me.

I went into a store selling kitchen equipment. They were closing down for the day, but were perfectly happy to sell me a G-2 Chef's Knife for a hundred and two dollars. The flash of anger I felt at having to overpay disappeared as soon as I held the knife. It was a perfect match for the sheath attached to my sacred thread.

I decided to take a walk. I was facing a fairly complex conundrum. I had cleansed my body. Now I needed to clear my mind.

An Alternate Use of Meditation

I decided to walk to the FDR. There, I could sit in the park next to the tennis courts. I could close my eyes and contemplate the identity of my next victim.

The park on the FDR was as quiet as it had been when I had last visited it in January. At the time, a white sheet of snow had covered the tennis courts. As I thought about the snow in the hundred-degree heat, the tennis courts from all those months ago seemed to be from another country. But the tennis courts were the same. It was the snow that had melted and gone away. It was exactly like how New York would stay the same. It was only certain people in New York who were about to go away.

I sat down cross-legged on a bench under a gingko tree. I began to meditate.

For the first fifteen minutes, my mind jumped around like a drunken teenager on a dance floor. Eventually, it sobered up. It settled down. With a singled-minded focus, it began to drill into the past. Midway through the meditation, forgotten grievances began to rise to the top like dead fish do to the surface of the lake. The Buddha had said that if one stared at these slights and viewed them with perfect equanimity, they would leave your being and dissipate into the universe. Eventually, your mind would clear itself of negative thoughts.

However, I would not allow these slights and grievances to escape. Instead, I would latch on the hurt. And I would magnify it a thousand times.

I closed my eyes. The first memory that floated to the surface was the sound of a woman oohing and aahing on Maná's *MTV Unplugged* album. This woman emanates the 'aah' just as Fher Olvera says that the band is about to play a ranchero composition by Alfredo Jimenez.

The woman's aah had irritated me. Hers was not the universal aah of appreciation that one bestows upon an artist. It was a jingoistic aah. It reeked of patriotism. It was similar to the aah I have heard middle-class Indians emit while watching a military procession during the Republic Day parade. These were the Indians who pretended day after day that the slums and the farmers in their country did not exist, who foolishly thought that their country was a rising superpower in the world.

Another memory surfaced.

I had just completed a year in New York. I had decided not to renew the lease on my apartment on 28th and Broadway. There were too many cockroaches in it. In addition, the apartment was situated in the garment district. The owners of the stores in the district were predominantly Indian. They had the characteristically sly eyes of the Gujarati businessman and were involved in the seemingly perennial pursuit of trying to decide if they should slot their fellow humans in the category of 'wholesale' or 'retail'. There are few things as disgusting as the sight of naked commercialism early in the morning.

I had walked to Central Park to look for a new residence. It was an area of Manhattan I particularly liked. There were trees. There were running trails. And the MET had a café with installations by Claes Oldenburg.

I had stopped by a building on 68th Street and Park Avenue. The doorman was Guatemalan. His name was Kevin Santiago. We talked about Rubén Blades, the 'El Cantante'. Kevin seemed to be a good-hearted man who would be sensitive to the needs of others. I had asked him about a vacancy in the building.

He had laughed.

'Why are you laughing?' I was surprised.

'What are you trying to say?'

'All I mean to say is that if you know of anything around…'

'Discount?' Kevin had looked away from me. He turned to an old man whose dog was whiter than his hair. 'Did you hear him? This man wants to stay in this building. And he wants a discount!'

'I never asked for a discount…'

'Go somewhere else, buddy. This building's not for you. It's for, you know, the men who…' He had caressed his thumb against his index finger and made the universal sign for money. He had then closed the door and gone inside to answer the call of another resident. Two babies carved into the gargoyles of the building stared at me with their dark eyes. I will never forget how they had mocked me.

I had waited for Kevin to come back. But he never did. In my entire life, I had never felt as confused as I had at that moment when the heavy door with gold borders had closed on my face. I could not understand what had happened. I could not also comprehend just how I should react to what had taken place.

When a white person is racist towards you, you know the stages through which your body and mind will pass.

At first, you will feel helpless.

After all, in so many ways, you are similar to the white man. You read Chekhov. You love Wimbledon. You don't want to blow up the Empire State building.

But how can you change the colour of your skin?

You brood and stew. The helplessness passes. After it does, you will feel ashamed.

After all, so many people have watched the incident take place. And most people have walked away without comment. The few that are moved to protest are seldom capable of constructive action. In most cases, they cannot feel any emotion that is stronger than pity.

You suppress the shame. You squish it into that black slab of tension that has never stopped pulsing in your body.

A few days pass. It is only now that you will feel angry. Anger is the emotion that receives the most attention in the newspapers and TV stations. But anger comes only much later. By the time you feel it, the world has usually stopped caring.

However, when a person of colour is racist towards you, you feel anger before you feel anything else. How can a person be so stupid to perpetrate the very stereotypes that were created centuries ago to justify colonization and keep the coloured man down?

I had meditated. And god had delivered Kevin Santiago's name to me on a platter. He would have to go.

In the distance, the orange rays of the sun fell on the majestic Brooklyn Bridge. I walked over to the footbridge on Delancey Street and crossed over to the Lower East Side. I stopped at the Starbucks on Allen Street. I took out my laptop from my Manhattan Portage bag, logged into the TOR client and performed a Google search with the terms 'Kevin Santiago MyFace'.

The probability of finding a doorman on a social network was low. But Kevin Santiago was on MyFace. The knave that he was, he had posted a photo of himself in his uniform. The last time I had met him, he had been wearing a purple uniform with gold stripes across the shoulder. In his photo on MyFace, he had on a navy-blue blazer. He had changed buildings. MyFace had automatically tagged the photo with his geo-location and had made it available to the public at large.

Kevin Santiago's photo had been taken in a luxury building near the West Side Highway.

I took the A train to the Columbus Circle station. Kevin Santiago's building was located near 11th Avenue. I would have to walk nine blocks north and cut four blocks west before I arrived at the building.

But before anything, I had to construct an alibi. My intuition told me that if all went according to plan tonight, I would be meeting with the detective tomorrow. I placed my hands on the sculpture of an elephant on Columbus Circle. My brain lit up with the spark of a memory.

One morning, after a meeting with a telecommunications client called Aruba Networks, Jeff Garner had told me about a bar near Columbus Circle. He said I would like the bar as it was 'frequented by a lot of Indians'.

I hadn't asked him any follow-up questions. But he had continued talking anyway.

'It's called the Volstead. It's on 56th Street.'

A bar full of Indians sounded exactly like the bar I needed to find. I walked east on 56th Street for two avenues. Midway through the next block, I saw a glimmer of hope behind a velvet rope. There was a bouncer standing outside what clearly had to be a club. He was gazing at the world with a detached air. He had his nose so high up that he could have been breathing mountain air.

'Excuse me,' I said. 'Do you know of a bar called the Volstead?'

'Yes,' he said. He didn't say anything further. To be fair to him, he had answered my question.

'And just how do you get there?'

'This is it.'

'I want to get in,' I said.

'ID?' he said. His face had hints of eyes, nose and lips. However, it was mainly composed of raised eyebrows.

'Yes,' I said.

'I need to see it,' he said.

I acted surprised.

'Oh, why didn't you say so? You know when people typically want something, they ask a question. A question is usually made up of more than one word. Sometimes, a question even has the word "please" thrown in somewhere.'

He showed human emotion. His eyes glowed.

'You trying to act funny, Mister?'

'No,' I said. 'I was never any good at acting.'

He took a close look at my driver's licence. He handed it back without looking at me. I had made an impression on him. He would remember me tomorrow when the detective showed him my photograph.

I left the pavement and stepped on to carpet. I reflected on just how much I had changed in the last few days. Just last week, I wouldn't have the confidence to even approach a club that was guarded by velvet ropes. But today, I had approached. I had dominated. And I had entered.

The bar didn't have as many Indians as there were Indians in India. But it came close. I sat at the bar. Jay Z communicated with us through tall speakers. He said that he had ninety-nine problems, but a bitch wasn't one. A white boy thumped a shot down next to me. He wore a blue, striped shirt. A tall Indian girl was draped all around him. Like Jay Z, he too seemed to have no problems with the opposite sex.

He asked the bartender for a gin and tonic.

He smiled at me.

'Indian culture is great man,' he said.

'Indeed, it is,' I said.

I waved at the bartender. I ordered a whiskey and soda. I put the glass to my lips and took a deep swig of Indian culture.

I waited till Biggie Smalls had finished saying how when he was dead broke, he had never thought he would be able to play Super Nintendo and Sega Genesis. My work here was done. I had conquered my fears. I had heard an uplifting story of a man coming out of poverty. I had also constructed my alibi.

I made my way to the exit. I pushed open the door. I stepped unnoticed into a cloud of perfume that floated down the block.

Kevin Santiago was on duty. Through the glass doors, I saw him smile in a servile way at one of the residents. I have always had sympathy for the poor people of the world. Their suffering lends the human condition a certain dignity. However, on most occasions when I actually talk to a poor person, I feel repelled. I dislike their overt obsequiousness. I find they are often loud, both in their speech and their music. I find the frank way they stare at the bottoms of women distasteful.

I touched my sacred thread and felt its reassuring weight. I opened my Manhattan Portage bag. I cursed at myself. I had forgotten to pack an 'I found you on MyFace' sticker. I needed to stick that sticker on Kevin Santiago after he died.

I would have to go back to my office to get a MyFace sticker. I did not look forward to the prospect. It was over ninety-five degrees. It was too hot for a man to walk across six avenues.

In New York, it is a far more pleasant prospect to walk in a northwards or southwards direction. Because the distance between the streets is small, the scenery changes often. Many a distraction captures the eye. As a result, the journey is often as pleasant as the moment of arrival at one's destination.

However, a walk eastwards or westwards along a street is an entirely different proposition. The avenues are far apart from one another. One views the different parts that make up the journey not as pleasant diversions, but rather as obstructions that have to be overcome. The effort tires both the body and the mind.

By the time I had walked to the office, I was drenched in sweat. I changed into a spare T-shirt I kept in my office drawer for client dinners. I packed a MyFace sticker in my Manhattan Portage bag and walked back to the luxury condominium. I was tired. The only emotion that fuelled me to further action was anger.

Unlike love, anger is a more amenable emotion. It can easily shift its focus from one object to another. I was angry at myself. A second later, I found that I was angry at the doorman. Now, I truly and really looked forward to killing him.

I threw a stone on the glass façade of the building. Kevin Santiago did not respond. I waited for ten seconds and threw a larger stone. For some reason, the phrase *People who live in glass houses should not throw stones at others* came to my mind.

Kevin Santiago reacted to the second stone. He walked towards the door and pushed it open.

I threw a third stone at the building.

'Hey, you,' he said. He ran at a brisk pace towards me.

I moved into the shadows cast by the trunk of a large tree. I was reasonably sure that I could not be spotted by any of the residents of the buildings around us. He came closer.

'Hello, Kevin,' I said politely.

He looked at me in a puzzled sort of way. He was trying to recognize me. I plunged the knife into the femoral artery of his left leg. For a few seconds, there was another man-made fountain in front of the building. However, it was one that was visible only to me.

But Kevin was a strong man. Most men would have fallen to the ground. Kevin merely stumbled like a drunk. He reached into his pocket and took out his iPhone. He pointed the phone at me and pressed on the screen. I heard the sound of a camera shutter. I stabbed him again, in a more indiscriminate way. He shouted loudly. If he were playing the role of a dying man in a movie, I would have said he was overacting. I slit his throat, not so much to kill him, but to kill his voice. This time around, he fell down. I caught him as he fell to the ground. I stuck the 'I found you on MyFace' sticker on his forehead. His fingers were curled tightly around the white iPhone, the phone that now had my photo in its image library. I needed to get that phone. However, even as I tugged at it, and tried to wrest it loose from his fingers, I heard people come out of the building.

Like a cab driver racing down a street, I broke into an indiscriminate run without any heed for who or what was in front of me. At the intersection with 10th Avenue, I turned around. There was no one following me. I turned right and walked south. The perpendicular change in direction helped me shift the incident that was Kevin's death to another place, another dimension and another point in time.

I entered an Indian deli on 48th Street. The owner was from south India. Before he could even ask me if I was a fellow Tamilian (I am not; I merely have dark skin), I went into the restroom. I wanted to make sure that Kevin Santiago had left no discernible mark on me. There were three small drops of blood on my Alfani leather shoe. But they had already dried in the heat. I scraped them off with my fingernails.

I ordered a glass of tea with milk and cardamom. The milk had been simmering at boiling point for at least a few hours. With the first sip, my body temperature rose at least five degrees above the ambient temperature. The law of radiation necessitates that heat must flow from a hotter object to a cooler one. I began to sweat. I cooled down.

Columbus Circle station was crowded. At first glance, I could see at least three people who looked more suspicious than me. I was ignored by the policemen on duty.

I wondered if Kevin had clicked a photo of me with his iPhone. The answer to this question bore repercussions that were as terrible and final as an earthquake or a tsunami.

I would not be able to sleep tonight.

I poured a generous amount of Famous Grouse into a glass. I made a checklist of things I had to do.

Before anything, I had to clean the Global Chef's knife.

I turned on the faucet. The force of the stream cleansed the blade of the day's events, as though they had never taken place. The lemon-scented detergent accentuated the feeling of goodness. If only Palmolive could also wipe a picture off another man's iPhone.

I had to hide Emily's scarf in a safe location.

The closet was out of the question. It was the first place the police would search. I reached for the top of my bookshelf and got down an ancient Chinese chess set that Mr Clarkson had gifted me as I was leaving for America.

I unlocked the dark-brown box with ornate floral patterns. The two halves opened out to form the chess board. There was a compartment underneath each of the halves. They housed an exquisitely carved collection of wooden chess pieces. The king was an exact likeness of Emperor Chengzu of the Ming dynasty.

Chengzu was the third emperor of the Ming dynasty. He was renowned for sending large fleets of ships around the world. These ships had sailed to south-east Asia, India and Sri Lanka. They had even gone across the Indian Ocean to Africa. They had returned with gold, jewels and artifacts that had been gifted by the kings and queens of the lands they visited. Most famously, they had once returned from Africa with a giraffe. With its long neck and gentle ways, the animal must have indeed been a wondrous sight to behold for the people of China.

I opened a hidden compartment located under the storage place for the emperor, his wife and retinue, and placed the ziploc bag containing Emily's scarf in it. I placed eleven 'I found you on MyFace' stickers over the bag.

I sent a text message to the boy. My flip phone lit up with a quiet and assured light in response.

'Northern and 72nd,' the message said.

I took the elevator down to the lobby of the building. I was about to open the door when I saw a most unexpected sight. Through the glass panel on the door, I could see Detective Crisafi. He was trying to blend into the shadow cast by the canopy of a gingko tree. But he was a white man in a brown neighbourhood. He stood out as clearly as the moon does in a dark sky.

He was clearly suspicious of me. But that did not mean I would change my plans for the evening. I would meet the boy.

In fact, it was now more important than ever that I talk to the boy.

I went back up to my apartment. My neighbour began to play his customary procession of mindless music. This time around, I welcomed the loud beats. They sounded like the soundtrack of a Hollywood action movie. They made me feel as though I was playing a starring role in a scene of consequence. They prompted me to act.

I opened the window and stepped on to the fire escape. It creaked loudly as soon as I put my foot on its black railings. I wondered if I was breaking a New York City law by using this mode of exit. However, I reasoned that the fire escape had been developed for emergencies.

And this was one hell of an emergency.

I descended the wobbly stairs till I was directly above a small space that passed for the garden of my Albanian superintendent. A daisy on the flower bed looked sad. A tomato had died. I backed up on the platform of the fire escape. I jumped over the width of the garden and the adjoining wall.

I landed into a patch of weeds that grew in the backyard of the neighbouring house. It was a large and dilapidated mansion that hadn't experienced human love and attention for what appeared to be hundreds of years. I fought my way through a large clump of rat-tailed grass. I pushed open the heavy gate with both hands and stepped on to 73rd Street. I was an entire block away from Detective Crisafi, who was presumably still staring at the entrance of my building with his eager, open eyes.

I had just finished dusting off the mud from my trousers when the boy arrived. Light travels faster than sound. However, the boy had managed to twist this fundamental law of nature. He played his music at such a loud volume that I heard him first. I only saw his red SUV much later.

'There's something else,' I said when we had finished our customary exchange.

He immediately sensed I had something important to say. He turned down the volume. I stared at his patent brown leather shoes.

'Tell me,' he said.

'I need a fake passport.'

'For what?' he asked. It was a reasonable question. I regretted I would not be able to provide an honest answer. I felt bad I couldn't say, 'You see, Fernando, the strangest thing has happned. I have made the unfortunate mistake of killing three people. For some reason, the police are suspicious of me. I want to be able to leave the country at a moment's notice.'

Instead, I gave that most Indian of answers.

'Just,' I said. 'Just like that…'

If one billion Indians are able to live with one another in that tightly cramped nation in relative harmony, it is because they have learned to answer pointed questions with this most non-committal and evasive of answers.

Why did you vote for the BJP?

Why did you covet his wife?

Why did you choose onion toppings for the pizza?

Just.

'I understand,' he said. 'You want a passport in case shit goes down… or has shit already gone down?'

'Precisely,' I said. I resisted the urge to take his multiple-choice test.

'I know where you're coming from,' he said. 'One country is too small for a man to call his home.'

He pulled over by a house. A dog whined from the yard. He lit a joint. The paper crackled and came to life for an instant. Then it too calmed down as it was numbed by the thick, sweet smoke that spread like a fog over the insides of the car.

'Hell, even one world is too small for a man to call his only home. Especially for people like us… who are battling with life… I can tell, man, you are battling through something.'

'Ah,' I said.

'The Aztecs,' the boy said. He coughed.

'The Aztecs?'

'Yes, you know, from my home town.'

'Ah, those Aztecs,' I said. 'Right on.'

'They felt that this one world was too small for them. So when they died, they went to another world.'

'Like up in the sky?'

'There's nothing up in the sky, yo,' he said. 'Except maybe B-52 bombers and shit.'

'Ah,' I said.

I dragged on the joint and handed it back to him. I looked outside the window. I saw a car gliding down the street as smoothly as an alligator does when going down a swamp.

'The best warriors among the Aztecs...you know, the ones that killed others and got killed, went to a land in the East after they died.'

'They did?'

'They called it the land of the shining sun. Isn't that where you're from...the East?'

'I am,' I said. 'Though I wouldn't go as far as to call India the land of the shining sun. There are lots of people in India on whom the sun doesn't shine. I estimate that number at around 700 million people.'

But the inequality of wealth distribution in India did not seem to interest him.

'The warriors that went to this Land of the East, they got reborn as hummingbirds.'

I tried to picture myself hovering over a flower looking for nectar.

The boy crushed the joint in the ashtray with a single-minded focus. It appeared as though he were extracting vengeance on the joint. When the last ember had died down, he made a smooth return to more worldly matters.

'This will cost you,' he said.

'I have the money,' I said.

'Bueno,' he said.

'I also have a question. How long does this take? For example, can you get it to me in the next two or three days?'

'That will cost you even more,' he said. He named a rather large sum, a number that would be most ungentlemanly to mention aloud.

'I have the money.'

'You'll need an Indian passport, I assume,' he said. 'If you ever want to return to your homeland in a hurry.'

'Can't I have an American passport?' I asked.

I wasn't being greedy. One should always look to fulfil one's aspirations through an alternate identity. Otherwise, what was the point? Clark Kent flew around the world. Peter Parker spun webs. I would be an American.

'No use having an American passport, bro,' he said. 'You'll need a visa to get back to India. And that shit's difficult to get. It takes a lot of time. The Indian government's really messed up in that way.'

'And in other ways too.'

I laughed. Tom Friedman always wrote about how India was competing with China and Brazil in the world economy. The truth was that the Indian government had a bad reputation for doing business, not only among major corporations, but even among the members of the underworld.

'Unless you want to go to Mexico,' he said.

'Would I stand out in Mexico?' I asked.

He laughed. 'With your dark hair, dark skin and shit, you could pass for a chola,' he said. 'But yes, you will stand out. Even though you speak Spanish and shit. Which is cool and all. I get a kick out of it. If you didn't speak Spanish, I don't know if I would really be helping you.'

It wasn't a ringing endorsement.

'Indian it is,' I said. 'When can you have it ready for me?'

'I'll text you,' he said. He pushed on a button that unlocked my door.

'You cool walking home from here?'

'Yes,' I said. I could not only walk, I could scale, jump and climb my way back home.

The doorbell rang a few minutes after I had jumped in through the window of the living room.

I closed the chess box and placed it back on the bookshelf. Had the detective observed me sneak out of the window and meet the boy? Was he here to search the apartment and arrest me for the possession of cocaine?

The doorbell rang again. There is no poet who has written a verse that yearns for the repeated rings of a doorbell. When it is sounded more than once, a doorbell threatens.

I looked through the keyhole. Blue fingernails threw black tresses of hair back over a long neck. There was a light scar near the chin. It was Michelle. I opened the door.

'What are you doing here?'

'Well, I've been texting you and calling you all day.'

'Really?' I said. 'I broke my phone. It was an unfortunate accident.'

'Oh?' she said. She didn't sound entirely convinced.

'Yes,' I said. 'It was a new iPhone.'

I must have succeeded in looking sufficiently dejected.

'I am so sorry.' She stood up on her toe and kissed me on the cheek.

'You are happy to see me, aren't you? Or would you rather I leave?'

I did not want to create a scene in the hallway.

'I am always happy to see you,' I said.

'Lies,' she said. She tried to sound angry, but she smiled. I could not help notice how pretty she looked. She had on a blue top with a green flower pinned at the chest. Blue diamond-shaped patterns were stitched along the length of her skirt.

'I'm sorry,' I said. 'It's just I've had a lot to think about at work.'

Her features softened. She ruffled my hair.

'You poor boy,' she said.

She hugged me. Then, she placed my hand on her breast.

'Does this distract you sufficiently? Or are you still thinking about stuff?'

If I were to be honest, I was still distracted. I was trying to imagine what the headline in the *Daily News* would be in the morning.

Michele was wearing boots with sharp heels. They made a hard, knocking sound every time she stepped on the wooden floor.

I was conscious I was losing the moral high ground with my neighbour. He would take the sound created by Michelle's walking not as a temporary aberration, but as a provocation. And he would retaliate.

I was right. By the time Michelle had walked the length of the hallway and sat down on the couch, my neighbour had increased the volume of the music to a level where it pulsed not with bass but with sheer revenge.

'Aiee, that's loud!' Michelle said. 'How do you put up with this music?'

'I just get angry and grow an ulcer inside.'

'Why don't you call 311?'

I had called 311 in the past. They called the police. The last thing I needed now in my life was the police in my apartment.

'I've tried. There's no point. The police come much later…or not at all.'

'Well, you shouldn't have to put up with this.'

She was right. I shouldn't have to, especially in a society of humans.

But the people below were divorced from the human condition. Like animals, they were living entirely in the here and now, with all their senses involved in the fulfillment of immediate pleasures. They did not have the mental capacity to move beyond the here and now and contemplate a future, where all humans were aware of their interconnectedness to one another and were sensitive towards each other's needs.

'Hey…' Michelle said.

'I'm sorry.'

'You're not listening to me,' she said.

'I am.'

'No, you're not,' she said.

'I think you're wrong,' I said.

'You know what I think. I think after last night, you're not interested in me anymore!'

'That's nonsense,' I said. 'You know that's not true.'

I sat beside her. With my lips and my tongue, I displayed active interest in her. She unzipped my pants. She did that thing with her fingers. Just as I thought matters were going to progress, she leapt away from me as though I had the smallpox.

'You've been with someone!'

'Yes,' I said. 'I've been with you.'

I should have agreed when the lady at the massage parlour offered to towel me down.

'That's not true,' she said.

'Michelle,' I said. 'What are you talking about? I got home early this evening. And I was you know, thinking of you…'

It was the right thing to say. She had been angry, even disgusted a moment earlier. But now she displayed that chameleon-like ability women have to change their facial expressions.

'You mean that?' she said.

'Of course,' I said. 'I am surprised you would even doubt it.'

'I wanted to ask you something,' she said. She had lost all interest in my penis. To its credit, it accepted this altered state of interest with a quiet and fading grace.

'But you'll probably say no.'

I felt the need to reach for my sacred thread. I resisted the urge.

'Tell me,' I said. 'I want to hear how you feel.'

I had once overheard a tall man talking to his friend on the subway. This man had a goatee on his face. He had been wearing a top hat. He was obviously a man who seemed to understand the workings of the modern world. He had told his friend that women love to be asked how they felt.

'Oh, Arjun,' she said, 'it would really be fun to get away for the weekend.'

'It would,' I said.

However, on cooler reflection, I saw why this would be a bad idea. If the *Daily News* picked up on the death of Kevin Santiago, I would have a short window of time to further the myth of the MyFace killer. I would only have a few days to connect with new people over MyFace. Then, over the weekend, I would have to meet my new friends. I would have to kill them. I could not put this plan of action off till the following weekend. I could not afford to fall out of the news cycle.

'Oh,' I said. 'I remembered something about this weekend.'

She had already begun to look upset. I had to talk fast. I could not let her disappointment harden into bitterness.

'I don't know if I ever told you this,' I said. 'I was in an orphanage for the first few years of my life.'

'I didn't know that about you,' she said. 'Are you serious or are you…'

'I am serious,' I said. 'I would never joke about anything like this.'

She moved forward so that she was now seated on the edge of the couch. She no longer seemed disappointed.

'The director of the orphanage was like a father to me. Unfortunately, he died when I was very young. And you know the strangest thing…his death anniversary falls on Friday. I'd really like to spend Friday evening alone. Just so that I could pray that his soul finds eternal peace and salvation.'

'Oh, Arjun,' she said. 'I didn't know you were in an orphanage… do you know how your parents died?'

'Oh,' I said. 'I don't know if they are dead or alive.'

Michelle embraced me. Her eyes glistened. I had become more than her lover. I was like a hungry child on a *National Geographic* special. I had become someone even more appealing than that. I was somebody she could actually touch and save.

'You were adopted?'

'Yes, my father was American, Mr Clarkson. He adopted me.'

'And he was married?'

'Yes.' I bit off a fingernail on my thumb so that it began to bleed. 'It's a long story, Michelle. I'll tell you about it some other day. I promise. I really do. I can see how it is important that you know about all of this. But for now, can we talk about something else?'

'Oh, of course.'

'So, I can't really leave town on Friday evening. And then on Saturday…they are holding a memorial for Raj and Emily…two of my co-workers. I don't know if I told you about them.'

'No, you didn't,' she said. 'But is this the same couple that's been all over the news?'

'Yes, the same.' I made a deliberate effort to keep my features impassive. I didn't want to appear like one of those commonplace people who get excited at being touched by celebrity, whose only differentiating quality is its sordidness.

'You knew them?'

'They were my co-workers,' I said.

'That's terrible,' she said. 'Raj was the man who killed his girlfriend and then took his own life?'

'Or possibly,' I said, 'they were both targeted by someone on MyFace. The police are working all the angles. At any rate, do you understand why I can't hang out on the weekend?'

'I understand. But I have one condition.'

'What?'

The world was a taxing place. Everyone wanted to play on your nerves as though they were violin strings. This is not a pleasing prospect when you consider just how many people don't know how to play the violin.

'That you lie down,' she said. 'I'll get you a drink. And we can have some tacos that I picked up from the Mexican stand outside the train station.'

But, of course, people who knew how to play the violin could play it really well.

'That sounds good,' I said.

She got us each a Pacifico beer. We took a bite of the most delicious tacos in New York. She laid her head on my chest.

'Arjun,' she said. 'I want to say something.'

'Sure,' I said.

'You know the other day when you said that you wanted to become a diplomat...and I mocked you.'

'Aah...no,' I said. 'I don't remember.'

I felt a dense rod of tension pulse within my heart. It was the kind that you could use to club other people to death.

'Well, in any case, I didn't mean it. I was only joking. I think you will make the most gentlemanly diplomat in the world.'

'Thank you.'

I felt a great peace. Through the window, I could see a big orange moon. It wobbled slightly in perfect rhythm to the heavy bass beats from down below. The entire world was in perfect harmony. I felt equanimous.

'Can I ask you another question?' she said.

'Sure,' I said.

'I know you said you wanted to talk about this later...'

'Go ahead,' I said.

'Mr Clarkson, did he have a wife?'

'Yes,' I said. I got up from the couch.

I needed a drink. I needed something with whiskey, something that Humphrey Bogart would knock off at the office desk before stepping out on Ventura Boulevard. I decided to make an Old Fashioned. I went up to the bookshelf and reached for my book with cocktail recipes.

'And how was she?'

'I didn't really know her well,' I said. 'Mr Clarkson wanted that I receive the best education. So he sent me to a boarding school in Dehradun. It was a Catholic school run by Jesuit priests.'

'God bless that man,' she said.

'He was a generous man,' I said. I wanted to lay it on thick just so that I could end the conversation. I quoted something that Austin had told me. 'The way you give to other people is the way god will give to you.'

'That's really nice,' she said.

That might have well been the case. But it wasn't an entirely comprehensive point of view.

Sometimes, the way god gives to you is also the way you give to other people.

An Up-and-Coming Executive

Kevin Santiago's collarbone snapped with a sharp click. A detective dressed in a dark navy-blue uniform placed handcuffs on my wrist. I sat up on the bed.

I walked the length of the hallway. I opened the door. There was no policeman. There was, however, a fresh copy of the *Daily News*.

The newspaper had taken a very literal approach towards reporting my actions.

There were no puns. It appeared as though their editorial team had been sufficiently stunned into going to press with a literal headline.

Serial Killer Surfaces on MyFace.

The journalist had reported that Kevin Santiago had been found dead outside his building. He said the cause of death was repeated stabs to the stomach. I sighed. The reporter had been careless.

I would never stab anyone in the stomach. It is too risky a method of trying to kill a person. There is a very high probability that a person who has been stabbed in the stomach will survive the incident. A man in north London had recently stabbed himself in the abdomen. He had called the police for help. As they had approached him, he had pulled out his intestines and thrown it at them. He had survived. He hadn't eaten for five hours. He didn't have enough poisonous bile in his stomach to die.

I would never have aimed for Kevin Santiago's abdomen. I might as well have stabbed his hair.

The article went on to say that an 'I found you on MyFace' sticker had been found pasted on Kevin Santiago's forehead. Officer Crisafi was quoted as saying they had plausible reason to believe that this was the work of a serial killer. However, he went on to add that it was still too early to be entirely sure.

He would be sure after the weekend.

There was no mention of any photograph that the doorman had taken. Was it possible I had imagined the sound of the camera shutter?

The article also had a quote from a spokesperson of MyFace. She had said that MyFace was committed to maintaining the highest levels of user privacy.

This was a lie.

Just last week, the company had supported CISPA, a programme that facilitated sharing of private data between the government and private companies. They had done this without the consent of their users. MyFace treated user privacy like an Indian family treats a daughter-in-law who hasn't been able to pay the dowry. That is to say, not very well at all.

On the next page, there was an article about another killing in South Jersey. Two teenage boys had lured a twelve-year-old girl into their residence promising her spare bicycle parts. They had then killed her and thrown her body in a dumpster. The boys had then bragged about the murder on MyFace. The mother had read the posts and turned the boys in to the police. If only the boys had stuck an 'I found you on MyFace' sticker on the girl's forehead.

The detective and his investigation would have been sucked into a whirlpool of confusion.

Michelle was still asleep. I decided to go out for a run. It was over a hundred degrees today. But the heat would help me tire my body sufficiently enough so that I would be too numb to think. My mind would be calm and free of worries.

However, no sooner than I had stepped outside the apartment, I found a huge worry staring me in the face. There was a black van parked outside my building. Garish red roses and the words 'French Bouquet Florist' were painted on its side.

I was being tracked.

There were people concealed in the flower van. They were members of the FBI who suspected me of being a terrorist. Or they were detectives of the New York Police Department, who did not believe sufficiently in my innocence.

I had my reasons for my suspicions.

Why would there be a flower van packed in Jackson Heights? In all my time in this neighbourhood, I hadn't seen a single person capable of expressing a romantic sentiment. Think of the taxi driver who has spent all his day honking and charging at pedestrians. Would he ever feel moved to experience a tender emotion and send a flower to his wife?

Even I didn't think so.

I walked up to Northern Boulevard. I glanced back at the van. The red tail-lights stared at me, still and impassive. I turned left on to the avenue and broke into a quick run.

The *Daily News* had said this was the hottest day in the history of New York. Records were going to be broken. However, the people on the street were not celebrating. It was only six in the morning. But the people of Queens were visibly fatigued. Their shoulders were slouched, as though they were hanging off a clothesline. They resented the moments when they brushed against each other. Everybody was tense. It appeared as though we were all at a well-lit nightclub, endlessly reliving the moment just prior to the gunshot.

I felt my knees wobble. I stopped outside a Volkswagen car dealership. Even as a salesman looked at me disapprovingly, I supported myself on his establishment's wall and stretched my legs. I began to think long, elastic thoughts.

The police were tracking me. They would soon get me. They would put me on an electric chair. And they would turn on the current.

Maybe it was time for me to return to India.

It would be very difficult to reconcile going back to a country with no public parks or libraries. I would have to return to a land where I belonged to a low caste. And India was home to Mrs Clarkson.

But at least, I would be alive in India. I could step out on a hot day. And I would be able to feel the sensation of relief when cold orange juice flowed over inch after inch of my parched throat.

A man and a woman stood at a bus stop. There were two children attached to each of their arms. The boy was shouting something in a language that wasn't English, Spanish or Hindi. The man ignored him. He kissed the woman and got into a bus. The woman now waited at the bus stop with the two children. When the Q32 bus arrived, she pushed her children inside. She got in behind them. The bus started with a heavy shiver and headed down Northern Boulevard.

I saw with an awful predictability how their lives had and would play out. They had met, married, procreated and moved to Queens. They spent their evenings with their children in sunlit parks. On one of those evenings, the boy had probably scored a goal from a free-kick, probably a spectacular one at that.

But what was the use of such lovely moments?

The children would reach puberty and try to establish their own identity in the world. They would find that they were still weak and incapable of doing so. They would become resentful. The parents, too, would feel resentful that their children did not recognize the sacrifices they had made. Eventually, the suppressed anxieties of the parents and the children would reconcile themselves in an uneasy harmony. The children would come of age. The parents would grow old and die.

I felt a hatred for these people, and how their fates had been irrevocably decided. I would not be like them. I would not let my destiny be decided by somebody else. I would not go back to the country that was the world champion in believing that all human beings were powerless in the face of their destinies.

I would be an exceptional, individual American. I would not go down without a fight.

I went back to the apartment. The flower van hadn't moved from its spot. The sun moved in the sky. The roses mocked me by turning a deeper shade of red. I walked slowly to see if there was a business name, URL or phone number painted on its sides. But the van was devoid of any advertising. I felt tempted to take a paintbrush and write some direct response advertising copy with a strong call to action.

An Indian spit red paan juice on the street. He wouldn't have the courage to do that in Manhattan. He could do that in only Jackson Heights because he was among his own. His was a classic exhibition of mob mentality.

There was exactly one month and three days left on my lease. I would then be able to leave this neighbourhood.

I had taken this apartment one day after Kevin Santiago had made fun of me for wanting to live near Central Park. I hadn't been thinking clearly at the time I made the decision to sign the lease. I had reacted emotionally to the real-estate agent when he said, 'Of course, I have another place. It's in Queens. It's rather large, but it might be out of your budget…'

'I'll take it,' I had said.

Michelle was curled up in a layer of bed sheets. She asked me to join her. She pointed to her computer screen. I looked at a YouTube video of two cats seated on a bookshelf. One cat tickled the other. It threw its paws back in the air and laughed.

'Isn't that adorable?' she said.

I did not think it was adorable. But I laughed. I was happy to see that even in our hyper-ironic world, there were people who could still take pleasure in simple things.

'That's really funny,' I added for the benefit of the people overhearing me in the flower van. Hopefully, I would convince them of my innocence. Happy people who laugh loudly don't go around the city sticking knives into people.

Michelle kissed my neck.

'You're sweaty,' she said.

She went into the bathroom. Taps opened. Water flowed. Toilets flushed. The morning symphony played.

'Come in,' she said.

The tub was full of water. The water was full of bubbles.

'Is Cleopatra paying us a visit?' I asked.

'Have you never had a bath before?'

'Well, I know I look dirty…but I do clean myself once every twenty-four hours.'

'No stupid,' she said. 'I didn't mean shower.'

She looked towards the ground and searched for the Spanish word for bath.

'Bath,' I said in English.

The English word seemed rude and unwelcome.

'Yes,' she said. 'Try taking one.'

'I don't know,' I said. 'It seems to be…too much.'

'Oh, come on,' she said. 'I insist.'

She insisted. I sat in the tub. At first, the water went into my ears and nose. I did not like the drowning feeling. I felt surrounded. I felt pushed at. I thought of Mrs Clarkson. But then I sat up. I felt the water roll back and forth over my shoulder blades. After a few minutes, I found myself wishing that I had a rubber duck. I knew I was truly relaxed.

Michelle came into the bathroom. She carried a bowl in her hand.

'Blueberries and yogurt,' she said. 'Eat it. You'll feel good.'

I ate it. I felt good.

I got out of the bath. I had arrived at a decision.

I would stay in America.

It appeared that the detectives really didn't have anything on me. If Kevin Santiago had indeed clicked a photo of my countenance, I would have been arrested by now. And if the NYPD didn't have a photo, they didn't have anything. On the evening Kevin Santiago had been killed, I was at the Volstead. As for the evenings when Emily and Raj were killed, I did not have an alibi. I could not prove I was not at the scene of the crime. However, neither could the detective.

I dried myself using a freshly washed towel that Michelle had hung on the hook of the bathroom door. She had picked up a copy of *La Casa de Bernarda Alba* by Federico García Lorca and gone back into the bedroom.

I roused my laptop from sleep. There was an email from Brett Cohen. He asked me to look into an ad campaign for a venture-backed start-up in New York. The company had developed a technology that allowed people to send messages to friends who were in their vicinity. The goal of the advertising campaign was to drive downloads of the app. However, the ad was not delivering click-throughs or conversions.

Brett's note was unusually curt. I wondered if he had become suspicious of me.

I doubted it. In his mind, I was a model Indian immigrant, the kind who played a starring role in Thomas Friedman columns. How could he think ill of me when I had just made him millions of dollars? It would be most un-American of him.

I logged in to the start-up's MyFace account. I clicked on the 'My Ads' link. The creative director at the agency had chosen an image of an iPhone map with a blue dot for the advertisement.

I went to istockphoto.com. I typed in the phrase 'smiling woman'. I purchased a photo of a woman with neatly parted hair and a smile as wide as Park Avenue. The photo had been shot with a wide aperture. The background was blurred and could be filled in with the user's imagination. I switched out the photo on the MyFace ad. It is incredible how often the creative personnel at advertising agencies forget the simple fact that people respond to other people. Sometimes, they even respond to geckos and swans.

I replied to Brett's curt note. I told him that I had swapped out the image on the ad. The click-through rates should improve. I forwarded my email to the creative director, so as to pre-empt the fit that he would otherwise throw in my office later in the day.

Michelle was lying on the bed supported on her elbow, reading. Her head was resting in her palms. She looked at peace with the world, as if the book was succeeding in giving her all that she had ever wanted.

'I have to leave for work,' I said. 'It's really very late.'

'Can I leave the apartment later? I don't have school till two.'

'Sure, you can,' I said. 'Just lock the door on the way out.'

'I'm going to play the radio,' she said. 'I want to listen to NPR.'

'Go for it,' I said. I enjoyed the mental picture of the people in the flower van struggling to stay awake.

'By the way,' I said. 'Do you want to come with me to the memorial on Saturday?'

'Do you mean that?' she asked.

'Mean what?'

'That you want me to come to the memorial?'

I did not understand. Why was she repeating what I had said and asking me if I meant it?

'Of course,' I said.

'Well…' She got up from the bed and sat with her feet planted firmly on the ground. 'Because, you know… that's just the sort of thing one asks someone they are dating. Like a girlfriend.'

This was good stuff. The term 'girlfriend' reinforced my appearance of normalcy. The people in the flower van would know I had a girlfriend. They would see that I was just like any normal, non-violent American.

'Sure,' I said.

'Oh Arjun,' she said. She hugged me.

'I have to get to work,' I said aloud to sound even more like an everyday American.

Being normal was so trite and difficult. I wondered how people suppressed all their anxieties and quirks and managed to appear normal every hour, every day and every month, year after year.

The flower van hadn't moved from its spot. I waved at it to let the surveillance personnel know that I was on to them. The van stood on steadfast, still and unblinking.

There were no policemen at the Jackson Heights station or, for that matter, the 23rd Street Station on 6th Avenue. On 5th Avenue, I decided to walk across Madison Square Park. I stopped in front of a giant installation in the shape of an octagon. The installation was made up of hundreds of transparent tubes connected to each other. Even in the bright daylight, I could see small pulses of pink light move across the length of the tubes. I made a mental note to visit this sculpture at night. In the dark, I would be able to see the pulses of light more clearly. However, even as I made the resolution, I was doubtful I would be able to keep it. The city was full of distractions. This installation was just one of them. In New York, there were simply too many things competing for attention.

On Park Avenue, a mother pulled at her heavy suitcase. She was accompanied by two children. The boy ran off towards a pigeon. The mother called out his name twice.

'Luis! Luis!'

But Luis was completely oblivious to anything that wasn't a pigeon, including the pedestrians and the oncoming traffic. The mother ran after him. The young girl, who was left behind, began to cry. The mother caught up with Luis. She dragged him back to where the suitcase and her daughter were. I braced myself for the slap. But all the mother did was kiss him. I was surprised.

I had four hour-long meetings in the morning. Three of them were set up just so we could reassure the marketing teams of our retail clients that their marketing plans would deliver a positive return on investment in the last quarter.

A marketing executive at Tommy Hilfiger had once told me that over 75 per cent of their annual sales took place in the period around Thanksgiving and Christmas. Industry reports suggested that the same was true for all the other major national retailers. If a retailer missed out on sales during the holiday season, it was next to certain that the company would go out of business.

I was confident we had a strong marketing plan in place for all our retail clients. I had taken the money out of the banner and rich media campaigns, and had reallocated the ad dollars towards email marketing. Brett had asked me if I was sure that investing our money against such an overused medium was a good move.

'Email is like that song "*RESPECT*" by Aretha Franklin,' I had told Brett. 'It may be old, but it always delivers.'

Hannah was at her desk when I arrived. She always arrived early on days when Brett's calendar was fully booked.

'There's a man waiting for you in your office,' she said.

'Who?' I asked.

But she had already begun talking to somebody else on the telephone.

I could see the man she had referred to through the glass walls of my office. He was going through the papers on my desk. His features were stern. His cheekbones were harder than my knuckles.

'Good morning, detective,' I said.

'I am sorry for stopping by so early, Mr…'

'Arjun,' I said.

'Arjun. I am a morning person.'

I did not believe him. If he were really a morning person, why was he hanging outside my apartment during the night-time hours?

'Do you have a few minutes?'

'Sure,' I said. 'But I am not sure I can help you learn anything new.'

'Maybe I'm not looking for anything new,' he said. 'Maybe I just want to talk.'

'I can talk,' I said.

I did the polite thing and asked him if I could get him some coffee and water. A gentleman is always hospitable even when under the duress of interrogation.

'You've read the newspapers,' he asked.

'Yes,' I said. 'I read about the MyFace killer…'

'So you think that the newspapers have got it right?'

'I think they are on to something.'

'So it doesn't strike you as odd that of all the people in the world who were on MyFace, a serial killer would randomly select two people who were dating each other?'

'Well,' I said, 'in a city of eight million people, coincidences are bound to occur.'

'I don't believe in coincidences,' he said.

'Maybe I'm using the wrong word. But surely, even a basic understanding of the binomial theorem will explain how seemingly unrelated events can occur. I don't know if you read the *Daily News* the other day. Two brothers were riding their bicycles on separate errands in Helsinki. One of them was killed by a speeding truck at 9.30 in the morning. The other one was killed eight minutes later – by a completely different speeding truck.'

'So what you are saying is that their selection as victims could be coincidental?'

'I am saying that we should not discount the possibility. But their deaths could also have played out in another way. Remember, we are talking about a social network. Maybe the killer saw Emily's profile. And then maybe she or he could have clicked on to Raj's page.'

He glared at me, as impassive as a stone carving of Abraham Lincoln. It took a lot of effort, but I continued to look into his eyes.

'Or maybe,' I said, 'what the *Daily News* reporter conjectured was right. That Raj killed Emily. And he killed himself because he was feeling guilty about her murder.'

'Think about it,' he said. 'If you were contemplating suicide, would you order Chinese food before taking your life?'

Actually, I would order Vietnamese. I would order the L28 peanut noodles from L'Annam.

'I don't know,' I said. 'I guess…I wouldn't. But some people have that notion of the last meal.'

'Okay, I'll give you that,' he said. 'But there was something else that didn't come out in the papers.'

'Was there?' I said.

He ran his fingers over his tie. His eyes were calm, like that of a boxer in the moment before he is about to deliver that knockout punch.

'Raj was found stabbed in the femoral region of his neck. Our criminal investigator seems to think it really odd…that a person who wants to commit suicide would stab himself in the neck. And you know what?'

'What?'

'I agree.'

I opened my mouth not to reply, but because I was surprised at my stupidity. He was right. People who committed suicide didn't go around stabbing themselves in the neck. I should have thought of this simple fact before I sent Raj to the fiery afterworld of hell.

'And there's one more thing, Mr…'

'Arjun.'

'Arjun, we followed up with the restaurant. It appears that the delivery was never made.'

'I see.'

'Yes, it appears that the delivery man kept buzzing the intercom to Raj's apartment. But he got no response.'

'Maybe Raj was already dead?'

'Or maybe he was being killed at that very moment.'

If we were playing a game, I would have said 'warm'.

'Yes,' I said. 'Maybe he was being killed by the MyFace serial killer.'

'Probably,' he said. 'But I have another theory.'

I sneezed. I was thankful for the particle of dust that had entered my nostrils. It allowed me to look away from him.

'I think someone killed Emily. Someone she knew. After all, there are no signs of breaking and entering into her apartment.'

'Interesting,' I said.

'And Raj wised up to the murderer's identity. He paid for it with his life.'

'Forgive me for saying so detective, but there's a big hole in your theory.'

I was surprised at my confidence. I raised my voice so that it matched the high degree of assurance that nowadays seemed to course perennially through my veins.

'A MyFace sticker was found by Raj's body. I read about a doorman who was found dead outside his building on the Upper West Side. It appears that the same sticker was found stuck on the doorman's forehead. If this is not the work of a random serial killer, how do you account for the doorman?'

'Which brings me to another point,' said the detective. 'What were you doing last evening?'

This time I had an answer.

'Well, I worked kind of late. I felt that I could do with a drink. So I went to a bar. It's called the Volstead.'

'And where is this bar?'

I told him.

'And I suppose you went alone?'

'I did. After all these meetings throughout the day, I felt the need to be alone.'

'And did anyone see you there at this place?'

I pretended to think. The Buddha moved across the width of my computer screen.

'The bouncer did. I even spoke to him.'

'Can you describe him?'

'He was big. He was rude.'

'The reason I am asking these questions, Mr Arjun, is because I know something that you don't know.'

'Ah.'

'Something that even the newspapers don't know.'

'Ah,' I said again.

He took out an iPhone from his pocket.

'At the time he was killed, the doorman took a photo of the killer.'

So this was it. This was the moment when the life and times of Arjun Clarkson would come to an end. I felt tired. My long and dreary existence would finally be over. I began to look forward to getting a new life, to being reincarnated as a hummingbird.

The detective leaned forward.

'Here is the photo.'

My chair shivered as I bent forward to get a closer look at the screen.

'The Buddha killed Kevin Santiago?'

'We believe that's a photo of the killer's T-shirt.'

'Ah,' I said.

'I notice your screensaver, Mr Arjun. You like the Buddha?'

'Yes, very much.'

'You wouldn't happen to have a T-shirt just like this?'

'Of course, I do,' I said. 'As does half of New York. Surely, you've seen the ads for the Uniqlo Buddha T-shirts on the subway?'

'Actually, I have,' he said. 'What were you wearing yesterday, Mr Arjun?'

I felt hurt he hadn't remembered.

'I was wearing a T-shirt with a bowling pin and a bottle of beer,' I said. 'And besides, as I have already indicated, I was at the Volstead.'

He closed his notebook.

'It does seem odd that on the night Emily died, you were in the area. It does seem odd that like you, the doorman's killer also had a Buddha T-shirt.'

'Unlike me,' I said. 'The killer was not at the Volstead. Unlike me, the killer was not wearing a T-shirt with a bowling pin and a glass of draft beer.'

'The facts seem to put you in the clear,' he said. 'But my intuition tells me something entirely else.'

'Do you know what my intuition tells me?'

'What?' he said.

'It tells me that the facts do seem to put me in the clear.'

'I'll follow up with you if I have any questions,' he said.

'I really hope you find out who's behind all of this.'

'I always do,' he said.

Brett knocked on my door. He smiled a long and patient smile as the detective gathered his belongings.

'Can you be a part of the Sears pitch?'

'I was planning on it.'

The detective gave us each a silent nod. He left the office at a slow and thoughtful pace.

'What's up with the detective?' Brett asked. 'Why does he keep coming here to ask questions again and again? You told him everything you knew, didn't you?'

'I did.'

'Then what's the point of coming here so many times? I mean, it's not like you are going to shed new light on the matter. It's not like you would lie.'

I did not reply. I respected Brett and did not want to tell him an explicit falsehood.

'Going forward, I need you to be on every client meeting,' Brett said. 'And I need you to hit it out of the park. We are behind our revenue projections for the agency. It's nothing to worry about, but we need to pull ahead in the last few months of the year.'

That afternoon, I hit several balls out of the park. By the end of the fourth meeting we had that day, all the retail clients had bought into my email strategy. The client from Dockers even sent Brett a text message after the meeting to thank him for having the courage to suggest a common-sense marketing plan that would actually work.

Brett was visibly surprised to see my new-found confidence. However, he was also visibly pleased.

'Arjun, about my questions the other day…'

'Yes?'

'I want to apologize if I suggested that you knew anything about Emily's …'

The sentiment was not one that was related to business. Brett could not express it without sounding awkward. He was like a man who was doing the foxtrot for the first time. He could not do it right. And it did not feel right that he should be doing it.

'There's nothing to apologize about.'

I meant it. Brett had sponsored my work visa. I had in him the simple faith that people invest in their deities. It was beyond my capabilities, leave alone desire, to blame him.

'It's now pretty apparent that this is the work of a madman.'

He showed me a photo of the building where Kevin Santiago was stabbed.

'The *Times* says he was stabbed by a stranger in the leg. 'Why would someone kill a person in such a barbaric way?'

I felt like telling him that there is nothing barbaric about it. It is very fast, efficient and American.

He turned the page of the newspaper. I hoped he wouldn't stumble upon some article by Tom Friedman on how Indians are five times faster than Americans when it came to using Microsoft Excel.

Brett shook his head.

'We all knew this was going to happen on MyFace. It's amazing how we spent the last three years pretending that such a thing would not happen.'

'Well, I hope it doesn't happen again.'

'I hope so too.'

Hannah interrupted our conversation. She told us the client from Overstock.com had follow-up questions from our meeting. I told Brett I had it covered. I went into the conference room and told the client the same thing.

People in the workplace don't want to hear about how much you worked, or how late you were in the office last night. All that your boss, or for that matter your client, wants to hear is, 'Don't worry about it. I got it covered.'

The client had a question about our recommendation. We had told him they should be investing their resources to generating user-focused content on their MyFace fan page as opposed to running a MyFace ad campaign.

'The click-through rate on a banner on MyFace is 0.04 per cent. However, if you get a friend to post your message on their wall, over 6 per cent of people click on the message.'

I quoted the CEO of MyFace, 'In today's socially connected world, the most persuasive ad is a friend's recommendation.'

'But just how do you get friends to post stuff on their wall?'

'Well, last year, we got people to post pictures of themselves wearing Tommy Hilfiger T-shirts and jeans on their wall. People liked the photos of their friends. The photos then appeared on their wall. The message spread. Tommy Hilfiger saw over 133 per cent ROI with the campaign.'

'What do we need to do?'

'You don't need to do anything. I've got it covered.'

He thanked me.

'You betcha,' I said.

I tensed automatically. But Raj Malik wasn't around to smirk at my pronunciation.

'What's come over you?' said Brett. He was standing at the door of the conference room.

'How do you mean?'

'You've made close to a million dollars for the agency in the last three days.'

'Well…'

'Whatever it is you've been doing,' said Brett, 'you should do more of it.'

'I plan to,' I said.

'I'm promoting you to vice president, Media. And your salary is now $150,000.'

I know it is not very gentlemanly to bandy about one's salary in public. But I had reached the big one-five-O in a little over two years. I probably now made more than Raj Malik had ever done. And I had done it on a work visa. He had been a bona fide citizen.

'Thank you, Brett,' I said. 'It's a big moment for me.'

'You should take the afternoon off. Celebrate with your girlfriend.'

'That's very nice of you, Brett,' I said.

But I would not spend the afternoon with Michelle. I would go to the Museum of Modern Art. I needed to create a new social network profile, one that would be the identity of the MyFace killer. I needed to be inspired. This MyFace page would soon receive a lot of publicity. It would probably live on for posterity. It deserved to be derived from the best works of our times.

As I was about to leave, Keith, the copywriter, came to my office. He handed me a piece of paper.

'It's the creative for FreshDirect. Can you get that live now?'

'Does it have to be now?' I asked.

'Yes,' he said.

He left the room, because my thoughts on the matter were of no consequence.

I looked at his ad. The headline said, You say tomato. The body copy said, I also say tomato. Get new recipes at freshdirect.com.

I was surprised. This was actually fresh copy. It planted a hummable melody in your head and got you to like the brand. The people who saw the ad would remember it. I made a minor change to the copy. I added the word 'now' to the end.

It is incredible how after all these years, copywriters still haven't fully realized the power of the words 'free' and 'now.' These words outperform every other word in the English dictionary when it comes to getting people to notice your ad and following your call to action.

Even people who aren't professional copywriters have recognized the power of these words. On the platform for the F train on the West 4th Street station, there is a sign outside a door that says 'Active Doorway! Step Out of the Way!' Using a magic marker, a subway employee has handwritten at the end of the message the word 'NOW!'

I pushed Keith's copy live. I walked down the hallway and knocked on the door to the CFO's office.

Rose Anderson seemed to have been promoted to the position of the CFO on the basis of a singular skill, the ability to smile and appear tranquil even when surrounded by payroll slips, account timesheets, vacation requests and other documents that expressed in sticky, black ink, the simmering discontent of the workers at the advertising agency.

As always, her room was cold. She smiled at me. She tightened the scarf on her neck as though attempting to strangle herself and put herself out of her misery.

'Congratulations!' she said.

'Thank you,' I said. I waited till she finished clicking on her mouse and looked away from her computer screen. 'I mean it. The raise is great. However, there is just one more thing.'

'Arjun,' she said, 'I can see how you think the money's not enough. You're an ambitious man. And you're bright. You're hard-working. Here's what I can do. I can increase your pay by a further five thousand dollars. But anything beyond that would be difficult. You see with the budget...'

'Wait,' I said. 'You're misunderstanding me. I'm really happy. I don't want a single dime more. I like one hundred and fifty thousand. It's a...'

I tried to think of the most appropriate words that could be used to praise a hundred and fifty thousand dollars.

'It's a round number,' I said. 'And I like round numbers.'

'Oh,' she said. She smiled for the first time in our conversation. She rolled her chair closer towards me.

'What did you want to see me about?'

'Well,' I said. 'I had a favour to ask, and I was wondering if you could help me.'

She nodded slowly, her eagerness to please tempered by a lifetime habit of caution.

'Rose,' I said. 'Now, that I am going to have a meaningful source of income, I want to be able to do a better job of saving money. I want to know at a physical level just how much money is coming in and how much going out of my account. With the whole direct deposit thing, the money goes into my bank so silently, I really don't have an idea of how much money I am working with at a given point in time. And I am too disorganized to log into my account daily and keep a track of my spending. I was wondering if you could…'

'Give you a cashier's cheque?'

'Yes,' I said.

Given that I had actually turned down her offer to increase my salary even further, she would have been amenable to fulfilling any request of mine. I could have asked her for all of the gold and perfumes of Arabia, and she would have logged in to her computer to check on the availability of camels that could be dispatched to the region.

'That's a great idea,' she said. 'Why don't we get started today?'

She rolled her chair to the desk in a noisy display of action.

'Why don't we?' I said.

She clicked on a button on her screen. What had to be the last surviving dot matrix printer in the world came to life. Rose and I stared at each other awkwardly as the printer went through its business, pixel after tortured pixel.

She handed me a cheque.

'Once again, congratulations,' she said,

I bowed graciously. I packed my bag and stepped out of the office silently. The sun fell on me from the side. My shadow fell behind me, as did the other people on the avenue. I marched ahead confidently.

At the Chase Bank on 27th Street, I performed a wordless transaction. I smiled and handed the cashier a cheque for over three thousand five hundred dollars. She reached out through the window and handed me a wad of dollar bills that was so thick that it needed to be counted by a counting machine.

I felt reassured at the weight of the green stack that rested on my palm. Now, Detective Crisafi could place a tap on my account. He could monitor my activity to see if I made unexpectedly large withdrawals. He could even get a warrant from a judge and insist that the bank freeze all my future transactions. But he would find it impossible to impede my access to the currency that is required to purchase goods and services in the capitalist market system. Goods such as a one-way airplane ticket to India should it be needed. Services such as those offered by a person who could make me a new passport with a new name.

I walked north on Park Avenue till I reached 42nd Street. However, I didn't enter Grand Central. Instead, I went into the Banana Republic store. The advertisements for Banana Republic featured outwardly ambitious and slightly morose-looking models. I had inferred from these ads that Banana Republic was where up-and-coming executives purchased their clothes.

I picked up a Classic-Fit ironed shirt. It was soft and had blue stripes racing down from the neck towards the torso. It cost $79.50. Today, I could afford it. I examined the label. It said, Made in India. I placed the shirt back on the shelf. I wasn't stupid enough to come all the way to America and pay eighty dollars for a shirt made in India.

I picked up a solid white shirt-sleeve shirt. It was made in Vietnam. Hanoi was the Paris of the East. That was good enough for me. I also picked up a pair of dark-blue boot-fit jeans that were made in Turkey. I walked up to the counter and purchased the shirt and jeans with a small portion of the cash I had just withdrawn.

I walked into Grand Central station. The giant arches and ornate chandeliers filled the station with their grandeur. However, now their majesty seemed to spring not from the craftsmanship of labourers more than a century ago, but from the contents of the Banana Republic bag I held in my hands.

I had spent all of my life in America feeling inferior to other people. But now, I felt at one with the old lady seeking a time table at the Information Desk, the young man who was talking to an Apple employee with headphones in his ears and the woman whose beauty made her far removed from everybody else at the Oyster Bar. I felt as though I could enter any of those places and start a conversation with any of these people.

This was an opportune development, for I had more than a few conversations I needed to start.

Hop-Frog's Revenge

On 51st Street a black man sat behind a police caution tape. He was sipping a cappuccino. He stared into his smartphone. He faced a faded yellow wall covered with neo-Cubist graffiti. A placard by the installation explained that this was a piece of the Berlin Wall.

It was hard to believe that this backdrop to a cappuccino had once taken so many lives.

Chris Gueffroy was the last person to die while attempting to cross the Berlin Wall. He had been shot by ten bullets as he had attempted to flee East Germany. He was just twenty years old at the time. If he had waited for a few more months, the wall would have fallen. He could have gone to work in West Germany. He could have even applied for a work visa and come to the United States.

He could have stood where I was now standing. He, too, could have sipped on a cappuccino. But he had died. The winter of his death had given way to spring. The Gulf Stream had carried warm waters across the Atlantic. The flowers had bloomed. Brooks had gurgled. The leaves had turned a deeper shade of green.

And Emily had died. Raj had died.

On 5th Avenue, smartly dressed mannequins stood framed against bright-red backgrounds in the Uniqlo store. Leave it to the Japanese to prepare your mind for modern art even as you walked to the museum.

A woman of Venice stared at me from the sculpture garden. A tall woman with high cheekbones and slender legs stood next to her. She brushed her nose with her index finger. She could have easily been mistaken for a sculpture that had accidentally come to life. A blonde woman walked through the exhibit space with a Lhasa Apso dog. Citizens like her didn't think twice before taking a dog to the world's premier modern art museum. As for an immigrant like me, I did not even have the courage to click a photo of the exhibits with my flip phone.

I walked through a room that had a collection of rugs. These handmade pieces of art had the outlines of every country and continent of the world embroidered on them. The Afghani women who had made the rugs did not know that the space between the continents was filled by blue oceans. Instead, they had coloured the oceans with the colour that was most readily available to them.

I thought the world looked like a far angrier place with red oceans. I wondered if a red ocean would smell as comforting as a blue one. The innocence of these Afghan women moved me. Or maybe, they were just being clairvoyant.

I was in this room for a reason. By placing me in the midst of this exhibit, the gods were asking me to select a country of origin for my MyFace profile. I pondered over every country on the map. The world seemed so full of colour and possibilities.

I thought briefly about selecting an East African country like Kenya or Uganda. However, I wanted to know what it was to be white, even if in a virtual life.

I didn't know Americans well enough to get away with impersonating a white American. The racist behaviour of Australian cricket teams rankled from my childhood years.

Europeans had a colonial past, one they glossed over in their readings of history.

I chose New Zealand.

I hadn't been to the country. However, I had seen an image of the Christchurch cricket grounds on TV as a child. At the time, I thought it was the most beautiful image I had ever seen. And it would have stayed that way. But then I had seen Emily.

I had met New Zealanders on two occasions in my life, once on a boat in Kerala and the other time, in an airport lounge in Hong Kong. On both occasions, they had struck me as being among the most polite and gentlemanly people in the world. If I were to be reborn, I would not mind being a Maori, a hobbit or, for that matter, a white person from New Zealand.

I stepped into a room bathed in a clear, white light. I felt hopeful that this was the room where I would receive illumination. I found it on the first wall I looked at.

An oil painting depicted eight monstrous-looking beings tied by a chain. They were suspended from a giant ceiling. They were on fire. The painting spoke to me as vividly as a vision does to a man who has just eaten a cactus root in the desert. It was deeply personal, real and prophetic all at once.

I wanted to get a closer look at the painting. But I found that a bespectacled brunette was blocking my view. She was taking notes from the sign that provided an explanation of the different exhibits in the room. The placard was filled with pretentious words like 'neo-modern' and 'contextuality'. I sighed. Why do human beings look towards priests when god is trying so hard to communicate directly with them?

When she moved away, I found myself overcome with a feeling of freedom. I stepped towards the painting. The line work was intricate. I could see that the artist had used a colour pencil. There were also watercolour additions.

The beasts that hung from the ceiling were aglow in the fire. The flesh was peeling off their bodies. They were beginning to develop the sameness of appearance that is characteristic of skeletons. The painting was called *Hop-Frog's Revenge*.

'Hop-Frog' is a story by Edgar Allen Poe. It is one of my favourite stories. I like it more than I do *The Hitchhiker's Guide to the Galaxy* and as much as I do *Anna Karenina*.

Hop-Frog was a jester in the court of a twelfth-century French king. The king was fond of practical jokes.

One day, the king goes too far and humiliates Hop-Frog in front of the entire court. Hop-Frog is deeply ashamed as he looks at the amused faces in the palace. The only face that is deeply saddened belongs to his beautiful lover, Trippetta.

Like any reasonable man, Hop-Frog is constantly on the lookout for the moment when he can seek revenge. One day, the king proclaims that he wants to throw a masquerade ball. Hop-Frog suggests that the king and his courtiers dress in orangutan suits, and that they cover these suits with tar. He also suggests that they be chained together. He persuades the king that this ruse will prove very effective when it comes to scaring the guests.

The day of the ball arrives. The king and his courtiers dress in the orangutan suits. They chain themselves together and await the guests. When the guests arrive, Hop-Frog's girlfriend Trippetta pulls the chain over a trolley so that the king and his courtiers are suspended from the ceiling. Hop-Frog sets them on fire. As the guests look on at the burning spectacle, Hop-Frog escapes with his girlfriend.

I wondered what Hop-Frog would have done to Raj Malik after a meeting.

I read the placard to find out more about the artist. His name was James Ensor. Mr Ensor was a Flemish Belgian painter associated with a group, Les XX. He was a man of decidedly 'anti-imperial, anti-clerical, pro-worker' leanings. The placard said that James Ensor had died on 19 November 1949.

However, Mr Ensor had not died. He would come back to life in the MyFace era. He would be reborn in New York City.

Mr Ensor was the most apt model for my MyFace profile. In the future, academics and students would make the link between two idealists who were fed up with the hypocrisies prevalent in society. The only difference between them was that one of them knew to paint, while the other...

I tried to look at the other paintings in the room. However, I was distracted by the sound of Mr Ensor's brush as he furiously painted those yellow flames of fire. I realized I had got what I had come for. I turned back and hastened towards the exit of the museum.

There was a policeman outside the station on 57th Street and 6th Avenue. However, he was standing in line at a coffee stand. He was not checking the bags of the passengers who entered and left the subway station. There was another patrol officer at the Jackson Heights station. I bought a churro so that I could look at it, instead of having to look into his eyes. I made my way out of the turnstiles with relative ease.

As I crossed Roosevelt Avenue, I saw yet another policeman in front of Patel's grocery. The officers of the law were certainly up and about in great numbers today like bees in a garden on the first day of spring. This particular policeman wasn't in uniform. He was dressed in a grey hoodie. However, I could tell he worked for the law. He stood unusually upright. The lamp post could have taken a few tips on good posture from him. When he stretched, his hoodie slid up the length of his torso. I could clearly see a bulge in his back pocket. It could have been a baton. Or it could have been the barrel of a gun. There was only one way to be sure. I would approach him. If he were a policeman in disguise, he would offer to sell me drugs.

'You want pot, man?' he asked, as I passed by him.

I laughed. He was a cliché of a policeman. He did not possess the quirks of imagination so necessary to entrap any criminal of diverse means and single-minded purpose.

'I am sorry,' I said. 'I don't do pot.'

'Really?' he said.

'Yes, really,' I said. 'And you shouldn't be selling drugs here. This is a respectable family neighbourhood.'

I raised my voice. People stared. The shadow of a large Sikh gentleman crept down the sidewalk towards us.

'Is this man troubling you, sir?' he asked. He didn't actually roar. But there was no denying that he bore a striking resemblance to a lion in a particularly bad mood.

The plainclothes policeman rushed towards the subway station. I continued to walk towards my apartment at a more leisurely pace.

The flower van had disappeared from the front of my apartment. Because I had waved at the van in the morning, the police had come to know that I was aware of their machinations. They had left. However, I still had to be careful, both in the offline as well as the online world.

I turned on my computer and logged on to the TOR client. I thought about making a cup of tea. But then I thought I wouldn't be able to sip on the hot concoction without making a slurping noise. I would get distracted. I needed to focus on the creation of the MyFace profile with all of my concentration.

Even though I was making a virtual profile on MyFace, I needed to make sure that its contents were drawn from the real world. People would instinctively see through anything that was made up. Anything on the profile that was purely imaginary would be like a plastic flower. It might succeed in drawing the eyes. But it would fail to entice.

I went to the Gutenberg Project. There was one listing for the life of James Ensor. Unfortunately, it was in French. I switched on the Google translate tool on my Chrome browser. And voilà! Or as the Google Translate tool would say, Bingo! Chrome translated the page into English.

The translation wasn't entirely fluent. It reminded me of the English of a newly arrived immigrant. I found it endearing.

By the time I had read three pages I knew that James Ensor was the ideal person to disguise the existence of the MyFace killer. After all, Mr Ensor was known as the 'painter of masks' to his peers. James Ensor loved painting masks more than he did landscapes, portraits or objects. He found them full of freshness and vitality. According to the book, they gave him the opportunity to dabble in wild, unexpected colours and revel in what he liked to call their 'exquisite turbulence'.

MyFace asked me to name my profile.

I chose Roger as first name. If I ever took up playing tennis, I would want to have a great one-handed backhand. Two-handed backhands were for sissies. I selected Diamond as my last name. It was the last name of the singer who had sung a song called 'Red Red Wine'. It was the first song I had ever listened to in the English language.

Making up a virtual profile had forced me to think of two things that I loved. As we run about our day-to-day lives, we never stop to think what makes us happy. But I had, and for this, I felt grateful towards MyFace.

But the feeling passed.

To register my MyFace account, I used the email address I normally used to access porn sites with premium content. For the first time, I would use this email address to view people who were not naked. In fact, the people on MyFace were more than fully clothed; they were overdressed with curated photographs, carefully braided likes and dislikes and elaborately manicured opinions.

MyFace asked for my email address and password so that it could automatically locate my friends. I bypassed this screen. I wasn't about to entrust a company like MyFace with personal information. Besides, enlargeyourmember@aol.com, the person who had sent the most emails to my backup email address, wasn't really that close a friend.

MyFace asked me for a profile photo. I selected Ensor's 1880 painting *The Lamp Boy*. The painting features a young man sitting on a chair. The man's facial features are concealed by the cap he has pulled over his face. He is swarthy enough to be brown.

MyFace asked me to select a school. James Ensor had come to America in 1861 to study civil engineering. Unfortunately, he couldn't acquire a degree, as his studies had been disrupted by the civil war. What could not happen then would happen now. James Ensor would not only be able to attend school in America, he would do so in an Ivy League institution.

I eliminated Harvard and Columbia from the list. The graduates I had met from these institutions were smug with their station in life. They were predictable. They were not slightly mad, nor were they despondent. James Ensor would not have liked them. I eliminated Yale. How intellectual could that institution be, if it had allowed George Bush to graduate?

That left Princeton. I looked up Princeton's civil engineering department on Google. I was glad to see that it was the top-ranked institution in the nation. Princeton was a school worthy of the man who had brought to life Hop-Frog's revenge. True, the school was located in New Jersey. However, James Ensor would not have minded this less-than-perfect setting. He had believed that a perfectly correct line could not inspire lofty sentiments.

In religious views, I wrote 'Occasionally'. James Ensor was clearly not a religious man. He had painted *Christ on a Donkey Entering Brussels* and *The Devil Leading Christ into Hell*. However, Mr Ensor was a superstitious man. He had composed an entire opera on the accordion using just the black keys, for he believed that the white keys would bring bad luck. A man could not be that superstitious and not believe in some greater Unknown.

MyFace asked me to select a home town. James Ensor was born in the Dutch town of Ostend, a small port city on the north-western coast of Belgium. The book said that waves and ideas from England rushed to this little port town at the time of his birth. I selected Dunedin as Roger Diamond's home town. It was the second-largest city in New Zealand. It was also home to one of its most beautiful ports.

It was essential that my profile be as opinionated as possible. James Ensor had said that tolerance was a flaw of middle age. A young man of twenty-odd years ought to have strong views.

I liked *The Daily Show* and *Colbert Report*. Mr Ensor would have liked the ability of both Jon Stewart and Stephen Colbert to regularly question not only the world, but also their own beliefs. I liked the Barack Obama page on MyFace. I did a Google search for the top twenty indie bands. I liked all of them. I like David Foster Wallace. I imagined that Mr Ensor would have really enjoyed *A Supposedly Fun Thing That I'll Never Do Again*.

I wondered if I should express mixed feelings on a complex issue such as abortion. But that would be too risky. It could result in Roger Diamond losing a lot of friends. On MyFace, it was important you had a definite viewpoint. There was no room for doubt. There was no room for the human condition.

Finally, there was an About Me section. Now that I was already pretending to be a white person in my virtual life, I could also pretend to have had a lovely childhood and a caring home.

I clicked into the text area MyFace had provided for the About Me section and wrote:

I grew up in the lovely port town of Dunedin in New Zealand. My grandparents owned a shop selling gifts by the beach. My earliest memories are of sea shells, stuffed fishes and novelty key chains. My father was a professor at the University of Dunedin. He was a man keenly interested in the concept of justice being made available to all levels of society. My mother was a jazz pianist. I was influenced by both of them. I am currently in New York. I am trying to make it here, so that I can follow it up by making it anywhere.

I scrolled up and down and reviewed my creation. Roger Diamond appeared like a human being.

Now it was time to find other human beings.

I then typed in 'Compost' in the search bar.

Earlier this summer, I had scrunched up my nose in Central Park.

'What's that smell?' I had wondered aloud.

'It's compost,' a blonde in her twenties had told me. She had a sincere and focused look on her face. I had tried to recall where I had seen that look before. The answer had come to me much later. I had seen that earnest look on the covers of albums of Bob Dylan, Jimmy Cliff and other musicians who had sung songs against capitalism and war in the 1960s.

I did not understand how it had come to be, but going by her utterly sincere look, compost must have become the equivalent of Vietnam for the modern generation. It was an issue that the public could easily gather around. And I was right. There were hundreds upon thousands of posts, groups and pages about compost on MyFace.

The first search result was for an event being held in Brooklyn. The event would demonstrate how to make compost, even in the small apartments of New York City. Apparently, New York needed more foul-smelling apartments.

I checked the box indicating that I would attend the event. I scrolled down the list of attendees. Jennifer Houston was attending the event. Jennifer wanted to learn how to make compost. But I couldn't find out anything else about Jennifer. She was an intelligent woman, who had taken care to make her profile visible only to her friends.

The notification bar on the top of my profile lit up with the number 1. Alice Reed had sent me a friend request. She was attending the event. I accepted her request and clicked on to her profile.

Sadly, like most MyFace pages, her profile was a caricature of a person. Every thought on the page expressed an opinion that was safe and predictable. There were no contradictions or imperfections that gave human beings their personality.

Alice was from Rochester, New York. She had studied Addictions Counselling at the University of Virginia. She liked books by Malcolm Gladwell, Stephen Pinker and someone named Ray Bradbury. Her favourite movies were *Spaceballs*, *The Secretary* and *Spirited Away*. She was interested in movies, '80s music and AIDS education.

And she liked to compost.

The event was in less than twenty-four hours. I had very little time to learn and perfect my social skills.

I went to Amazon.com and downloaded a copy of *How to Win Friends and Influence People* on my Kindle. My cell phone lit up before I had the chance to begin reading the book. It was Michelle. I ignored her call.

Dale Carnegie and I shared that perfect understanding between author and reader. He spoke clearly and simply, and I understood what he had to say. An hour passed, maybe two, when my cell phone rang again. It was Michelle calling again. I thought I had better pick up the phone. Else, she would pay me another surprise visit. I was feeling a little tense of late. I did not think I would be able to cope very well with a surprise.

'It's Thursday,' she said.

'So?'

'We should go out tonight.'

'Why? What's so special about Thursday?'

'Haven't you heard?' she said. 'Thursday is the new Friday.'

'Is it?'

'Yes.' She sounded confident. I felt glad to have learned something new about American society. I memorized this bit of knowledge for future reference.

'Let's go out,' she said.

'And do what?'

'It's New York City, you know? There are tons of things to do. Great restaurants...'

'I've eaten already.'

'So have I,' she said. 'But that's not the point...there are also so many nice bars.'

'I have a whiskey right next to me.'

'You might even get to meet all kinds of interesting people.'

'You're all the interesting people I want to know.'

'Oh come on, Arjun,' she said, stretching each vowel to the fullest. She sounded exasperated. If she had owned a cat, she would have kicked it.

'All right,' I said.

I had to finish reading the book. And there was so little time left till the event. However, if I turned Michelle down today, I could be sure that I would have to go through a tiresome conversation replete with reprimands in the not-too-distant future. The irritants posed by this conversation were both threatening and ambiguous. I was not entirely sure that I would be able to cope with them.

'Great,' she said. 'I'll see you at your place in a bit. And we can head out from there.'

'Head out where?'

'Well, let's see. We'll go to a bar where you can have a Manhattan. Or an Old Fashioned. And listen to some really good jazz.'

She was a teacher. But she could have easily pursued a career in sales.

I changed into my grey shirt and dark-blue boot-fit jeans from Banana Republic. I buttoned my shirt with a beleaguered air. But as I examined myself in the mirror, I liked what I saw. My slouch had disappeared. I stood tall and upright like a glass of whiskey.

I imagined the stirrer leaning against the glass with an almost military bearing. I inhaled the sharp whiff of bitters. I heard the tinkle of a piano note. Maybe going out for the night would not be such a bad thing after all.

Michelle had on a long white dress that flowed down to her heels. Her earrings were each made up of five yellow sunflowers arranged along the sides of a pentagon.

'You look great,' I said.

'I try,' she said.

'Let's get out of here,' I said. 'I can't take any more of this music.'

'What music?'

'You're kidding, right? Don't tell me you can't hear that.'

'I really can't.'

'Whatever,' I said, but only to myself. I do not think that it is gentlemanly to say words like 'whatever', 'weird' or 'gross' aloud.

As soon as we stepped on the pavement, Michelle took my arm.

'Admit it,' she said. 'Going out is so much better than having to sit at home and worry about your neighbour.'

I saw this line of thought couldn't be allowed to develop. I spent ten hours a day at work with people. That's all the people I could take in a day. I needed to be able to spend time in my home in the evenings.

'The Buddha has said that solitude is essential for the nourishment of the human soul. He has said that one should leave the dark state of being and enter the bright life of the bhikshu. Just like well-makers lead the water where they like, fletchers bend the arrow, carpenters bend a log of wood, wise people fashion themselves. Just like…'

I spoke for a while.

'I can totally see what he means,' Michelle said when I had finished. 'By the way, what's a fletcher?'

'I guess it's someone who makes arrows,' I said.

I was amazed. Unlike most people, she hadn't gotten annoyed by the words of the Buddha. Instead, she had actually listened to my speech, absorbed my words and distilled their essence.

We got off at the West 4th Street station and walked to 7th Avenue. At the corner of the block, the garbage had begun to sweat. A tired-looking banana peel curled over a discarded cup of coffee. Removing this stench now seemed to be beyond the powers of the New York sanitation department or, for that matter, any man-made organization. God would have to step in and take care of the cleaning operations.

But the skies were cloudless.

Michelle stopped at a newspaper stand.

'What's that painting?' she asked.

'That's a depiction from India's most famous epic, the Mahabharata,' I said. 'The guy in the chariot is Arjun.'

'Like you,' she said.

'With a name that's just like mine,' I said. 'But definitely not me. That Arjun was from a high-caste family. The guy on the ground is Karna. Both Karna and Arjun had the same mother. But Karna had been born out of wedlock. His mother had given him away to a low-caste family as soon as he was born.'

'Because she was ashamed?'

'Precisely. Society would ostracize her for having a child out of wedlock. So she gave him away. Karna grew up in a low-caste family. But even as a child, he was ambitious by nature. He wanted to belong to the upper strata of society. However, in order to gain access to the best schools that taught archery and warfare, he had to pretend to belong to a high-caste family.'

'Was that such a big deal?'

'Yes. It was a pretty big deal. When his teacher found out the truth, he was furious. He placed a curse upon Karna. He said all the knowledge that Karna had acquired would fail him when he needed it most. And that's what this painting shows. It depicts the moment his brother is about to kill him. Karna can't fight back because he has forgotten all that he knows about warfare. And, if you can permit me to indulge in a spoiler alert, he dies.'

'That's really sad.'

'Karna was incredibly grateful to the people who had accepted him. Outwardly, he never argued with his benefactors, even when he didn't agree with them. He remained silent just so that he could fit in. But, internally, he was governed by a rock-solid value system that the external world could never touch with their actions or even their condescending ways. You know, in many ways, Karna reminds me of an immigrant.'

'Or even a woman,' Michelle said. 'We have to put up with the same thing.'

She had a point.

'Do you think Karna succeeded in fitting in?' Michelle asked.

'He failed miserably,' I said.

The traffic ran along the length of 7th Avenue. A girl ran towards a taxicab. The seconds ran on the screen of my flip phone. But the bouncer stood perfectly still underneath the archway of the door.

The bar in the basement was small, so that you could see the candles flicker on the faces of its patrons. The walls met each other at right angles behind the bar. However, at the front of the bar they rushed towards each other and stopped just short before they culminated at the apex of a triangle. The polygonal shape imbued the Little Branch with an aura of eccentricity.

I could hear cymbals tapping in a room hidden behind a gaggle of elbows. The waitress guided us towards a table that had been magically squeezed between the drum set and the wall.

The lead singer sang in a hoarse undertone. The waitress brought our drinks to the table. We tapped our glasses softly. The light played with Michelle's face. It bathed the right side of her with a soft glow, and cast a shadow on the side that was further away from me. Michelle sipped from her Pisco Sour. It appeared as though she had been drinking from the fountain of eternal youth.

She looked at the band. Her face lit up in recognition. The singer waved to her. She came up to the table, took Michelle by the arm, and just in the middle of a riff, gave her the mike.

Michelle began to sing. Her voice wavered for an instant, after which it became as sure as the path of the sun. It touched everyone who heard it and filled it with its warmth.

'Oh I love to climb a mountain,' she sang. 'And reach the highest peak.'

She came closer to me.

'But it doesn't thrill me half as much…As dancing cheek to cheek.'

The bartender started to clap. A woman in her fifties smiled and closed her eyes. The people on the adjacent table were visibly mesmerized. Michelle smiled at me. I felt as though I was touched by celebrity.

'To heaven, to heaven,' she said. I smiled.

But I could hardly speak.

She finished the song to great applause. When the people in the bar had left their homes that morning, they didn't know they would encounter something special. But they had. Something special had socked them in the guts harder than a mugger could ever have in Central Park.

'How did you know that singer?' I asked her later as we walked to the E train.

'Oh, Alex and I took singing classes together at the 92nd Street Y…it was ages ago. We stayed in touch, off and on, via email. You know the funny thing…even Alex does not have a MyFace profile.'

I felt tense at the name of the social network. I remembered that I had to finish reading *How to Win Friends and Influence People*. The composting event was in less than twenty-four hours.

'I meant to ask you,' I said. 'How come you don't have a MyFace profile?'

'Because what I do and don't do, what I like and don't like, is none of MyFace's business.'

The children in her maths class were in good hands. I saw bright prospects for their future.

Michelle tapped me on my shoulder.

'See, that wasn't so bad,' she said.

'No, it wasn't,' I said.

I was surprised. Sometimes, you think the world is one way. But then it shows you that it is capable of being something entirely else.

'Remember, how I told you I was part of a band in Taiwan?'

'The campus school rock?'

She stopped to look at me. She was impressed that I had remembered.

'Did I ever tell you why I started singing?'

'No.'

'My mother made me. My mother used to sing very well. But she was from a poor family. Her father never had enough money to invest in her training. As a result, she never fulfilled her dreams. She was quite determined that I didn't miss out. She invested in my training from an early age.'

'Which is a great thing,' I said. 'I mean there are so many parents in India who force their children to become doctors and engineers. You had a mother who actually encouraged you.'

'You would think that,' Michelle said. 'I mean which girl doesn't want to go out on stage and be adored by thousands of people.'

'I do not know the answer to your question,' I said.

'Arjun, it's every young girl's dream! But my mother took that dream and made it her own. She kind of took it away from me.'

'That's too bad,' I said.

Like a boxer in the sixteenth round, Michelle was in her zone. She wasn't even listening to me.

'My mother is a very dominant woman,' she said. 'She has a very definite idea of what's right and what's wrong. She didn't approve of the people I used to associate with at these singing events. That man's hair is way too long, this woman smokes, that guy is clearly gay...'

We passed through the turnstiles on the subway.

'I began to do things I didn't even want to do. I guess I did them just to show that she couldn't dominate me. I started to smoke... I began to read Flaubert. I even started going out on dates with men in nightclubs... of course, I wasn't really interested in them. And because I was so disinterested, I thought nothing would happen. But...'

She said something. But she was forced to repeat it loudly so that she could be heard over the percussionists on the subway platform.

'Something happened…'

I didn't want to ask her what that something was. I know just what a suffocating experience feeling awkward and ashamed can be.

'It was quite a scandal. For an unmarried girl to…sometimes, I think my mother feels happy at what happened, just so she could tell me that she was right.'

Two seats opened up at the Queens Plaza station. We sat down.

'Before he died, my father had inherited a two-bedroom apartment in Taipei. It was a big enough apartment for just the two of us. But my mother's presence was so large that I remember feeling squeezed into a corner all of the time. I used to think that I would die an old and disgraced lady in that very apartment.'

'But something happened.'

'Yes,' she said. 'My luck changed when I started taking classes with this professor in high school. Unlike the rest of our faculty who had never left their home town, Mr Chan was savvy in matters of the world. He had secured a degree in nuclear physics from the University of Berkeley. After spending many years in San Francisco, he had decided to come back home. He recommended that I apply for a degree in America. Using his connections, he helped me get a scholarship at the University of Texas at Austin.'

'And that's how you got here.'

'That's exactly it.'

She rested her head on my shoulder.

'But it's so strange. I could never let go of that shame…I never even dated anyone, you know, until I met you.'

'Really?' I said. It was a word that sounded sufficiently empathetic and non-committal at the same time.

Michelle and I disliked our native countries. We shared a love for jazz music. We both loved the Spanish language. And she had something of a Mrs Clarkson in her life too.

I supposed it was a good thing she did not have a MyFace profile.

'What are you doing tomorrow?' she asked.

'Nothing much,' I said.

I was lying. However, I had no other choice. I could not afford to have her next to me when I met Alice Reed at the compost event in Brooklyn.

Brooklyn

The MyFace killer had not killed anyone yesterday. However, the impact of his actions had been strong enough to survive two days of the news cycle. The *Daily News* had reported that one of MyFace's earliest investors had sold more than twenty million shares of the social network. He had denied that his decision was related to the MyFace killings. The article quoted an analyst from Gartner saying that MyFace would disappear in a few years. Even if it didn't go away entirely, it would evolve into something like Yahoo! It might be around, and it might still make money, but nobody would really care.

The *Daily News* had carried another MyFace story on the same page. An ex-military man in downtown Pittsburgh had taken a hostage in an office building. He had posted a message on MyFace saying that he had lost everything.

Whatever had happened to the more innocent times on MyFace? Nowadays, people were killing each other on the social network. They were kidnapping each other. They were driving people to suicide. Didn't anyone poke their friends and throw pigs at them anymore?

On my way to work, I encountered a policeman at the Jackson Heights station. He asked me to open my bag. He looked at my Kindle and my notebook. I asked him if he wanted to read my notebook. He shook his head and told me that he really didn't care.

As I walked to the platform, I wondered why he had not wanted to read the notebook. Did he already know of its contents through the surveillance cameras placed by the people in the flower van? Or did they already have so much on me that they didn't need a notebook to bring the case to trial and prosecution?

It is very difficult for the mind to let go of all of its worries. There are just too many of them. They are all tightly interlinked, dancing an endless procession of tangos with each other. You let go of one worry, and soon enough, another one dances right to the centre stage to take its place.

No sooner than I had stopped worrying about the policeman, I started worrying about work. I had feared that our clients would begin to write in to ask that we pause their campaigns on MyFace. If that were the case, I would have to stop the MyFace campaigns for each and every one of our clients. At the same time, I would have to ensure that the agency did not lose revenue. To prevent this from happening, I would have to find alternative media venues to replace MyFace. I would have to issue detailed memorandums on how each of these alternatives aligned with the client's marketing objectives. I would then have to secure client approval for these recommendations and book available inventory. All of this would entail having to work well after midnight, which meant that I would have to miss the compost event.

However, luckily for me, our clients had decided to adopt a wait-and-see attitude.

I had just one question from the client at M&Ms. He wrote in to ask if they should be worried about the negative publicity MyFace was receiving in the media. I wrote back saying that this was not the first time MyFace had received negative publicity. I added that I hoped there would be no more murders linked to MyFace and that all of this would soon pass. I attached a screenshot of the latest MyFace campaign performance report. It showed M&Ms getting over 200,000 Likes in just the last day. I added it would be a shame to pause the campaign just as it was gathering momentum. The client wrote back to say that he agreed with my recommendations.

Other than this one email, it was a quiet day at work.

I opened the Amazon Kindle App on the Chrome browser and began to read *How to Win Friends and Influence People*. Dale Carnegie is an engaging writer. As soon as I dove into a paragraph, I was able to swim on page after page without getting distracted. After I had finished reading the book, I jotted down all of his principles on a small card. I made a mental note to laminate this card and place it in my wallet.

At one o' clock, my body gave me a programmed response. My stomach rumbled. It was time for the L28 peanut noodles.

As I took the elevator down, I decided to practise a principle of Dale Carnegie on Austin. I decided to try and take a genuine interest in him and find out just what had happened in the course of his life that had got him so interested in Jesus Christ.

But I wasn't given a chance.

'You're looking tired, sir,' he said.

'You are right, Austin,' I said. 'I was out very late last night. I think I need some sleep.'

'Sleep is important, sir,' he said. 'It is sleep that knits up the ravelled sleeve of care.'

'Shakespeare?'

'Yes, sir,' he said. 'But I fear it is not sleep you need, sir.'

'I don't?'

'No, sir. If I might say so, sir, it is peace that you need. Heaven's forgiveness and peace and love in the soul. Money cannot buy it, intellect cannot procure it and wisdom cannot attain it. In short, sir, you cannot by your own efforts hope to reach for it. But god, sir, He offers it to you as a gift.'

'Maybe so, Austin,' I said.

I walked to L'Annam in a contemplative mood. On my way to the restaurant, I stopped by the Chase Manhattan Bank. I made a healthy withdrawal from my account to add to the money from the day before. The sight of money inspired belief in the promise of a near Utopian world. It would not be a perfect world. In this society of tomorrow, there would still be inequality between the different classes. Key members of Al-Qaeda would still be at large. However, I would still be breathing and alive. I would be inhaling entire lungsful of air, entire continents, away from the machinations of the suspicious detective.

I sat down to eat the noodles in a relaxed state of mind. The deep-fried peanuts induced that state of mild comatose that helped me get through the afternoon.

The sun dimmed outside my office window. On Park Avenue, an entire minute passed without a car sounding its horn. I decided to go home before going to Brooklyn, so as to change into a nondescript T-shirt. I wanted to wear something that was a simple black, something that did not have any distinguishing imagery. The Buddha had nearly got me arrested on the night Kevin Santiago had died. I would not allow the Benevolent One to get in my way again.

There were no policemen on the 28rd Street station. However, I was surprised to see none other than *the* policeman, my very own policeman at the NYPD, Detective Crisafi, at the Jackson Heights station. He was seated in the passenger seat of a dark-blue sedan, being driven by his colleague who had a scar running along the length of his nose. Detective Crisafi was not dressed in his customary suit. Instead, he was wearing a plain white T-shirt and blue jeans. He was trying his best to be inconspicuous. But in the midst of the Indians, Bangladeshis and Pakistanis, he stood out as clearly as a pearl onion does in a basket of potatoes.

He began to follow me when I crossed the intersection at 34th Street. I did not turn back to look at the car. Instead, I turned on my flip phone and stared intently at it, as though it were a device capable of displaying the weather, showing the news or, for that matter, allowing me to throw birds at thieving pigs.

My nerves were too agitated to be able to wait for the elevator. I ran up the stairs. I resisted the urge to have a drink and calm myself. I had to remember the principles of Dale Carnegie and deploy them in a precise manner. At the end of the evening, I would have to wield a knife. I could not afford to have a foggy mind.

I changed into a new T-shirt, and brushed the wrinkles down with the palms of my hands. After a minute of gentle patting, I found that the motions served to ease out the furrows in my troubled brain. I decided to take the alternate exit, even if it involved wobbling on a shaky fire escape and leaping over the dying garden of a drunk Albanian man. A few minutes later, I found myself pushing at the iron gate of the old mansion. I brushed the dust off my trousers. Instead of going to the Jackson Heights subway stop, I walked to the station that was further off on 68th Street.

I transferred to the F train and took it to the Bergen Street stop in Brooklyn. Outside the station, I observed that god's cleaning crew had begun to move over the borough. Sweaty grey clouds had begun to congeal in the sky. Like subway passengers, they seemed to react with anger upon coming in contact with each other. They thundered.

I was struck by the incredible diversity of people on the street.

A Puerto Rican man blasted Rubén Blades' '*El Cantante*' from a store selling T-shirts, pajamas and women's clothing. Half a block ahead, an African American man advocated loudly that I follow the way of Jesus Christ. He said that if I didn't do so, my soul would be damned to eternal condemnation. I ignored him. He lacked Austin's courtly politeness. A Hassidic Jewish gentleman strolled down the street with his son. I wished I could accompany him to his home and have the bowl of matzo ball soup that J.D. Salinger had talked about.

The compost event was being held at 61 Local. As soon as I entered the bar, all of the diversity disappeared. Everyone was white, with the exception of three Asian girls and a black man in a yellow shirt. I saw instantly that I couldn't stay here for another second. If I did, I would be easily identified by more than one person when the detective came calling tomorrow.

I stepped outside the bar. From the pavement, I scanned the crowd. I saw Alice. She was standing with a girl who wore a NYU sweatshirt. She laughed at a joke with a practised ease. She reminded me of an actress on Broadway who was rehearsing a familiar line in familiar settings.

Alice had a tattoo of a hydra on her forearm. I had read about the mythical creature in a book on Greek mythology. Every time you cut off the head of a hydra, it grew two new ones. I hoped that Alice would be easier to kill than the creature depicted on her tattoo.

A tall girl with dark eyes handed me a cup.

'Want a free sample of kombucha?' she said. 'It's really good for you.'

'I'll try some.'

I wished I hadn't said that.

The drink had a bitterness that stuck to your tongue. Like a bad memory, it refused to leave my being. I moved my tongue over my lips and caught the whiff of urine. If drinking kombucha was what it took to live a long life, living a long life was overrated.

An exceedingly thin, almost two-dimensional man rolled a barrel in through the door. It had to have contained a rotting human body. He opened the lid of the barrel with a flourish.

'Compost!' he said.

Barrels that smelt like faeces. Drinks that reeked of urine. Were the people of Brooklyn in training to be third-world slum-dwellers?

'Creating your own compost pile is easy...' he began.

I threw the kombucha in the trash can where it belonged. I walked across the street to a Dunkin' Donuts. A Bangladeshi working at the counter smiled at me. He was suffused by a sudden fit of patriotism. He addressed me as 'brother' and gave me a large-size coffee, even though I had paid for a smaller portion. I stared at the oversized container with distaste. I could have watched my nails grow in the time it took to drink such a large coffee.

A graphic on the glass said that *America Runs on Dunkin'*. But I didn't want to run. Sometimes, a man needs to sit down and think. I sat down on a long-legged bar stool. I had a clear view of the people entering and leaving the bar across the street.

A homeless man lay twitching on the pavement. A young couple, an old woman and a dog stepped over him. I purchased a bottle of water and went over to him. I threw a few drops of water on his face. He opened his eyes. I gave him the bottle. He clasped his hands around it and went back to sleep.

After two hours, Alice came out of the bar. She was surrounded by a small group of people. She was talking to a white man with a long beard. It struck me as unfair that in post-9/11 America, white men were the only people allowed to have beards. Not that I would ever grow a beard. But shouldn't I be allowed to pursue every available happiness, including that of growing a beard? After all, wasn't that the whole point of the American Dream?

Alice said something. Her friends laughed at her. They walked into the subway station. I followed them. This time, I stepped over the homeless man.

A gust of air caressed our cheeks. A train was approaching. Everyone ran towards the platform, as though it were not a subway train that was approaching, but an ice-cream truck. The F train entered the station. As it slowed down, Alice began to embrace her friends. They hugged each other with great feeling and depth. They gave the impression that they would not be seeing each other for the next twenty years.

In this case, they wouldn't see her – ever again.

Her friends got on to the F train. I prepared to enter the train. But Alice stayed on the platform. She was waiting for the G.

The ghost train.

The G was the only train that ran directly between Brooklyn and Queens. Brooklyn and Queens were adjacent to each other. Between them, they had a population of four point seven million, more than four times the number of people who lived in Manhattan. Even so, there was only one train line that ran directly between the two boroughs. All other routes led through Manhattan.

The F train left the station. I took a deep breath. I recalled the first rule of starting a conversation.

It is important to have a big smile.

I stretched the muscles on my cheeks so that my lips were pulled in either direction. The only problem was that this gesture did not feel natural. My lips felt like unwilling dogs being pulled on a leash by their owners.

Dale Carnegie had said that it was important to be genuine. I needed to smile from inside. I thought of a scene from *The Simpsons* where Homer is told that scholarships at a particular private school are available only to minority students.

'Muchas gracias señorita,' he begins. 'Don't even try,' the dean says. 'Aso,' Homer then says in Japanese.

I began to laugh. You couldn't have removed the smile from my face with a pair of tweezers. Dale Carnegie was right. A warm smile was every bit as contagious as smallpox. Alice smiled back at me.

'You enjoyed making compost?' I said.

She stopped smiling.

'I was there,' I said. 'I saw you.'

She relaxed. She smiled again.

'It was difficult, especially in this heat. But it was worthwhile,' she said.

I agreed with half of her statement.

'True,' I said. 'But it's just the sort of thing that you need at the end of a day of yoga.'

Alice had listed Iyengar Yoga as one of her 'passions' in the About Me section of her MyFace profile.

'You do yoga?' she said.

'Oh, I teach it,' I said. 'I travel to different countries around the world with teachers from the Iyengar School of Yoga.'

'I love the Iyengar method of yoga,' she said.

'You know of it?'

'Sure,' she said. She lit up with pride even before I had the chance to look impressed.

'A daily practice of yoga is essential to maintain the perfect union between body and soul,' I said. But then I thought that this sounded too serious. So I added, 'I am a world-renowned expert in the corpse pose.'

'You're funny,' she said, instead of laughing.

I introduced myself. She did the same.

'Alice,' I said. 'Nice to meet you.'

I had just put into action the second most important rule of Dale Carnegie.

It is important to get to know the name of a person and use it often. There is no sweeter sound for a person than the sound of their name.

Alice was thinner than I would have liked. She seemed to have been influenced by the models on the catwalk who try so hard to acquire that third-world look. There was very little of the roundness that I like to see in a woman.

But she was attractive. Her eyes were black and intent. Her nose ended in a gentle curve that made me want to touch it. As for her body, I couldn't really tell. She had on a loose-fitting top and a pair of loose trousers that billowed in the wind. They were so old that they were evolving into sweatpants before my very eyes. She had gone out of her way to look unattractive.

A rat scampered down the length of the platform. Alice placed her hand over her mouth. Her body shook visibly, but all that made its way to her mouth was a muffled shriek. She stepped closer to me. I walked towards the rat and stomped loudly. It went behind a pillar and was swallowed by the darkness.

'Please excuse him,' I said. 'If he seems irritable, it's only because he's waiting for the G train.'

She laughed. It was an awkward and strained sound. I could actually hear the words, Ha, ha, ha. If I were to get Alice to spend time with me, she needed to feel more comfortable in my presence. I deployed another tip from Dale Carnegie.

The best way to move a person along to your course of action is to get them to say 'Yes' as often as possible. If a person agrees to what you have to say more than once, she or he will fall in line with your suggestions.

'Do you live in Brooklyn?'

'Yes.'

'Me too,' I said. 'I live in Williamsburg.'

'Shut up,' she said. I had been in America long enough to know that she wasn't saying that because she was offended.

'Me too,' she said.

But I already knew that from her MyFace profile. She lived in an apartment building near a bar called Moto. Moto was housed in a triangular building. It had been featured in a documentary called *Eat This New York,* a film about the business of food.

'Do you like jazz music?' I asked.

This was another safe question. Even if one found jazz music boring, it is socially unacceptable in America to say so.

'Yes,' she said. 'A lot.'

I said that I loved jazz music too. I spoke about John Coltrane's '*A Love Supreme*', and how I had first heard it played in the Hong Kong airport during a transit connection on my way to America. I told her about how I listened to '*Freddie Freeloader*' whenever I needed energy to begin a run. I mentioned how I had discovered '*Watermelon Man*' after finding out it was the favourite song of a sixteen-year-old son of an acquaintance, a boy who had been accidentally burned to death by his electric razor.

Alice nodded 'Yes' on four separate occasions. I could feel the gust of wind that announced an oncoming train. Now was the time to ask the big question. I asked Alice if she had heard about Moto. She said yes. I asked her if she wanted to go and listen to some jazz music at Moto.

The train had arrived at the platform. It was slowing down to a halt. Alice seemed uncertain. However, she was powerless against the momentum of all the 'Yeses' that had come before this moment.

'Yes,' she said.

I saw that we had arrived at a crucial point in the story of our acquaintance. If I allowed the conversation to lag now, she would change her mind as soon as we got off at the Broadway Avenue station. She would remember an early morning meeting. Or she would complain of a headache. She would go home. Her interest in me was so new that it could die as easily as the flame of a candle.

I asked Alice if she liked to travel. It was a rhetorical question. She had installed the 'Places I've Visited' app on her MyFace profile.

Alice responded eagerly. She said that she had been across Europe on a backpacking trip. She said that she would like to travel to Africa.

'I love those handcrafted baskets from Ghana. It would be great to buy them, mark them up and sell them on Etsy.'

I nodded. I was confused. I wasn't sure if she wanted to travel to Africa or colonize it.

The train had arrived at the Broadway Avenue station. I had succeeded. We had completed the journey without any awkward silences. When we were getting off the station, Alice was still in the midst of a story of how she had once been kidnapped by a cab driver in Poland.

Her story might have been very exciting. I wouldn't know. I had tuned out. I was distracted by the large number of people on the avenue, each one of them a potential eyewitness. I would have to put off what I had come here to do. I would have to wait until after Moto.

The building that housed Moto was in the shape of a triangle. It appeared like a miniature version of the Flatiron in Manhattan. The bar was small at the entrance and large at the rear, so that the notes that filled its interiors appeared to be pouring forth from the throat of a gramophone.

Alice sat at a table towards the back. It was sufficiently in the dark.

'We'll have a bottle of that,' I told the waiter, pointing to a wine listed on the menu. It saved me the trouble of having to pronounce its name.

I did not look at the price. It wouldn't have been the socially acceptable thing to do, now that I was a vice president at a New York advertising agency. Alice ordered an organic chicken leg dijonnaise with mashed potato and cabbage.

'I hope that chicken was free range,' Alice said.

'Free range?'

'Yes, you know. Chickens that aren't cooped up in little cages or anything. They're allowed to run around free.'

'And then they die?'

'Yes.'

'And that's a good deal for them?'

'Yes, of course,' she said. 'It's a great deal.'

Obviously, she wasn't seeing this issue from the point of view of the chicken. However, I was glad she thought that the chicken was getting a great deal. Because that was exactly the deal she was going to get. She had led a free-range life. Now, it would be coming to an end.

'Hey you,' a voice said over my shoulder.

Alice looked up. Her face lit up as though it were an iPhone screen.

'Simon,' she said.

Simon was six feet tall. He had eyes that twinkled even in the darkness. He had the carefully manicured stubble of an actor.

'What are you doing here?' he said.

'Oh,' she said. 'Just having a drink with a friend.'

He looked at me closely before he shook my hand. I felt like a paramecium on the other end of a microscope. I had no doubt that he would be able to describe me in great detail to the police sketch artist tomorrow.

I grasped my fork tightly. I fought the urge to stab it down on the table. I had put in a lot of hard work and research into planning a perfect evening. I had read Dale Carnegie. I had implemented his teachings. I had managed to be courageous and suave at the same time. It wasn't easy, but I had done it. And now, it was all for nothing.

'Watching the Olympics?' he asked.

'Trying to,' she said. 'But the five-hour time delay takes the fun out of it. I can successfully manage to avoid looking at websites to see, you know, who won and who lost. But the bank has TVs all over the place. And CNN puts out the results every fifteen minutes. So there are no surprises waiting for me in the evening.'

I had planned a surprise for her. But now, she would never know.

'Really?' he said. 'And I thought to watch CNN, you had to be on a treadmill. Or an airplane.'

She laughed. It was quite literally a knockout display of humour. I gasped. I realized I could never come close to him in delivering comments that were so subtle and yet laced with irony.

He picked up a purple-coloured beet from Alice's plate. He looked at it with the care of a jeweller inspecting a diamond. He placed it on his tongue. Having demonstrated his familiarity with Alice, he looked at me with a superior air.

'I thought of you the other day,' Alice said.

'Yeah?'

'Totally. I was walking by the bookstore on Bedford Avenue. And I saw this book by Sartre … Simon loves Sartre,' she said.

He nodded while chewing on the beet.

'Really?' I said. 'So in the world of fiction, on a scale of one to ten … 1 being, you know, the *New York Post* and 10 being Tolstoy…'

'I choose to turn Sartre all the way up to eleven.'

Alice began to laugh.

'That's the best movie ever,' she said.

I did not understand what she meant. I did not like existentialism before. I glared at the superior smirk on Simon's face. I liked it even less now.

'Well,' I said. 'I think existentialism is a deeply flawed theory.'

I had their attention.

'I think of existentialism the same way I think of objectivism. You know, the rational self-interest theory that's espoused by Ayn Rand.'

I did not know that it was illegal to take the name of Ayn Rand in Brooklyn. They seemed shocked, almost as if I had grabbed a blond child and flung him underneath a speeding car.

'What I mean to say is that both theories stress individualism to an inappropriate degree. I think it is essential to have one set of morals for individuals and for society as a whole.'

'You mean like the Ten Commandments.' Simon sneered. He had been spewing and sputtering even as he was silent, for there was spittle in the air.

'Or the American Constitution,' I said. 'But we can't each just do what we want to do and ignore what our society as one collective body is up to. I know many of us in America are against war. However, we choose to look the other way when America just goes around bombing children in downtown Baghdad. And why just stop at America? We should have a universal moral code for the entire world. As one of my favourite writers once said, as a human race, we have to give birth to new fruits and flowers under the sunlight of united hearts.'

'Dude, that's so cheesy.'

'That might be so,' I said. I wiped my lips slowly with the napkin. 'But the guy who said it won a Nobel Prize in literature. Rabindranath Tagore said these words when warning the world about the ill effects of the rise of nationalism in Europe.'

I took a long and slow sip of water.

'You know Tagore, don't you? He's India's greatest poet and Nobel laureate.'

They didn't know who Tagore was. Simon looked irritated. He clearly didn't like to be put in situations where he appeared ignorant.

Dale Carnegie tut-tutted in my ear. He had said that one should never point out another person's mistake directly to their face. I realized I should have said, 'Totally, dude. These words are so cheesy, especially when you think of them being used in a speech. Or, for that matter, a song. However, Tagore had used these words in quite another context, in a treatise on the evils of nationalism, where he implored Japan not to become like the West.'

I could tell I had lost Alice. Just a few seconds ago, her eyes had been bright. Now, they had dimmed. They appeared not like love lights, but like malfunctioning lighting fixtures at Penn station.

'Sorry, if I sounded rude,' I said.

I pointed to the bottle.

'Wine on an empty stomach,' I said.

They did not seem mollified. I was compelled to go Buddha on their asses.

'The Buddha says that a man speaking in a foreign tongue is often apt to be misunderstood.'

The Buddha hadn't actually quite said anything even remotely approaching that. But I thought saying 'The Buddha said' added weight to my sentence.

Simon still looked as though he had been force-fed a particularly sour lemon.

I saw that merely going Buddhist wouldn't suffice. I had to go Buddhist and helpless.

'Like, for example,' I said, 'I had no idea what you meant when you said, I have to turn Sartre up all the way to eleven. I totally didn't get that.'

Of the three of us, I had taken on the role of the ignorant one. Now that Simon had relinquished the position, it took him no time to return to his animated self. He told me about a movie called *This Is Spinal Tap*. He pulled over a chair and joined us by the table. He then puffed his chest out and spoke about *The Big Lebowski*.

Austin worshipped Jesus. Simon worshipped the Dude.

Alice too joined in to say something about hating the Eagles. Simon mentioned a group called Arcade Fire. Within a few minutes, their words began to flow together, and they were one gushing river of perfect synchronicity. As she spoke about her likes and dislikes, Alice no longer appeared awkward or uneasy. She didn't seem to be like a person struggling with the human condition. Now, she was a caricature of a person. She had devolved into a MyFace profile.

The waitress cleared away our plates. Alice began to tabulate the items on the bill to calculate who ate what and who owed how much. I always find this exercise tiring. Why bother to drink wine if you are not going to be magnanimous? I told Alice I would get the bill.

'I asked you out for dinner,' I said. 'I insist.'

'I didn't realize that this was a date,' she said.

'You'll be surprised just how many women have said that to me,' I said.

She laughed.

'Thank you,' she said. She smiled. The gesture touched me. She had felt happy that someone had taken her out for dinner. It had meant something to her.

The band began to play. We stepped out of Moto. The air felt warm on my skin. The street lamp had taken over admirably from the sun. Simon's cell phone rang. He crossed the street and stood in front of a deli. A red car pulled over in front of the store a few minutes later. Simon got into the car. Like me, he too had his own version of the boy. I wondered if his boy supplied him with marijuana or cocaine.

Alice followed the path of the car with her eyes as it disappeared around the block.

'We used to go out last year,' she said. 'Simon can seem a little stand offish. But deep inside he's a really sweet guy.'

Really, really deep down, I thought. You'd have to buy a ticket, call in some vacation days and make a journey to get there.

'You know, he once left me a message at work, saying he really missed me and loved me very much.'

Alice didn't see the irony in her statement. She had hit upon a fundamental truth of the human condition. People need cheesy sentiments. They need to be told they are wanted. Ironic declarations are like protein bars. They can nourish our souls. But they cannot satisfy it.

Simon joined us. He rolled a joint. We crossed over to the other side. Simon walked slightly ahead. Alice walked at a slower pace alongside me. The sounds of the cars from the Brooklyn–Queens Expressway came to our ears in an indistinct hum. Simon offered Alice the joint. She puffed on it delicately and released a small cloud of smoke. She passed it over to me. I refused. He seemed surprised.

'Yo, man,' Simon said. 'You don't partake.'

'No, I don't,' I said.

'You don't approve?' he asked.

'Look, man,' I said, 'I don't care if you do marijuana. I just don't approve of me smoking it. I find that when I do, I get distracted and I end up wasting a lot of time.'

But he wasn't listening to me. He was already thinking about something else.

'Wasting time, huh? Let me show you this great passage by Sartre.'

Simon knelt on the ground. He opened his backpack. He pulled out a bottle of kombucha and set it on the pavement. He fumbled in the insides of the bag as he looked for the book. I was surprised. Why have kombucha during the day to extend your life, if you are going to be out binge drinking at night?

'I thought I had it,' he said.

'No worries,' I said. 'You can always email the excerpt to me. I'll give Alice my email address.'

He didn't seem to care that I wanted to further intimacy with his former girlfriend. He stepped into a handball court on Rodney Street. He faced the wall and waved his hands in the arc of a forehand.

'Handball,' he said. 'Squash for the poor people.'

I saw that I had erred. I was being as unimaginative as an online marketer. I had abandoned the mission to kill Alice because there was an eyewitness present. But in this case, the witness deserved to die.

I looked outside the court. A dog barked into the night. But there was not a single human being on the street. I looked again. I could not afford to be even remotely linked to this incident after the fiasco with Kevin. The church opposite the court was solid and silent. It would be able keep a secret.

'Simon,' I said. 'You know Tagore, that Indian guy I was talking about? He said something else. He said that freedom cannot be about slavery to taste. Real freedom is the freedom of mind. And today, I'm setting you free.'

I cut the carotid artery on his neck and then a little more. He began to gush like a fire hydrant. He reached for me. I stepped a few feet away. He fell to the ground.

I turned back, prepared to run after Alice. But she hadn't moved. She was looking at me with wonder. She did not blink. Her lips were open. I thought I had achieved the feat that Simon had spoken of earlier that evening. I had turned it up to eleven.

'I am sorry,' I said.

She gasped as I caught her by the shoulder. It was the last sound she made.

I stuck an 'I found you on MyFace' sticker on Alice's white top. Beauty taken away in youth always made for a sad image. The *Daily News* reporter would be able to write a poignant paragraph. I stuck another sticker on Simon's forehead. The joint smouldered next to his open hand. The reporter would feel bad for wanting to laugh.

Raindrops began to fall from the sky. They were heavy and fat. They cleansed the earth of garbage, sweat and fingerprints. The drops were warm to the touch. I felt as though I had turned on both faucets of the shower.

I turned to the church. I knelt down and made the sign of the cross. I walked up Rodney Street till I reached Broadway. This particular avenue was so different from the Broadway in Manhattan. It was silent. There was me. And there was my shadow. There was nobody else. I smiled. The gods were continuing to blot out my transgressions.

A Fat Cat

For the first time in six days, the *Daily News* did not have a write-up about MyFace. Alice or Simon hadn't died in time to make the print edition. There was an interesting story about an Indonesian man who had spent eight months hiding in a New Jersey church. The immigration officials had caught up with him. They had kept him under questioning for twelve hours, at the end of which, they had decided to let him go. Apparently, the man belonged to a persecuted Christian minority in the Banda Aceh region of Indonesia. I felt heartened to know that there could be a compassionate side to the Department of Homeland Security.

It was a sunny day. The sky was blue without a single cloud. It might have been posing for a painting at the MoMA. Now that the heat had passed, the people of Queens had lapsed into a relaxed state of mind. Even the cars on 37th Avenue didn't honk. They stood patiently in front of Rajbhog, even though three taxis had double-parked on the avenue to get food.

People milled around stalls selling samosas and life insurance. They sauntered lazily in non-linear paths on the streets. A yellow butterfly tapped lightly against a bus and, making a graceful arc, flew away into the sky.

I was the only person hurrying along the street. I was also the only man who was dressed in a suit. Emily and Raj's parents were holding a joint memorial for their children at a church on the Upper East Side.

A police car made a right turn by the entrance to the subway station. I had no doubt they were following me because they suspected me of murder or terrorism, possibly both. The officer in the passenger seat was speaking into his car microphone. I could lip read what he was saying without having to make too much effort.

'Charlie to Victor. Charlie to Victor. Suspect on 37th Avenue. Suspect is dressed in a suit. Suspect has wires in pocket. Suspect is on his way to a mosque.'

They were way off the mark. The suspicion that I had wires in my pocket was ludicrous. I did not have wires. I had earbuds. The suspicion that I was on my way to a mosque was inconsistent with prior evidence. While speaking to Michelle, I had had the foresight to explicitly mention that the memorial would be held at a church. I had spoken loudly. The police personnel in the flower van had to have heard me.

There were two policemen outside the 86th Street and Lexington Avenue station. They were providing directions to a woman with a curvy ass and a sleek poodle. The officers of the law seemed to be completely engrossed by her guiles. However, I could tell from the corner of my eyes, they were looking at me.

The church was located on Park Avenue. There was a flag that fluttered outside the church. I knelt down and made the sign of the cross. I hoped that the FBI officers observing me were taking notes.

Michelle was wearing a black dress. Her arms glinted in the sunlight. I felt aroused. I saw she was speaking to the once-compassionate Detective Crisafi. He had changed out of his casual Friday wear. He was wearing the same dark-grey suit and red-and-blue striped tie that he had worn on two prior occasions to the office. I was fairly confident they were talking about me.

I kissed Michelle on her cheek. I looked at the detective after a delay as though he were an afterthought.

'I was just speaking to your lovely girlfriend here,' he said.

I was glad. I had wanted to appear normal. There is nothing more normal in the eyes of a white man than having an Asian girlfriend.

Michelle's smile did that zero to sixty thing. The detective smiled appreciatively as he saw her light up. I placed my hands lightly on the small of her back. A group of Indians opened the door of the church. A grandmother in a sari shivered. It was dark and chilly inside.

'It's so tragic,' I said. 'Have you made any progress on finding out how these deaths occurred?'

'Well,' he said. 'Both died of knife wounds.'

I saw that he didn't want to say too much.

'I see,' I said.

We entered the church. Fanciful arches swooped towards the ceiling. Haloes of light manifested themselves around every stained-glass window. The gold on the pillars shone mutedly in the dark. Decade after decade, this church had borne witness to the births, follies and deaths of millions of lives. And yet, it stood stoic, silent and forgiving. If only Jerry Springer and Dr Phil could learn from its example, America would be a much more tolerant and understanding country.

The body of Jesus Christ was nailed to a cross on a wall with floral patterns. He looked thin and distressed. Like some tired immigrant being turned away at the border between America and Mexico.

Emily's parents were seated in the first row. Her father had a square face. Jowls hung from the sides of his cheeks. He had his arms around Emily's mother. Her eyes were expressionless and completely detached from the proceedings.

'Are you Arjun?' her father said.

'Yes,' I said, surprised.

'Emily told us a lot about you,' he said.

I did not reply. I did not want to say anything that might sound disingenuous. Emily had told me that her father had once been a judge in the supreme court for the state of Wisconsin. He was a man who didn't suffer fools gladly.

Besides, I was in the grip of a new physical condition. I found that I had tears in my eyes. I could not remember the last time I had cried. I was unsure of how to guide and control my body, as though it had recently switched from an automatic to a stick-shift mechanism. Michelle grasped my arm.

We walked a few seats down the front row to meet Raj's parents. His mother was wearing a white sari. It was in stark contrast to the black clothes worn by Emily's parents. Emily and Raj were from two cultures that were so diametrically opposite that they used completely contrasting colours to symbolize both life and death. How could such romances ever hope to survive?

I hadn't brushed my tears away. Raj's father took one look at my eyes and embraced me. He told his wife I reminded him of their son. My teeth rubbed against each other. I felt a spark of anger. I passed out of my state of solemnity. I wasn't anything at all like Raj. Besides, I don't like the word 'son'. Raj's father said that I should visit them sometimes. He spoke to me in Hindi. This simple shift in language made the invitation sound familiar and welcoming.

The priest was a tall and lean man. His voice was deep and resonant. He asked us to take solace in the fact that Emily was at home with her god. I closed my eyes and thought of where Emily might be. I pictured her perennially optimistic spirit mingling with the breeze, blowing over tulips and turning windmills.

The priest began to talk about Raj. Now, his words failed to move me. All I experienced was curiosity. What happened to people like Raj after they died? Were they given a short tenure in heaven because they had died in their youth? Or were they sent directly to hell?

As the priest continued to talk about Raj, I began to wonder what Michelle and the policeman had been talking about before my arrival. Had she told him about the repeated text messages and calls that had gone unanswered? Had she told him I was alone at home on Friday evening?

People rose to their feet. The priest reassured us that Emily and Raj had gone to a better place. I wanted to ask Michelle about her conversation with the detective. But I didn't dare. In these cavernous chambers, I feared that even the smallest whisper would echo like a giant confession.

I waited until we were outside. I waited until I had made sure that we weren't being followed. We had reached the reservoir at Central Park. The pond sparkled in the sunlight. A fountain gushed in its midst. A small flock of birds rested on a stone by the fountain.

However, the world will just not let you be. A bicyclist came down the road at a speed that was more suited to the takeoff of an airplane. He braked in front of Michelle. He cursed at her. I took out my flip phone and clicked his photo. I stared at him till he looked away.

'Why did you click his picture?' Michelle asked.

'Just to report him in case we run into a cop,' I said.

Google had recently announced a new feature for their images section. You could upload an image to Google Images. The search engine would tell you the name of the person in that photo. The search results would also include a link to that person's MyFace profile. I had a photograph. I would proceed to link it to a profile as soon as I got home.

'What did you think about the ceremony?' I asked.

'It was beautiful,' Michelle said.

A golden retriever grabbed at a tennis ball that had landed dangerously close to my feet. It held it in its mouth and ran back to the owner.

'I noticed how moved you were when speaking to Emily's father.'

She didn't say anything else, as if this were the only moment that had taken place all morning.

'I don't know how that happened,' I said. 'I'll be honest. I was so embarrassed...'

'Stop,' she said. 'Don't be stupid.'

'I guess I never thought I would run into all these people there... her parents, Raj's parents, the detective...'

'Ah yes, Detective Crisafi... he is such a nice man.'

'Is he?'

'Yes... he was telling me a very interesting story...'

He had told her a cat that had gone missing from the terrace of an apartment in the Upper East Side. The patrol officers had gone to the building to look into the incident. They had made enquiries in and around the building. But they hadn't been able to find the cat.

After a few hours, they received a call from the superintendent of another building three blocks away. The cat had been found on the terrace of that building. It had been carried away by a hawk. However, it was so fat that the hawk could not carry it very far. The hawk had been forced to let go of it.

'Can you believe it?' Michelle said. 'Being fat actually saved that cat's life.'

'We should go to McDonald's right away,' I said.

She laughed.

'It's quite a life these police inspectors lead,' she said. 'Of course, it's not always this fun. Sometimes, they have to deal with super grisly stuff too.'

'Like Emily's and Raj's murders,' I said.

'Yes, we were talking about that too,' she said.

'What did he say?'

'Apparently, he is not sure that a serial killer is behind all of this. It seemed to me they are still in the process of getting the basic stuff straight … like who died when and where, and who was where on which night.'

'Ah,' I said.

'But I don't want to talk about it,' Michelle said.

I was convinced she was hiding something.

'Should we go home?' I asked.

'No, why would we do that? It's such a beautiful day.'

'You are right,' I said. 'Let's keep walking.'

'This has been such a difficult weekend for you,' she said.

'It has?'

'Yes, with three memorials …'

'Three?'

'Well, we had the memorial for Emily and Raj today. And you had your memorial yesterday for the director of your orphanage.'

'Yes, of course.'

'Do you want to talk about it? About what you did last evening to commemorate his memory?'

'Orphanages. Homicides. Detectives. Is this how you want to spend such a beautiful day?'

'You're right,' she said. 'Let's talk about something else.'

We walked down the Bridle Path listening to the breeze play with the leaves. When the sun set, we wanted to continue to surround ourselves with beauty. We took the train to Grand Central. We gazed at the ceiling. It was green, just like the trees in the park.

My phone rang. The caller ID did not show up on the screen. I wondered if it were someone trying to blackmail me. I picked up the phone. It was Mr Clarkson.

'Arjun,' he said in a soft, effeminate voice.

How in the world did the man manage to get a job at the Voice of America? Austin had once told me that Jesus had identified three kinds of eunuchs. Eunuchs who had been born as eunuchs. Eunuchs who have been made eunuchs by men. And eunuchs who had made themselves eunuchs. Sometimes, I felt that Mr Clarkson was this third kind.

'I was just calling to check up on all these MyFace murders.'

'What do you mean?' I asked.

'You know, I was just calling to make sure you were OK.'

'Ah,' I said.

'All the murders are taking place in New York,' he said. 'You should probably get off MyFace.'

'I will,' I said. 'I hardly use it much anyway.'

I did not say much after that. He was a reserved man. He was not able to introduce new topics that would extend the conversation. We hung up.

A policeman and his dog walked by me. The dog sniffed at the ground. I stepped away. The Department of Homeland Security and the New York Police Department were probably working closely together to get me on the first pretext that became available to them. They had found they would need more than the help of mere humans to incriminate me for the MyFace murders. They had enlisted the assistance of animals.

At this moment, they were probably reporting on my every move.

Suspect has just entered Grand Central.

Suspect has just fidgeted with keys in pocket.

Suspect has looked up towards the ceiling.

Michelle has suggested to suspect that they have a cocktail.

'A cocktail sounds great,' I said.

I could indulge in an all-American activity under the watchful eyes of the police.

I looked at my feet. I was wearing my formal shoes made by Alfani.

'I don't have my sneakers on,' I said. 'We can go to the Campbell Apartment. What do you say to cocktails from another era?'

'That's wonderful,' Michelle said.

'What is?'

'The way you put that…cocktails from another era.'

'If this was at work,' I said. 'I would have taken the credit. But all I'm doing is reading that sign.'

She punched me on the elbow. I laughed.

A voice in my head told me I had work to do. I had to go home and upload the photo of that bicyclist in Central Park to Google. However, I had spent the day ensconced in magnificent enclosures. The cavernous church, the canopies of the park and ceilings of Grand Central had induced a sense of freedom in me. They had liberated me from the burdens I had been carrying. The presentations that were due at work, the loud music played by my neighbour and the machinations of the detective now appeared as inconsequential as the 7.39 train to Poughkeepsie, whose platform information lit up the monitors scattered around the terminal.

Michelle ordered a Cosmopolitan. I asked the waitress for an Old Fashioned. I sank back into the leather armchair. Etta James sang, '*I just want to make love to you*'. With its couches and coffee tables, Campbell Apartment felt like a very comfortable residence. It was a residence that always played my kind of music.

We had nearly finished our drinks. My breath felt as warm as my chest. My mind was conscious only of the last drops of whiskey that clung to the ice. The cocktail had magically transformed all of my preoccupations into a mild and gentle fog, a hazy reminder of life.

'I have been thinking about what you said,' Michelle said.

'About?'

'About doing something to fill the time in the evenings. I think I am going to start singing again…'

'That's excellent.'

'And maybe take up something else…some yoga, some chess…I haven't really thought about it.'

She was speaking fast, rushing from one thought to another, as though in a hurry to get to the point that really mattered.

'But I'd like to spend this evening with you.'

'That goes without saying,' I said. 'Why would we want to break the flow of such a nice day?'

She smiled. Her earrings sparkled.

'But didn't you want to purchase some coffee for your apartment? Oren's Coffee is probably a good place to buy it.'

'You're right,' she said. 'I had forgotten.'

She brought her face close to the drink, as people do when they are drinking from a martini glass, and took a sip.

'You know what,' she said. 'Over the last few days, I've noticed something different about you. You're not as forgetful. You're really…really put together.'

'Really?' I said.

'Yes, really. You seem to be more sure of yourself.'

'You might be right,' I said. 'You know, I've always been absent-minded. I think that's why I've always had this feeling that I am on the verge of screwing something up. It made me a very tentative person.'

'Really?'

'Yes, really. When I used to smoke, no matter where I saw a fire engine, I used to think that the firemen were on their way to put out a fire caused by a cigarette that I had forgotten to extinguish. But you're right. Over the last week, I don't feel as tentative anymore.'

'I wonder what changed during the last week,' she said.

'I wonder,' I said.

'Well, we started, you know…'

'That's just it,' I said.

I spoke intently to Michelle as we walked by policemen both at the Grand Central Terminal and the Jackson Heights station. Once home, we stayed awake for two hours. After she had gone to sleep, I powered on my Lenovo laptop. I opened up the TOR client and logged into MyFace.

I uploaded the photo of the bicyclist who had bumped into us at Central Park on the Google Images website. Google helpfully displayed the links to his LinkedIn and MyFace pages. The biker's name was Matt Fleming. He was thirty years old. He was originally from Orange County. He worked at AMC. Like me, he was an online marketer. Unlike me, he was heavily into networking among the marketing professionals of New York. He was a part of the Mobile Monday Association, Digital DUMBO, Shake Shack, nextNY and the New York Internet Marketers Meetup. I clicked on to the Meetup page. They had a meeting tomorrow at reBar in Brooklyn. I decided to stop by their event after work.

I went into the bedroom. García Lorca's book lay open beside Michelle. She was awake.

'Come here,' she said.

I jumped on to the bed. I got on top of her. She giggled. I nibbled on her neck. I bit her ear and kissed her. She began to cry.

'What did I do?' I asked.

She continued sobbing. She wrapped her arms around me and continued sobbing.

'Oh Arjun,' she said. 'I am so happy with you. I don't want this to end …'

'And why would it end? It's not like we are in a movie.'

'It's just that …'

But she never completed her sentence. And how could she?

There is never just one grievance that we can clearly pinpoint as being the cause of our sadness. Instead, there are a thousand little hurts, all intertwined and crawling over one another like worms over the surface of our brains. Memories of Taipei. A dominating mother. An unfaithful lover. A scandal.

So many worms, meshing and gnawing and grinding their teeth.

'Don't think about it,' I said.

Sometimes, all thinking does is give you a thoughtache. When you get thoughtache, you have to stop thinking. The only way to cease all thought is to pursue a course of clear and direct action.

I looked forward to the next Meetup of the New York Internet Marketers Group.

Of Narnia and New Jersey

The MyFace killer had once again made it to the headlines of the *Daily News*. The newspaper had printed a large picture of a blurred MyFace profile page. The caption read: Two People Found Dead On MyFace.

The report stated that the bodies of Simon Hennessy and Alice Reed had been found on a racquetball court in the South Williamsburg area. Unlike the last time around, the journalist had reported the stabbing accurately. He reported that Simon had been killed by a wound to the carotid artery, and that Alice had died as a result of suffocation from a perforation to the throat area.

The report also quoted Jon, a friend of Simon and Alice. Jon stated that Simon and Alice were dating until recently. The journalist noted that Emily and Raj, two prior victims of the MyFace killer, had also been dating each other.

Detective Crisafi was quoted as saying, 'We have every reason to believe that the killer is finding and hunting his victims on MyFace.' On being asked if he recommended that people delete their accounts on MyFace, the detective said, 'All I would say is that people be careful about the kind of information they share not just on MyFace, but on any public forum.'

The article also quoted a MyFace spokesperson as saying that the social network was extremely committed to user privacy. As an immediate measure, the network was proactively making the email addresses, phone numbers and mailing addresses of people on the social network private.

'This was something MyFace should have done all along,' said Mr Kahn, chairman of the Consortium for Internet Privacy. 'It's unfortunate that five people had to die in order to get MyFace to take consumer privacy seriously.'

The MyFace spokesperson refused to cast light on whether people had begun leaving the MyFace network as a result of the killings. The head of Nielsen research said that data on any change in MyFace usage would be available in the next three days. The article finished by quoting Jon, who said that he 'would be continuing to stay on MyFace', because 'he refused to bow down to terror'.

I switched on my TV. I turned down the volume so as not to wake up Michelle. But I needn't have bothered. I was finding out that she could sleep through the sound of an eighteen-wheeler truck fighting its way through the potholes on Northern Boulevard. What gave some people the ability to sleep soundly? Was it because they were not as anxious as the rest of us? Or was it because they were so anxious that they were frightened to wake up and face the world?

I switched to channel 78.

The channel aired two hours of Indian programming on Sunday mornings. The shows featured old Bollywood songs and a thirty-minute news programme. Today, I wanted to see if they were going to cover the MyFace murders. After all, an Indian had been the second victim of the MyFace killer. Raj Malik would have denied his Indianness. But even though he didn't watch Bollywood movies, or follow cricket, one couldn't deny that he had sprung from the loins of the motherland.

The TV channel was showing a replay of a cricket match between India and South Africa in Cape Town. I reached for the remote. There was no other activity more Indian than watching a cricket match. In America, it was only Indians on work visas who wasted their time watching cricket; time they could have instead spent on drinking, inhaling cocaine and fornicating.

Just as I was about the change the channel, Mohammad Azharuddin appeared on the screen.

Like most other sports, cricket is rife with clichés. Players dazzle, shine, sparkle, take the game to new levels, and electrify the crowd with their teamwork. They are ebullient, daring, confident and brash enough to defy the odds. They play with their bodies, their hearts and their souls and yet remain content to be unsung heroes.

But none of these words could be used to describe Azharuddin. As I saw him raise his bat and work the ball through the midwicket region in a wristy follow-through, I realized that no adjective could ever do justice to his batting.

Waterfalls are not described for possessing genius for the ways they fall down the faces of cliffs. Rainbows are not described as brilliant for the way they stretch colour across the sky. Azharuddin batted as though every stroke was an act of nature. He batted without visible human effort.

I hated him for making me watch cricket. I hated him for making me feel so Indian. When he unleashed a straight drive down the ground, he made me realize that cricket wasn't just an interest or a hobby. Like my sickness, it was something that was a part of me. I could never expel it from my being.

My phone rang. It was Raj's father. He wondered if I wanted to visit them that afternoon. He told me they lived in Rahway, New Jersey.

Since I had arrived in the United States, I had stayed away from New Jersey. I had heard that New Jersey was home to the greatest number of people of Indian origin in the entire United States. I had heard of a town called Edison with so many Shahs and Patels that the post office did not make deliveries to individual houses.

Instead, they dumped all the mail in one central location. They left it to the Indians to separate and distribute the mail to their individual homes.

However, I couldn't refuse Mr Malik's request. He had recently gone through a profound change in his life. Visiting him in New Jersey and making him feel better was the least that I could do. I told him I would see him there at two.

'Text me when you are on the bus,' he said.

The news came on. The anchor wore a sari. She spoke Hindi with a strong anglicized accent, as though she had just come back from India after a colonizing mission. She did not cover the MyFace murders. Instead, she focused on events that had taken place two weeks ago. I admired her obstinacy. She had refused to bow down to the expectations of fresh and timely news that her viewers might have of her in the Internet age. Her reporting might have been untimely. However, it was a relief to be able to watch a news programme without the words 'Breaking News' flashing on the screen.

Michelle woke up at noon. She said that she had no time for lunch. There was a Parent–Teacher Association event at her school.

'They normally do it on the weekdays,' she said. 'But this is their big annual event. They planned it on Sunday so that the entire family could attend.'

I changed into a new-age kurta that Mr Clarkson had sent me from India. It looked sufficiently traditional to make a good impression on Raj's parents and sufficiently modern so as not to alarm the patrol officers at the Port Authority.

I bent down to tie my shoelace at the intersection of 34th Avenue. I looked carefully down the length of the tree-lined boulevard in either direction. The sunflowers were yellow, the orchids were red, and the Gerbera daisies were blue, as blue as the sedan parked one block away in the sunlit avenue.

I felt a deep empathy for these officers of the law. The Buddha had said that if a man were to rouse himself, if he exhibits control

and displays earnestness, he can make for himself an island that
no flood may overwhelm. Detective Crisafi's retinue of men had
followed the path of the Buddha. They had roused themselves.
They had followed me in right earnest. They had exhibited great
self-control when it came to arresting me and reading me my
Miranda rights.

And what had I given them in return? Uneventful trips whose
trails led from my workplace to my apartment. That was all. By
living a life that was exceptional in terms of its very ordinariness, I
had flooded their island.

But today, I would light the candle of hope in each of their
hearts. I would give them something to talk about, in hushed
whispers to their partners and near-incomprehensible crackles on
their walkie-talkies. I would imbue their boring field reports with
small, interesting, even tasty and aromatic details.

I turned left on 34th Avenue. I entered the wine store by
Maharaja Sweets. It was run by the only angry-looking Tibetan
woman in the entire world. I battled through her scowl and
purchased a bottle of 2008 Pinot Noir wine. I crossed the road
and went into Raja Sweets. I bought six samosas. Once outside the
store, I knelt down on the ground. Slowly, yet surely, I placed my
purchases in my North Face backpack.

The blue sedan had followed me. It had crawled its way down
to Roosevelt Avenue. The officers had seen me purchase wine.
They had seen me order samosas for these New Jersey parents
who had recently been separated from their child. I hoped they
would now think of me as a compassionate American, one who
was thoughtful enough to buy the aged wine and deep-fried food,
the best antidotes for grieving souls.

The Port Authority was like Bihar. There was lawlessness
everywhere. A man urinated against a pillar. A police officer
and his dog ignored him. A boy ran up an escalator in the wrong
direction. Two palms touched each other and drew quickly away.
The Port Authority was steeped in urine and hopelessness.

If it were a country, it would perennially be on the agenda of conferences that focused on international aid.

I caught the Number 192 bus towards Clifton. We passed through the Lincoln Tunnel. I moved to the aisle seat. I did not want my face appearing on the TV cameras in the Lincoln Tunnel. With the advances in face recognition technology, my whereabouts would instantly be broadcast both to the flower van and the offices of Detective Crisafi.

A black SUV tried to hustle its way in front of our bus. When passing through the Lincoln Tunnel, every New Yorker becomes a Republican. Every man acts in his own self-interest. But our bus driver plowed through the tunnel with the realization that he had the largest vehicle. It wasn't even a contest.

Mr Malik was waiting for me at the bus stop in a gray Toyota Camry. He smiled and said hello. He asked me how I was doing. He did not start the car till I had finished giving my answer. He asked me the questions that Indians ask each other at the beginning stages of their acquaintance.

Where was I from?

What was my last name?

What was my income?

I said that I was from New Delhi. Nobody wants to admit that they are from Bihar. I was thankful that my last name was Clarkson. With my American last name, Mr Malik would find it impossible to discern my caste. I told him I made $150,000 a year. It was a number that had to be higher than what Raj had made at the agency. I pushed back into the car seat and relaxed.

I had never been in a large American home before. But I had imagined living in one of them often. I had seen them on television. They were places where every room was large enough to be its own world. Every closet led to Narnia.

'You don't have to remove your shoes,' he said. But he looked glad when I did.

There was a statue of Ganesha in the hallway. It led to a large living room. Another passage branched off into even more rooms. A staircase curved and ascended towards even greater possibilities. I wondered what it must be like to stroll from one area of the house to another, with your feet at times on tile and at others on carpet. These were homes spacious enough to think big thoughts. These were the kind of homes that must have shaped Internet technologies and Russian novels.

'It's a beautiful house,' I said. 'It's so big.'

'Yes, maybe too big for just two people,' he said. He turned to his wife as she came down the staircase.

Mrs Malik was wearing a white salwar kameez. She reminded me of a woman I had seen in a painting at the MoMA. The woman in the painting had long hair. She had a face that had achieved a perfect balance between length and roundness. That painting was called *Madonna and Child*. However, unlike the Madonna in the painting, Mrs Malik's eyes were red. She had been crying.

She asked me the same questions that her husband had asked me in the car. I answered consistently.

She led me to a big table that had eight chairs. The table was located in a section of the house that Mr Malik called 'the dining area'. Mr and Mrs Malik had hung the certificates they had received upon graduating from medical school on the wall behind the dining table. Every other object in the room had something or the other to do with Raj.

In one photo, Raj was dressed in a Luke Skywalker outfit. In another, he was seated on top of a horse. There were snow-capped hills in the background. Raj was smiling. The horse looked sad. There was another certificate on the wall. It had been awarded to Raj for receiving a black belt in karate.

'He even won the national spelling bee contest when he was just eight,' Mrs Malik said. She had been following the movements of my head with her eyes.

She reached up to the wall and detached a newspaper clipping surrounded by a heavy black frame. The article featured a photo of a young Raj in front of a mike. The caption said that he had correctly spelt 'guatepens'.

'The word means "ambush",' said Mr Malik.

There was a sepia-toned photo of a young Raj rubbing noses with his mother. They were on a beach. There was a caption underneath the photo. It said, 'The most beautiful thing in the world is to see your parents smiling, and the next best thing is to know that you are the reason behind that smile.'

It was an honest statement. However, it was one that was devoid of all irony. I thought Raj would have sooner died than upload that photo to his MyFace profile.

The food was simple. It was devoid of the excessive turmeric, chilli powder or the hodgepodge of spices so often used to mask the taste of bad Indian cooking in New York. Mrs Malik was like a confident virtuoso, who was content to play a simple C major when no other chords were necessary. I nearly cried with delight upon tasting cumin with the first mouthful of dal. The potato was as soft as the fenugreek was crisp.

Mr Malik barely touched his food. Save for a spoonful of rice and yogurt, Mrs Malik's plate too was empty. I protested every time Mr Malik piled a fresh serving of food on my plate, but we both saw through the façade of my good manners. He asked me to eat more. I obliged.

So this is what it must feel like to grow up with a father and a mother in a loving home. People were attentive. They were tender towards one another. The smallest action was worthy of praise. A misdemeanour was deemed innocent and devoid of malice.

'You know Raj spoke about you at home?'

'He did?'

'Yes, he told us once that an Indian had joined the office. He said that you were the rising star of the media department.'

I was surprised.

'That's very generous of him. I must be honest and tell you that there's only one person in our media department.'

'It says a lot about your work that they don't need any more people. Raj was right,' Mrs Malik said. 'He was always a very perceptive boy. There was this time when he was young when he,' she pointed at her husband, 'had wanted to invest in some business. We had argued about it for days. Even though he was so young, Raj could make out we were having some problems. That night, when I was going to sleep, he came to my bed. He kissed me on my cheeks and told me that everything would be all right.'

She smiled at the memory. Then she became sombre again as if she felt guilty for smiling. I put my spoon down on the table. I suspected that it would have been impolite to ask for a fifth helping.

Mrs Malik began to clear out the dishes. I offered to help.

'All I want to see you do is sit down and relax,' Mr Malik said.

Mrs Malik brought out three cups of tea.

I like the taste of ginger. Even though the glass was hot, I sipped deeply.

'So this Emily,' Mr Malik said. 'What kind of person was she?'

'She was a very good girl. She had a good nature.' I didn't precisely know what having a 'good nature' meant, but I knew that Indian elders prized it as a quality in a human being.

'And how was their relationship?'

'Well, Emily had left the company,' I said. 'And Raj had been very tight-lipped about the whole thing. But from what I know of both of them, they had to have had a very loving relationship.'

'So what people are saying about Raj, that he…'

'It's a lie,' I said. 'Raj had nothing to do with Emily's death.'

It felt wonderful to be able to tell a truth. I was able to look both Raj's father and mother in the eye. They relaxed visibly. I felt delighted to have been able to bring comfort to these people, who could have so easily been my own parents.

'I am sorry,' Mrs Malik said. 'I'll be back.' She got up. Her chair screeched against the floor. The staircase creaked. A door closed.

'I am sorry,' Mr Malik said. 'This has been really difficult on her.'

I offered to leave.

'You must want to be with her,' I said.

'You can't just eat and leave,' he said. He said this in a matter-of-fact tone as though it were a commandment in a religious book. It was impossible to refuse him. To his credit, he initiated a new conversation.

He began to tell about how he had come to America after John F. Kennedy had passed the Immigration and Nationality Act in 1965.

'The law was primarily meant to increase the immigration of people from Europe…East Europe, but we Indians were quick to take advantage of it.'

'How very Indian of us,' I said. He laughed.

Mr Malik and his wife had moved to Rutgers because they had been awarded scholarships. They had moved to Clifton because 'there were many Indians and it was sufficiently close to Rutgers'. They had continued to live in New Jersey because it had the best schooling in the entire country. All their life, they had done nothing more than ensure that Raj grew up in a loving family that was able to provide for his every need.

I asked Mr Malik if he was actively involved in politics. He looked at me with a puzzled air. Then he laughed.

'Oh that sign on my lawn! It was put up by one of Raj's friends. I couldn't say no to him. And besides, it was blue. I thought the colour went well with my lawn.'

I laughed.

'I don't care much about politics. I don't let it bother me.'

He sipped his tea.

'Though I really liked Bill Clinton. He is a really intelligent man.'

He asked me if I watched Hindi movies. I told him that I did not care for movies very much. He asked me if I ever watched cricket. I told him that except for tennis and chess, there was no sport that interested me.

'Incredible,' he said.

The alarm on my phone went off. I had set it to remind me to make a checklist of the things I would require prior to my meeting with the Central Park bicyclist.

'I should be going,' I said. 'Tomorrow is Monday, and I have to get ready for work.'

It was a Puritan sentiment and one that was readily appreciated by an immigrant.

'Keep in touch,' I said. 'Are you on MyFace?'

He laughed.

'Just email or call me,' he said. 'My wife is on MyFace. She showed me Raj's MyFace profile once. I couldn't understand head or tail of it. No doubt you get all the references.'

I smiled.

'MyFace has memorialized Raj's profile,' he said. 'They've handed over the username and password to us. I go there once a day and write to people who have expressed their condolences.'

He coughed.

'You know, once MyFace memorializes a profile, they block a person from showing up in News Feeds, birthday notifications and suggestions for friend recommendations. But the funny thing is that they don't stop showing the ads. Just the other day, I was on Raj's profile. I saw an ad for a kitchen knife. The ad said that this knife could cut through anything.'

'No,' I said.

'Yes,' he said.

'I am sorry,' I said.

I got up to leave.

'Why are you limping?'

'It's nothing,' I said. 'It's just my knee. I think I might have hurt it when running.'

'I think I have some painkillers. Let me see.'

And before I had a chance to protest, he went up the stairs. He came down with a yellow pillbox. Mrs Malik accompanied him.

I thanked her for the food. She smiled. I told her I would come and see her again. It was the least I could do.

'How often should I take this tablet?' I asked.

'Whenever it hurts,' she said.

She smiled vacantly. I could see that she didn't really care about my knee. My mind went back to the memory of only an hour ago, when our conversation at the dinner table had seemed imbued with a certain familial intimacy.

And now, she hadn't even warned me that I should not take that tablet on an empty stomach. She hadn't said that I should not take it more than once every four hours, or with alcohol. She had not expressed a single irrelevant or redundant thought that betrayed maternal concern.

'Don't take it more than once every eight hours though,' Mr Malik said. But it was too little, too late.

We walked towards the car.

'Come see us again,' he said, as he dropped me off at the bus stop.

I nodded. But I doubted that I would. Parents and families were a soft spot for me. And that's the thing about soft spots. Should the slightest thing touch them, they flare up. Just like that.

A British Lord Reincarnated

The top story on the *Daily News* featured a research report that estimated 100 million people had left MyFace in the last thirty-six hours. The journalist had interviewed a cross section of New Yorkers on why they were leaving the social network.

A CUNY student said that she was deleting her profile because she liked how she felt when she was alive. An old Asian lady in Queens said that she would most probably close her account because she felt scared. However, she would miss seeing photos of her three-year-old grandson in China. A coffee stand worker said, 'What's MyFace?' He added that life was too short to bother with such nonsense.

The next page featured an article about a man in Secaucus. His wife had been suffering from cancer. He had prayed with great devotion to a crucifix at a local church. His wife had been cured of the disease. The man was overcome with devotion for the crucifix. He was a construction worker by trade. He decided to renovate the crucifix to its former glory. However, as he approached the crucifix to begin work on it, it fell on him. The doctors said that they would have to amputate the man's leg. The man had tried to get the church's insurance company to pay for the operation.

However, they had refused to return his phone calls. He was now taking them to court. The journalist had drily remarked that the man was now praying for judgment, not from a higher authority, but from a civil court.

I thought there was a moral to this story. Maybe god, like a hurricane or a volcano, was ultimately indifferent to what happened to all men and women, good or otherwise. You can feed a beggar. Or you can kill a beggar. God really doesn't care. I decided to ask Austin his views on the matter later in the day.

I called Dr Firstein's office. The receptionist answered with a hello. I was surprised. This was the first time she hadn't answered the phone with a 'Can you hold?' I told her that I would be unable to make my appointment for later in the day. I asked if we could make up the session next week.

She grunted because 'OK' was such a long word. She suggested a new date and added that I should give more notice in the future. She was making an exception just for me just this one time.

She grunted again. If she didn't watch out, it would become a habit. She disconnected the phone. She wasn't happy. When Dr Firstein heard of the change, she wouldn't be happy. And when she emailed Mr Clarkson that I had cancelled the therapy appointment, he wouldn't be happy. My cell phone would start ringing as soon as it was morning in India.

It started to ring now.

'Arjun,' Brett Cohen said, 'what time were you thinking of coming in today?'

'I was just on my way in.'

'Take a cab,' he said. 'Expense it to the company.'

'Is everything all right?' I asked.

'It's the detective again. He has a few more questions.'

'Of me?'

'Yes, of you. And strangely enough, he spent a good fifteen minutes with Rajiv.'

Rajiv was the only other (living) Indian in the company. Like most people from India who weren't involved in agricultural pursuits, Rajiv was a software engineer. He was your typical middle-class Indian. He was quiet. He spoke softly. Most things either scared or shamed him. I had once accompanied him to an Indian restaurant on Curry Hill. He had hesitated for an entire five minutes before asking a waiter for a clean plate so that he could go to the buffet table for a second helping.

I combed my hair without looking in the mirror. I rushed out of the apartment. All the taxi cabs of New York were parked outside Rajbhog. The street was awash in yellow. It seemed like the first day of spring. I got into a cab with a Sikh driver.

'28th Street and Park Avenue,' I told him. 'Please take the shortest possible route. I have to get to work quickly.'

He nodded. He burped. He started the car. I like Sikhs. They are clean. They are self-sufficient. They never beg for food.

He had graduated from the Brake and Horn School of Driving. Within two blocks, I noticed he seemed to be possessed by a perennial desire to belong to a lane that was not his own. To this end, he darted his car repeatedly and unexpectedly between gaps.

I began to feel car sick. I rolled down the window. I tried to fix my gaze at the horizon, but my line of sight was obstructed by his turban and the taxi medallion. I sat back in my seat, closed my eyes and played jiu-jitsu with my nausea.

I am used to traversing New York by foot. As it always happens, I lost all sense of perspective within minutes of being in a car. I did not know which route he was taking. I abandoned myself to the mercy of the cab driver.

The Queensboro Bridge was long. Second Avenue was uncooperative. By the time we got to the office, I felt sea sick. I wondered how those immigrants of old managed to look so hopeful when they first saw the Statue of Liberty. If I had been in their place, you would have seen a painting that depicted me throwing up into the Hudson.

'Was that the fastest route?' I asked.

'No, sir,' he said. 'But it was the cheapest.'

'What do you mean?'

'Sir, I could have taken the Midtown Tunnel. It would have come straight here. But you would have to pay a seven-dollar toll.'

'So?'

'Sir, you are a brother from India. I was trying to save you some money.'

I inhaled deeply.

'This ride was expensed to the office. I told you I didn't care about the cost. Just the time.'

'Ah, office expense,' he said. 'Do you want a receipt for a greater amount? My last passenger didn't bother to collect her receipt.'

It was futile to continue this discussion. Tom Friedman could continue to inhabit his fantasy land. India would never progress.

I took the receipt for the correct amount and got out of the cab.

Austin opened the door with a benevolent smile. He had the look of a man on the verge of reciting a Biblical parable having to do with a mustard seed.

'A mustard seed…' he began.

'I have to run, Austin,' I said.

The detective was sitting in my office. He was looking at some papers strewn over my desk.

'I am sorry to keep you waiting,' I said. 'The traffic was terrible at this time in the morning.'

'I can believe that,' he said, as though everything else I had told him till this point in time had been a lie.

'I understand you have a few questions?' I asked, tapping on my keyboard and rousing my computer out of sleep mode.

'Yes, regarding Friday evening. Do you remember where you were?'

He knew where I was. I was at home.

'Didn't you already ask my girlfriend Michelle the same question?'

'Ah...Michelle. A lovely girl.'

'Thank you,' I said, even though I had no role to play during her formative years and early education.

'But I wanted to check something all the same. You wouldn't have happened to visit Brooklyn on Friday?'

'No,' I said.

'I don't know if you've read the newspapers over the weekend,' he said. 'But there were two people found dead at a handball court in South Williamsburg.'

'I think I might have read about it in the newspapers. And this pertains to me because...?'

'And this pertains to you because there was a homeless man on Bergen Street. He came to the police station to say that he recognized Alice from the newspaper. He said that he could never forget the tattoo of the hydra on the girl's arm. He said that the hydra had visited him in his dreams last night.'

'I am sorry to repeat myself,' I said, pressing on the stapler and wasting a staple pin. 'But this pertains to me because?'

'The homeless man said that there was a man standing next to the girl. He said that he was convinced this man was an Indian. He said that the man sounded like a person who worked at 7/11.'

I felt hurt. I had been nice to the bum. At the very least, he could have said I sounded like an Indian doctor.

'And that's why you came to me,' I said. 'Because I am the only person of Indian origin in the entire continental landmass of the United States. I was the Indian who helped architect the TARP bailout. I then dressed up like a woman and took a space shuttle to outer space. I also invented Hotmail and designed the world's first Pentium chip. In fact, I am responsible for over 40 per cent of Silicon Valley's startups.'

He didn't react. He wasn't as up-to-date as I was on the achievements of Indians in America.

'I see what you are trying to say,' he said in a voice that was as dry as a glass of Cabernet Sauvignon. 'You are not the only Indian in America.'

'That could be it,' I said.

'We showed the homeless person your photo,' he said. 'And he made a positive identification.'

'That man was high. You could have shown him a picture of Gandhi and received a positive identification. Don't even tell me that you are going to believe a hopped-up heroin fiend over the words of a school teacher.'

'A school teacher who happens to be your girlfriend.'

'A school teacher who is choosy about the people she dates.'

'Well…I hope you can forgive me for being suspicious,' the detective said. 'You were in Harlem when Emily was murdered. The person who murdered Kevin Santiago had an image of the Buddha on his T-shirt. And now this. You do understand that I have to ask the questions. I have to be thorough.'

'I understand,' I said. 'Real detective work involves having to follow up on leads, and working each one to its logical end. The police can't be like Poirot, relying solely on the psychology of the individual and all that nonsense.'

'Poirot?'

'Oh,' I said. 'This gay Frenchman I used to know.'

'Aren't they all?' he said.

'That sounds like the story of a very dirty movie,' I said. 'Even by French standards.'

He laughed. I laughed. A discussion that was in danger of becoming acrimonious had ended on a pleasing note. I felt the ghost of Dale Carnegie giving me a solid pat on the back.

Brett came into my office.

'We're on the WebEx,' he said. 'The client's getting irritated.'

This seemed to be a big morning for irritated people. The receptionist at Dr Firstein's office was irritated with me. I was irritated at the cab driver. The detective was irritated with the

MyFace killer. The client was irritated at the agency. And if I were to take a guess, Brett was irritated at the detective. It was almost as though he now resented having another authority figure in the office – and if one were to judge power by the ability to pull people out of meetings, an authority figure that was more powerful than him.

'What's the deal with this guy anyway?' he said. 'Why does he keep coming back to you?'

'Well, he came here today regarding a MyFace murder in Brooklyn. He specifically wanted to talk to Rajiv and me because a homeless person said that he had seen an Indian man with the girl who had been murdered.'

'And he came here because the two of you are the only Indian men in America?'

'Exactly.'

'Well, he's gone now,' he said. He put his hand on my back and guided me towards the conference room.

But he wasn't gone. He was closer to me than he had ever been. I would have to commit another murder and do it in such a way that he would be forced to remove me from his list of suspects.

The client was calling in from GAP's new creative headquarters on 5th Avenue in New York. They wanted to cancel their MyFace advertising programme.

'This killer is making advertising on MyFace a very bad proposition.'

Brett frowned. GAP planned to spend over five million dollars on MyFace in the fourth quarter. This translated into a seven hundred and fifty thousand dollar commission for the ad agency. I too was unhappy at this development. A loss of this magnitude would ensure that I didn't make a bonus at the end of the year. The MyFace killer was hurting my take-home income.

'Wait,' I said. 'It is true that one hundred million people have left MyFace. That still leaves an audience of nine hundred million.

This is the kind of reach you can't get on any other display advertising network.'

'But…'

'And the nine hundred million people on MyFace have remained on the network because they want to. They are tuned in. They are high-intent prospects for GAP.'

'Arjun, I appreciate the argument, but our brand can't afford to be seen in a venue where people are being killed.'

GAP advertised on NASCAR. But this was not the time to quibble.

'How about we take the money for MyFace and allocate it towards email and direct mail-list marketing? We can buy lists of people who have shopped at Aeropostale, Uniqlo, American Eagle and all the stores that belong to your competition.'

Surprisingly, there was no notion of user privacy in the offline world. With direct mail, highly sensitive information like a user's home address, phone number and recent purchase history were sold and resold between thousands upon thousands of list brokers. However, nobody seemed to care.

'That's a good idea.'

He sounded more relaxed. His voice no longer reminded me of a taut clothesline. He was obviously relieved that he didn't have to put in the work to find a way to spend the five million dollars.

'Let me get back to you with more specific recommendations,' I said. 'If we have money left over, I can recommend some search advertising keywords and some in-app mobile ad units that can really move the needle for GAP this holiday season.'

'That was well done,' Brett said. 'But it's not the last such conversation that we are going to have. You do realize that other clients are going to be asking for the same kind of thing.'

'Well, hopefully, the killings will stop,' I said.

Or maybe they wouldn't.

However, this time around, I had a plan. After the next MyFace murder of the Central Park bicyclist, Detective Crisafi would have no option but to eliminate me from his list of suspects.

Unexpectedly, the one person instrumental to the success of my plan was Jeff Garner. The Buddha was right. Every being, no matter how big or how small, how fat or how thin, how silent or how loud, played an important role in the functioning of the universe.

Jeff's office was empty. But I heard him at the reception.

'I'm going to grab a quick lunch. I'll be back in twenty minutes,' he was saying to Hannah.

Jeff always spoke in a loud voice. Even if you couldn't see him, you could always hear him.

His MyFace profile too was loud and overbearing. It was full of words like 'winner', 'surge' and 'triathlon'. Jeff liked competitive bicycling. Seven of his friends were in biking gear. All the photos he had been tagged in involved competitive bicycling. Jeff was competitive. I knew this because, on his MyFace profile, he had written the words, 'I am competitive'. He liked something called the Audio Tour, the White Plains Downtown Criterium, a law firm called Lucarelli & Castaldi LLP and an email service provider called Movable Ink. He had studied philosophy at the Occidental College in Los Angeles. I was surprised. He had never said anything thoughtful in all the time I had known him. His favourite quote was, 'He who makes a beast of himself gets rid of the pain of being a man'. He was an atheist.

I took the elevator downstairs. I gave Austin that 'I am in a rush, can't be proselytized now' look. I squeezed myself in the gap between two pillars outside the Starbucks on our office block. Partially hidden from the view of people exiting the building, I waited for Jeff Garner.

I realized that was the first time all day I actually had a moment to stop and take in the world. It was a beautiful day. The air was crisp and cool. The sun was gentle. It was almost as if god had switched on a giant air conditioner in the sky.

Jeff crossed Park Avenue. He entered Dean & DeLuca. It did not surprise me that he would go to the gourmet market. Dean & DeLuca was the most expensive delicatessen in the neighbourhood. In Jeff's dictionary, 'expensive' translated to 'the best'.

And Jeff liked nothing but the best.

He wore calfskin boots with rubber soles designed by Salvatore Ferragamo, dressed in shirts designed by Bottega Veneta, drank Van Gogh Blue vodka and red wine from the Ramey Pedregal Vineyard Cabernet Sauvignon 2008, owned a Dana Bourgeois acoustic guitar (just in case he ever began to play) and on casual Fridays, wore a sport navy stripe T-shirt designed by Prada.

I have neither the desire nor the ability to remember and pronounce European-sounding names. If I am able to do so, it is a testament to the powers of repetition by a very loud voice.

He was staring at the Mexican who was preparing his sandwich.

I greeted him.

'One second,' he said. 'I want to make sure he gets this right.'

People in America often complain about the drudgery of day-to-day life. However, if they were less exacting about what they were going to receive, they would find that their life would fill up with more variety.

'How are things?'

'TGIM,' he said. 'Thank god it's Monday.'

Jeff's wife had recently given birth to a child. I had seen the baby when he had brought it to the office. It had shrieked like the 4 train coming to a halt at the Union Square station.

'No sleep, huh?'

From this point on, I knew exactly how the conversation would play out.

'Yes,' he said. 'I could really do with some…'

'Uninterrupted sleep at a Caribbean Resort?'

'Cocaine.'

'Ah.'

'Do you think you could call … what's his name?'

'The boy?'

'Yes, the boy.'

'And then we go could to The VIP Club.'

'That sounds good,' I said.

'You're still single?'

'No, I've started seeing this girl called Michelle …'

'Great,' he said. 'Going to strip clubs is one of the best things about the single life. You're a good man, Arjun. I'll see you at 7.00 at the restaurant? We could grab a bite at Prime Steak House and head down to the VIP Lounge.'

'I'm vegetarian,' I said.

'They have excellent potatoes.' He grabbed at the sandwich. I thanked the Mexican on his behalf.

He paid for his lunch. 'You know,' he said even as the cashier was handing him the change, 'I am really looking forward to this evening. We'll have a nice steak, do some coke in the bathroom and head on to the VIP Lounge. Of course, when Jeanne comes to the office, you'll have to tell her that we spent the evening discussing client strategy at Desmond's. I don't want her to think her husband is a coke fiend who goes to strip clubs.'

A young girl, who could not have been older than seven, stared at us. A memory that would last forever, one that would be recounted in future therapy sessions was being formed before my very eyes. A teenage boy in a red cap was sitting on a revolving stool. He made a complete revolution and smiled. An old lady coughed. She opened her mouth to protest, but found that this simple act of democracy was beyond her.

'See, old lady,' I wanted to tell her. 'It's not just the immigrants who are destroying the social fabric of America.'

Jeff dug his nose.

'I think you're a nice guy, Arjun,' he said. 'You don't judge people.'

'Believe me,' I said. 'I'm not in a position to judge.'

'Why's that?'

The good thing about talking to people like Jeff is that you didn't have to lie, because you didn't have to speak. He had already moved on to his next thought.

'Did I tell you about what happened in Prospect Park? So I was going on my bicycle at 40 miles per hour...' He told me a story at a faster speed than that.

I pretended to walk around for five minutes, evaluating my options for lunch. I then went to L'Annam and ordered the L28 peanut noodles. I also ordered a deep-fried eggplant starter. I needed to have a heavy lunch, considering potatoes were all that I was going to be eating for dinner.

Austin greeted me as I entered the building.

'Have you deleted your MyFace account, Austin?' I asked.

'I was never on MyFace, sir,' he replied. 'I am not that young. So I don't have that much to say.'

'You'll be surprised, Austin,' I said. 'People of all ages can say quite a lot. At any rate, Austin, it's a new day. I think we are about to see a new world. A new way of living.'

'Ah, that is good to hear, sir,' he said. 'If I might say so, sir, please do not let yourself be fashioned by familiar lusts. Let them pass you by.'

'What do you mean, Austin?' I said. But he was now nodding politely at an old man who had just come out of the elevator.

I spent the afternoon making Plan Bs for all our clients. These outlined alternative media venues should they decide to pull out of MyFace. I found that there was a total of eight million dollars that needed to be moved out of the social network. I wondered how much larger the amounts would be at global advertising agencies like Ogilvy & Mather and MediaCom.

I received a text message at four in the afternoon. The boy was in the city. This could only mean that my new passport was ready.

The only other vehicle on 3rd Avenue which was as large as the boy's car was the M 101 bus.

I got into his car. I could not discern the presence of any policemen in my vicinity.

I wasn't surprised. Like the rest of the world, the NYPD presumably operated on a tight budget.

The *Daily News* had recently reported that the average salary of a NYPD officer was in excess of ninety thousand dollars a year. The people at the top at the police department no doubt ensured that every hour of these highly skilled professionals was put to the most optimum use. All the MyFace murders had taken place during the evening hours. In the daytime, plausible suspects such as myself were involved in no other task than to advance the many goals of modern commerce. There was no reason to follow us during the morning and afternoon hours.

The boy smiled uncertainly. He seemed disoriented like an owl that has been asked to go out on an important mission during the daytime hours.

'You want the cocaine today?'

'Not during work hours,' I said.

'Just the passport then.'

On the front page of the blue document, a Sikh smiled back at me. He seemed self-conscious and uneasy as though the chicken biryani he had just eaten prior to the photo shoot had not agreed with him.

'Dude,' I said. 'This is a Sikh man.'

'That's great, right?' he said. 'Put on a turban and a beard, and you'll disappear. Like a...' He made the sound of a cloud going *poof*.

'That's true,' I said. 'But surely you can see that he is so fair. And look at me...' I pointed to a patch of skin directly above the scar on my forearm.

The boy smiled.

'With our busy work schedules, day after day, month after month, and year and year,' I waited for the boy to finish because I saw that he was going somewhere with this, 'with the stress we encounter every day in the workplace, who couldn't do with a vacation in Florida? Tell me this … can you do with a vacation right about now on South Beach?'

'Yes,' I said honestly.

'So could I,' said the boy. 'And so could this Sikh gentleman. He went to Florida. And he got a tan.'

'I see …'

'And besides, dude, for the white security man at the airport, we are all as black as Malcolm fucking X. We are all one colour. The only time these motherfuckers can tell darker shades apart is when they are picking colours from a paint catalogue.'

'You have a point,' I said. 'And this new passport will work? It will go through the computer system?'

'It will go through with just the one beep of approval,' the boy said. I must have appeared reassured, for he relaxed visibly. He slouched back in his seat. He took out his iPod. He pressed a button. The music began to hit the glass windows with a pulsing ferocity.

'Can I ask you a question?' I shouted over Calle Trece, who had just started performing the '*Baila de los Pobres*'.

The boy nodded his acquiescence.

'How exactly do you get these fake passports?'

'You know this Sikh gentleman,' he said.

I didn't know him personally. But I nodded anyway.

'So this Sikh gentleman … he goes on this vacation to Florida. He comes back to his normal life, works hard for a few months and feeds the family and shit. Then he decides to take another vacation. This time around, he decides to go to Toronto.'

'Makes sense,' I said. 'Toronto has a huge Sikh population.'

'Right on,' said the boy. 'So this overworked gentleman goes to visit his relatives in Toronto. He stays at a hotel in the city …'

'And he has to. I mean he couldn't stay with his relatives. I'm sure the apartments in Toronto, like those in New York, are very small.'

'You're probably right,' the boy said. 'Our friend goes to a hotel. In his relaxed vacation mood, he is not his usual, watchful self. He is standing in the lobby talking to his wife. Or ogling at the receptionist's tetas. Whatever be the case, he leaves his luggage unattended. Someone sneaks up to him. Someone steals his bag.'

'You are no doubt referring to the bag with the passport...'

'Precisamente.' The boy smiled knowingly like the Buddha must have after having shown an ignorant disciple the light.

'Makes sense,' I said. I placed the passport in my pocket. I handed the boy an envelope.

'You might want to count the money,' I said.

The boy shook his head.

'I know where you live,' he said.

He pointed at the passport.

'Or now maybe, I don't.'

He counted the money. He smiled. We knocked fists.

I stepped out of the car feeling like Clark Kent must have the first time he put on that cape in a telephone booth. He must have felt like a new man. He must have felt like he wanted to fly around the world. I certainly did.

But all I did was return to my desk. It was seven o' clock by the time I had finished drafting the proposals and issuing revised recommendations for all of our clients. I went into the restroom and made sure that I had everything I needed to make the evening a success. Sacred thread with concealed knife. Cocaine. MyFace sticker. Check. Check. And check.

I joined a stream of people walking down Park Avenue. They were rushing towards the subway station with a single-minded intent like animals running away from a forest fire. I turned over my shoulder and looked quickly at the multitude of people behind me.

I had seen that nose before. I had seen that scar that ran down the entire length of the left nostril.

I turned forward and continued walking at the frenzied speed of my fellow human beings. At 28th Street, the entrance to the subway station sucked a significant portion of the crowd into its insides, quicker and more effectively than the best vacuum cleaner on the market. I continued walking along Park Avenue. After I had crossed the intersection on 27th Street, I slowed down just a little. I stared into a glass window of a storefront selling wine. I saw the scar and its accompanying nose reflected back at me in tinted hues.

He was following me.

I continued to walk at a leisurely pace till I reached the restaurant on 23rd Street. I stretched my arms into the air. I sighed deeply to affect an air of deep relaxation. I moved my neck from side to side. The policeman with the scar had stationed himself one block away on 22nd Street.

The restaurant was large and dark. Jeff was waiting for me at the reception. The warm, heavy and welcome fragrance of wine greeted us as soon as we walked inside. There was a mirror over the bar. Jeff checked himself out with a quick glance as he walked to our table. He combed over his hair with his hand.

He ordered a bottle of wine whose name I could not begin to pronounce. The waiter brought the bottle to the table and showed Jeff the label. Jeff examined the label closely. It appeared as though he were making sure that there were no spelling mistakes.

The waiter poured a small amount of wine into Jeff's glass. Jeff looked at it. He ogled at it. He swirled it, sniffed it, and gurgled it. He did everything short of removing his trousers and making love to it on the table. Finally, he approved of it.

He ordered steak tenderloin. I ordered potatoes. The waiter raised his eyebrows at me in a restrained manner that reminded me of Austin.

'Why aren't you eating steak?' Jeff asked after the waiter had left. 'Are you gay or something?'

'Oh,' I said. 'I thought you were gay when you wanted to stick your penis in another man's arse.'

'No, really. Why don't you eat steak? Is it some kind of religious thing?'

'No,' I said. 'I just find meat to be very chewy. It's got nothing to do with religion or anything. I just don't enjoy it at a physical level.'

'So you don't think it is wrong to kill animals?'

'No. I don't think it is wrong to kill anything.'

'But if…'

'You know, you are making me break one of my most important principles with this conversation.'

'Making you talk about killing animals?'

'No. By making me sound like one of those annoying vegetarians.'

He laughed. The light danced on his face. I could see the wrinkles underneath his eyes. He seemed tired. He had to be. This was probably the first time he had spoken for so long about something that was not related to his life.

The steak arrived. Like so many Americans do when involved in the pursuit of pleasure, Jeff became a temporary Buddhist. He was completely immersed in the here and now of the experience. He oohed and aahed with great feeling as he cut the dead cow into tiny squares and placed each piece into his mouth.

The skins on my potatoes were surprisingly crisp. They were plump. They squirted out juice when I stabbed my fork into them. They were delicious. But a man can take only so many potatoes at a time. I sensed that two were sufficient.

I flipped my cell phone open and talked into it.

'When did this happen?' I said loud enough so that Jeff could hear, but not so loud that the white couple at the adjoining table would think of me as a loud and boorish working-class immigrant.

'I have to leave,' I told Jeff. 'I am really sorry, but it is an emergency. That was the client from GAP. He is flying out to Minneapolis tomorrow. And he needs some data for his presentation tonight.'

'I guess you are not going to the strip club now.'

'I can't,' I said. 'I really wish I could, but I can't.'

He looked morose, even more so than an immediate friend or family member of the cow that was on his plate.

'But you can go,' I said.

'You don't know Jeanne,' he said. 'She'll kill me.'

'I'll say I was with you,' I said.

'Really?'

'Really. I'll tell Brett, the people in that office, even the detective…'

'The detective?'

'Yes, the guy who keeps coming by the office…I'll tell everybody we were at…'

'Desmond's.'

'Till?'

'1.30 a.m.?'

'Got it.'

I left sixty dollars on the table.

'You don't owe that much,' Jeff said. 'You hardly had the wine.'

'But I would have had a lot more if this goddamn client hadn't called,' I said. 'I am really sorry to leave you alone here.'

'Don't worry about it,' Jeff said. 'Aren't you forgetting something?'

'Look under the money,' I said.

He was an extrovert. I was an introvert. But we had one thing in common. We were both capable of being perfectly happy by ourselves and the company of a bag of cocaine.

The waiter stepped away from me as I walked towards the exit of the restaurant. He looked at me with a disapproving air. I had committed the faux pas of ordering the potatoes while ignoring the steak. I had also left a diner alone at the table. This is what happens when you let immigrants into the country. The silk-like threads that keep the fragile fabric of civilization together begin to be torn asunder.

'Excuse me,' I said to the waiter.

He jumped like an upper-caste zamindar who has just been approached by an untouchable. I plowed on in the face of his icy demeanour.

'I'd like to speak to the manager, please.'

'Is everything all right, sir?'

'Oh yes,' I said. 'Everything is more than all right. The potatoes were excellent. They were so juicy. So crisp. So succulent...' I paused. A man can go only so far in his praise of potatoes without appearing suspicious.

'At any rate, I'd like to meet with the manager. You see, I am a journalist for a food magazine based in Asia. I've already sampled the food here. I would love to do a write-up on the restaurant.'

I took out a small notebook from my pocket. I thought it made me appear more like a journalist. There was a pen by the cash register. He was sufficiently impressed. Till this point in time, he didn't strike me as someone who possessed a military background. But now I had second thoughts as he snapped hasta pronto to an upright attention.

He disappeared into the steam cloud emanating from the kitchen. He came out with a man dressed in a sharp navy-blue suit. I was particularly struck by his companion's cheekbones. They were so lean and angular. The chefs in the kitchen probably used his face to cut hard cheese and grate lemon zest.

'Adam Demby,' he said, proffering me a hand.

He gave me a greeting that is so particularly American. He crushed my hands and had the temerity to smile at me at the same time.

'Sam here was telling me you are a reporter for a food magazine.'

'Yes, we are based in Hong Kong...'

'And what's the name of your publication?'

'*Bon Appétit*,' I said. '*Bon Appétit Asia*.'

The brightness of his eyes visibly grew in amplitude till their luminosity bordered on greed.

'And what would be your name, sir?'

'Venkatpathy Balasubramanian,' I said.

Good luck googling that name.

'I would give you a card,' I said. 'However, I ran out them at this conference...'

The Buddha had said that those who imagine truth in untruth and see truth in untruth never arrive at the truth but follow vain desires. And he was right. Desire had clouded Mr Demby's ability to reason clearly.

'That's not a problem,' he said. 'Not a problem. Not a problem. Now, how can I help you?'

I closed my eyes and invoked the spirit of Mr Carnegie. He asked me to ask Mr Demby about himself.

'Tell me about yourself,' I said. 'How did you get into this business?'

Mr Demby told me about his work on a poultry processing farm. He said that by the time he was twenty-one, he had become a manager of five hundred workers.

'I was making a difference in the daily lives of people,' he said. 'And I liked that. It's what I have always wanted to do. I've always wanted to help others. I guess it comes from being the son of a fireman.'

He took me through the entire arc of his life, heroic deed by heroic deed, till he landed up as the manager of a steakhouse in New York City.

'That's fascinating,' I said.

But I had been fascinated to the end of my tether. I couldn't take any more fascination. For Mr Demby's continued well-being and mine, I needed to change the topic.

'Now, can you tell me a little bit about the kitchen? Tell me what makes it unique when you compare it to other kitchens in the city?'

'Ah, the kitchen,' Mr Demby cried. 'Follow me, follow me...'

We entered the room saturated with the smoke and sizzle of steam. Mr Demby told me they had gutted the old kitchen and built a new one from scratch. He pointed at an immigrant who smiled at his boss, even as the hair on his forearm was being singed by a hot flame.

'This is a new six-burner Garland stove,' he said. 'We got one with a standard thirty-inch oven. We still retained the hood from the original stove.'

'What's past is prologue,' I said.

However, Mr Demby didn't seem to be in the mood to discuss Shakespeare. He seemed to want to focus on matters that had more to do with the cleansing of our physical bodies, rather than the nourishment of our souls. He took me to a sink.

'New York State law requires that every kitchen has a sink where employees can wash their hands,' he said. 'However, we also have this additional sink that supplies pasta water.'

'Wow,' I said. I pretended to jot down a note.

'The ingenious L-shape design of the alleys allows us to have as many as six chefs. Alternatively, we can accommodate five chefs and a pig,' he said. 'Or maybe even a cow.'

He found this observation amusing. I feigned appreciation as his half-smile evolved into a full-throated laugh.

'And what's that?' I asked.

'Why it's the door...the exit,' he said.

'And it exits on to...'

'Twenty-first Street,' he said.

The most beautiful street in all of Manhattan. Twenty-first Street was an entire block away from the policeman with the scar on his nose. A policeman who would be asked by his superiors to explain just how I managed to get away from the restaurant unobserved. A policeman who would chide himself during a quiet moment of reflection for not being alert to his surroundings, for perhaps being too entirely engrossed with the insides of a chicken salad sandwich.

'Mr Demby,' I said. 'It's been a pleasure. I will send a copy of the magazine as soon as it is out in print.'

'You have no further questions?' he asked. He seemed dejected.

'You, Mr Demby, have given me all of the information I need and more,' I said. His was of a simple nature. He cheered up at my easy praise.

I did not wish to have my hands crushed twice in one evening. I gave him a distant wave and stepped out on the street. I was instantly cooled by a pleasant breeze that coursed down the length of the street. I watched it tickle a candy wrapper that lay on the pavement.

I found myself having to go to Brooklyn for the second time that week. This time around I had to go to an area called Dumbo. I had performed a Internet search for Dumbo earlier that day. Dumbo stood for the Down Under the Manhattan Bridge Overpass.

I had found several blogs that extolled the virtues of Dumbo. These included handcrafted tote bags, handcrafted goat cheese and even handcrafted cappuccinos. In this respect, Dumbo was different from the rest of the world, where coffee shops used Chinese power looms to make their cappuccinos.

Dumbo was at the York Street station of the F train. It was the first stop in Brooklyn. The bar was a block away from the station. There was a coffee shop on the ground floor. The bar was located on the upper level. This design seemed counter-intuitive to me. I had heard of more people tripping on stairs after they had drunk alcohol as compared to after they had sipped coffee.

The menu was mounted on the wall. The names of different beers were written in chalk on a black slate. Most of the beers had names that were difficult to pronounce. Only two weeks ago,

I would have gone to another bar and ordered a Budweiser or Amstel Light.

But today, I told the bartender, 'I'll have an Ommegang Scythe and Sickle, please.' She complied. Confidence was a forward-moving emotion, one that allowed you to experience new things and partake of new adventures. If we were in New Zealand, I would have stepped out of the bar and bungee-jumped.

I saw that the bar was well designed for my mission. Three ornate chandeliers came down from the ceiling. But all they did was cast a dim light. There were many areas of the bar that were sufficiently in the dark. I sat on a table underneath a heavy, grilled iron frame.

I looked around to see if I could spot Matt Fleming, the Central Park bicyclist from Orange County.

On the table next to me, a fat man in a black T-shirt thumped his hands hard on the table. Conversation in the bar ceased. Even the music stopped. The fat man was seated in front of an Asian gentleman. He moved his thick neck slowly to take in the entire bar. He raised his hands in apology. The Asian made the peace sign. People began talking to each other again. The alternative rock band began to play.

'That was uncalled for,' said the Asian.

'You deserve my anger,' the fat man said. 'Frankly speaking, what other people make at the company is none of your business.'

The Asian adjusted the spectacles on the bridge of his nose. It was an endearing gesture, one that emphasized the need for thought before argument. He too was visibly agitated. But whereas the fat man's anger had culminated in a loud and vulgar display, the consternation of the Asian served to make his voice more measured and forceful. He was no longer conscious about his accent.

'Look,' he said. 'You asked me to take a pay cut. At the time, you told me that I should take the pay cut because everyone else was doing the same. I agreed. Today, I learned from our CFO that Ray is not taking the cut. I hope you see the irony in this ... Ray is after all the head of sales. And the sales team is responsible for the huge revenue drop.'

'Well, frankly, what Ray does or does not do is none of your business.'

'But it has become my business because ... because when asking me to take the cut, you said that I should comply because everyone else is doing it.'

'I am running a small business,' said the fat man. 'Everything can't be perfect. Sometimes, things will fall through the cracks.'

'And that's why I am pointing it out. I am saying, Hey look there, there is a crack, and there is stuff falling through it.'

I didn't know who this Asian was. But I thought that his photo should replace that of Che Guevara on every T-shirt in the United States.

'This is a capitalist system,' said the fat man. 'And everyone is treated differently.'

Fair enough. I could see the fat man's point of view. America was not a socialist country. Nor did its people have a socialist mindset like the populace of India. In America, you didn't have to be ashamed if you owned a house on a hill.

'And Ray has three daughters, whom he has to support. You—'

'Ray belongs to one of the richest families in America,' the Asian said.

'Don't interrupt. Remember that it's one of the founding rules of our company. Never interrupt someone while they are talking.'

He sipped deeply from his beer. The Asian man festered.

'So like I was saying, there are two factors at work here. One, this is a capitalist system. And two, Ray has three daughters. He needs the money. You, on the other hand, are staying with your girlfriend in a rental apartment.'

The fat man was exhibiting an ability unique to the American businessman. He could make an unfair decision and rationalize it to himself by whatever means possible. He could do so without experiencing a shimmer of doubt, even if that rationalization involved defending capitalism by invoking the principles of socialism.

The British had rationalized their way through history for three hundred and fifty years. In the 1840s, there was a British admiral who felt betrayed by 'the ungrateful Indians'. He could not understand how 'Indians had failed to see that colonialism was a necessary stage for maturation in their society'. The admiral had then impaled an entire village of Indians and mounted their heads on wooden stakes.

Blatant colonialism was out of fashion. But the British admiral hadn't disappeared. He had been reincarnated as a fat man in a black T-shirt, a man who hadn't lost the penchant for exploiting people of Asian descent.

The Asian finished his drink. He powered on his iPhone and read a text message. He told the fat man he had to leave. The fat man waved him adieu with an imperious nod that was so detached and impersonal, it made me yearn for the early days of the French Revolution.

Matt Fleming would live to see another day. The fat man would die tonight.

'That's a lovely carving,' I said after the Asian had left the bar. 'From Bhutan, yes?'

The fat man seemed surprised. He caressed a small carving of a dragon between his fingers.

'Yes,' he said. 'That's the Thunder Dragon.'

'The Druk Dragon,' I said. 'I know it well. You know the jewels on its feet. They signify wealth.'

'Interesting,' he said. His pudgy chin sank towards the table as he moved to take a closer look. I sidled over to his table.

'That orange piece of cloth symbolizes the Buddhist religion,' I said. 'And the yellow colour pays homage to the ruling dynasty.'

'Interesting,' he said again. 'You seem to know a lot about Bhutan.'

'I know I don't look Bhutanese,' I said. 'But I have family from there.'

I wasn't lying. Mr Clarkson's sister had adopted a dog she loved very much. She treated the dog just like a family member. The dog was from Lhasa, the capital of Tibet. Tibet bordered Bhutan along its northern borders.

He said he ran a startup in the mobile advertising space. I pretended to have heard of the company. I could tell he was pleased.

'It's quite a task to grow a business,' he said. 'But I'm sticking with it. I think our solution will actually help small businesses in America grow. It will help small businesses get new customers. You know, that's why I founded this company in the first place.'

'Ah, I wasn't aware that your company was a not-for-profit organization.'

'We aren't,' he said. 'But I am always thinking about how I can help other people improve their lives. That's kind of my raison d'être, you know?'

'That's really noble,' I said. 'At a time when even the politicians have given up on the people, businessmen like you are doing all they can to help.'

The conversation drifted into politics. Politics in America is very similar to caste in India. If you belong to the wrong caste or support the wrong party, you might very well end up being ostracized. I was careful not to put forth any opinion. I merely nodded my head in agreement to whatever he had to say.

'And those people in the middle states, if they want to vote for Romney, and he wins and screws them over…they can…' The fat man searched for words, but all that came out was spittle. '…they can come over to my house and do the dishes. Polish my shoes. I will make them work at below minimum wage and…'

He went into a list of things he would do if the poor of the country voted for Mitt Romney. He had a very detailed list of items. He had given this matter a lot of thought.

'…they can pick up my dog's shit, and not get paid anything in return.'

I didn't particularly care who won the presidential race. After my salary raise, I had been placed in a twilight zone where either of the candidates winning the election would have a positive impact on my life.

Upon entering the country, an American immigrant goes through three phases of life.

During the first phase, the immigrant is a Democrat. After all, it is the party that is more accepting and inclusive. The immigrant then makes a lot of money and moves on to the second phase. In this phase, the immigrant supports the Republicans. How could those lousy Democrats redistribute her or his wealth and stifle the flow of free enterprise? If the immigrant makes more than twenty-five million dollars, she or he moves on to the third phase. In this phase, the immigrant stops caring about humans. All she or he worries about are whales.

As a vice president of a New York ad agency, I was between phases one and two.

The fat man was close to finishing his beer. I feared he might get up and walk away. It was still before midnight. The citizens of Brooklyn and the policemen that guard them would still be up and about. It was essential that I kept him interested in the conversation until a later hour of the night.

'So tell me more about your startup.'

He looked at me with a sour expression on his face. It was almost as if he had just realized that it was getting close to midnight and that he was sitting in a bar with an immigrant with a strong accent.

'It's getting late,' he said. 'I should ask for the cheque.' He beckoned to the waitress.

'So,' I said again. 'Tell me more about your startup.'

'I told you … we work in mobile advertising,' he said.

He yawned widely. If Captain Ahab were in the bar, he would have thrown a harpoon into that mouth.

'Yes, I know. But I want to know more. You see, I work in the mobile advertising department at Google.'

And just like that, he became alert and interested. You could have sent him to hunt a tiger in the Indian jungle.

'In what department?'

'Mergers and acquisitions,' I said. 'More specifically, I am tasked with buying startups that fit in well with Google's long-term strategic roadmap.'

The waitress came over with the cheque.

'Actually,' he said, 'my friend and I were going to have another beer.'

He used the word 'friend' on three subsequent occasions. After he had called me friend for the fourth time, the nature of his confidences began to change. They began to deal with topics that were more personal in nature.

He told me that every New Year's Eve, he spent the night alone on a cold mountain up in Vermont. He owned a cottage there. The last time he had gone up the mountain, he had come to the realization that his wife was growing further and further away from him. He told me he had never shared these confidences with anyone else and he was telling me all this because I was a friend.

'So tell me,' he said. 'Why exactly did Google acquire Wildfire?'

I told him a story.

He sat back in his chair and nodded to show me that he was paying attention. But he was as distracted as a bee in a garden. He kept looking at the waitress, trying to get her attention. However, she was busy flirting with a customer. She did not pay him any attention. Even in the candlelight, I could see the fat man's face getting red, as red as the glass of wine that Jeff had ordered earlier that evening.

'We should go to another bar,' he said when the waitress had begun to kiss the gentleman she had been flirting with. 'Let's go to this place called Boat.'

He said it was the best place in the world. I said I was eager to see it.

It had rained while we were inside. On the street, I could hear the ripple of a bicycle wheel pass through a puddle. A creaking and clanging garbage truck approached us from far, far away.

'The subway is that way,' I said.

'Let's pick up my car,' he said. 'I get claustrophobic in the subway.'

He made it sound like a medical condition.

A small alley ran towards the bridge on the left side of the street. It was dark and full of shadows.

'Is that the Manhattan Bridge?' I asked.

'Ya, man,' he said in a Jamaican accent.

'Do you mind if we walk down there to see the bridge up close?'

'For a friend…' He patted me on my back. 'Anything.'

The N train went on the bridge directly above us. There was a loud rumbling sound. I wasn't sure if it was the train or thunder in the sky. The fat man began to walk ahead of me. His voice was loud and full of enthusiasm as he described the bridge and the neighbourhood. I realized I did not know his name. He must have told it to me, but I must have tuned out then. Just as I was tuning out now.

I slowed down. I took out my chef's knife from its sheath. We had now walked under the arch of the bridge. It had been built out of heavy brown stone. I marvelled at the bold imagination and daring of the people who had once thought these heavy blocks could soar so high. Tonight, I had to draw from their confidence.

'What car do you drive?' I asked him.

'A Land Cruiser,' he said.

'The British car,' I said. 'The big one?'

I must have appeared disapproving, for he became defensive.

'It's a big car,' he said. 'It's not so fuel-efficient. But I make up for it by purchasing carbon credits in other countries, like Mexico, Guatemala … and India, come to think of it.'

'That's really nice of you,' I said.

I would kill him, and I would kill him now. It would be my contribution to reducing carbon emissions in the world.

I stuck the 'I found you on MyFace' sticker on his forehead. I grasped my knife. I would stab him in the femoral artery. The blood would gush into the air. It would pour down upon these wizened cobblestones that had seen blood spilled for centuries upon centuries. It would be the most poetic of the MyFace murders to date.

And then I stopped. It is difficult to stop stabbing someone right in the middle of the act. It is akin to stopping a fart or a sneeze mid-emission. However, I was sufficiently distracted to accomplish this difficult feat. I saw a face bob in and out of the corner of Front and Pearl Street. The face manifested itself only for an instant. However, its countenance was as clear as the outline of the bridge that stood before me.

It was Michelle.

Another train began to rumble on the bridge. It spurred my CEO friend into action. He planted one foot on the pavement for leverage, and leapt with an extraordinary agility with the other. Now, he seemed highly athletic, like a deer jumping over a rock on a mountain.

The momentum of his leap carried him out of the archway and into the street. His jump was full of life. He reminded me of a young man of twenty competing at the Olympics. He landed on the cobblestones with a terrific sound that could be heard over the rumbling of the train. A garbage truck hit him. He fell on to the ground.

And just like that, a voice materialized. It was as if the moonlight falling on the ancient stone had caused a ghost to awaken from a deep hibernation.

'Oh my god,' a lady cried.

'Stop! Stop!' A man ran behind the garbage truck. It screeched to a halt.

I wondered if my CEO friend was dead or alive. But I had no time to check on his medical condition. I ran to the intersection of Front and Pearl Street. Michelle had disappeared. I turned right on Jay Street to take the F train back to Manhattan. However, I realized it would be awkward if I found Michelle or for that matter a policeman waiting on the platform. I began to walk towards the Manhattan Bridge.

I stepped on to the staircase at the entrance of the bridge. I sighed with relief. It would take me to the other side.

An Unexpected Tornado

The CEO's name was Scott Harpin. He had made it to the cover of the *Daily News*. The article stated that he had been hit by a garbage truck and was now in a coma. The article also stated that he had been found with a MyFace sticker stuck to his forehead. The drivers of the garbage truck had been taken in by the police for questioning. The doctors in the hospital said that Mr Harpin was in a critical condition.

I liked the sound of the words 'critical condition'. I did not have to book my return trip to India just yet.

There was more bad news for MyFace. Their CEO's personal account had been hacked. A photo of his wife cooking in the kitchen had been made public. The journalist conjectured if this was the work of the MyFace killer. A computer programmer (who was not Indian) said that it did not appear that the MyFace serial killer was a technically skilled person.

'If he were a programmer,' the person said, 'all he would have to do was make a mobile app that pulled the public information of users from MyFace and, come to think of it, even Twitter and FourSquare. The app would then combine this information with available geodata. The killer would be able to find and kill his victims easily. In fact, it would be as easy as shooting frogs in a bucket.'

The journalist had pointed out that the CEO of MyFace had recently said that the desire of human beings to have a private life came in the way of a more open society. And yet, he hadn't made his own MyFace page public. All a person could do was subscribe to posts that he had chosen to make public.

What a hypocrite the man was! I would bring down his social network. There were still seven hundred and fifty million people on MyFace. I would be surprised if by the end of the day there were more than a million.

A brown face stared at me from the next page of the newspaper. My thoughts that had been so coherent only a moment ago began to grow disconnected. The words on the page appeared out of focus. I walked to the kitchen and made a glass of tea. I breathed deeply.

A Bangladeshi had been arrested by the FBI for wanting to blow up the New York Federal Reserve building. He had been working with a partner who he believed was a fellow disgruntled soul, but who was in reality an undercover FBI agent.

I wondered if I would be able to leave the apartment today.

Wouldn't the superintendent push me to the ground? Wouldn't the coffee cart owner poison my coffee? Wouldn't the subway passengers form a mob and claw at my face?

However, my fears did not materialize. It seemed that all anyone on the street wanted to talk about was MyFace.

Are you getting off the network? Do you know anyone who deleted their account? Is it even possible to delete your account?

I looked up to the heavens. I thanked god for the MyFace killer. In the popular imagination, he had taken the place of the brown-skinned terrorist as the most feared entity in America.

A Sikh gentleman leapt out of an establishment playing loud bhangra music.

'Do you want to buy gold, sir?'

This wasn't the first time this particular gentleman had made me this offer. I recognized him by his eyebrows. The hair rose from them noisily and as plentifully as leaves from a mulberry tree. If there was a goat in our vicinity, it would have nibbled on his face.

Normally, I would have curled up my right nostril in distaste at this display of vulgar commerce and walked on. However, today I needed something from him.

'I need a turban,' I said.

'A turban?'

He appeared suspicious. In a post-9/11 America, it was passé to ask for turbans, and that too in public.

'It's not for me,' I said. 'It's for a Sikh friend of mine in North Dakota.'

'There are Sikh people in North Dakota?'

'There are until they leave,' I said.

He chuckled.

'Come with me,' he said.

We crossed the street and entered a door. It opened up unexpectedly into a mall made up of small stores that were crowded tightly together. I followed the Sikh man into the basement. We entered an establishment that was to the immediate right of the staircase.

The storekeeper, who was also Sikh, sat next to an idle photocopier. Without any customers for company, the man and the machine stared morosely at each other. I thought of the astronaut and HAL playing out their end game in *2001: A Space Odyssey*.

'Meet Gurpreet,' my Sikh companion said.

'I don't need photocopies,' I said.

'He also sells turbans,' the man said.

'Hello, Gurpreet,' I said.

My companion told Gurpreet there was a Sikh man in North Dakota. He shook his head in disbelief.

'The world is changing,' he said.

Having offered his pronouncement on modern times, he bent down and reached into a shelf by his knees. He placed four turbans on the table.

'I like the red one,' he said.

'I like the blue,' I said. 'It goes very well with a Banana Republic relaxed-fit shirt that my friend likes to wear.'

The sky had turned black when I got out of the subway in Manhattan. It was almost as if god had tipped over an ink bottle and watched it move slowly all the way to the horizon.

Michelle called me on my cell phone. I let the phone ring. I wasn't entirely sure I wanted to talk to a person who spent her evenings following me around. But I remembered what Sun Tzu had said about keeping your enemies close. He would have wanted me to take this phone call. I flipped my phone open just as the call was going to voicemail.

I said hello. It was all that I was prepared to say.

There was a long silence. The person who was overhearing the call at the National Security Administration must have felt a little bored.

'Hey,' she said finally. 'I just called to tell you that there's a tornado in Queens. I can see it from my window.'

I wondered what else she had seen in the recent past.

'How come you're in Queens?'

'Oh, I took the day off from work. I wasn't feeling so well after last night.'

Maybe it was because she was hanging out late in Brooklyn.

'It's probably nothing,' she said even though I hadn't asked how she was doing.

'Oh, you won't believe what's happening!'

'What?'

'The tornado has just picked up a car. And it's tossing it down the street.'

I heard a loud clanging sound in the background. But I still didn't believe her. Belief is a slippery slope. Once you give someone the benefit of the doubt on one matter, you soon end up believing everything they say.

Brett was at the door of my office.

'I have to go,' I said. I disconnected the phone.

'Do we have alternative plans for our clients?' Brett asked. 'All of them … and I mean each and every one of them want to get off MyFace.'

'We do,' I said.

'Good. Email me the plans in separate emails so that I can forward them on to our clients. Print out the plans. And see me in my office. We have calls to make.'

Every client we called picked up the phone with that prompt liveliness that is often the first symptom of panic. We assured them that we had already designed alternative plans for their brands. We recommended that they pause their advertising efforts on MyFace with immediate effect.

'You saw the headlines,' I said. 'The account of the MyFace CEO was hacked. Who knows if this has anything to do with the killer? But believe me, you do not want your brand to be featured in a screenshot that illustrates the moment when everything went wrong.'

I followed this statement of warning with a more reassuring one.

'But we believe that the alternatives we have laid out will help you achieve your 4Q marketing objectives.'

The last phone call ended at noon. There was a click. The world fell back into place. CJ&R would meet its fourth-quarter revenue goals.

'What were we doing without you? Brett said.

'Making even more money?'

He laughed. He scratched at the stubble on his chin.

My body gave me a programmed reminder to eat the L28 peanut noodles from L'Annam. I ignored it. I had to undertake a task of paramount importance. I caught the Q32 bus from Madison Avenue to the New York Public Library.

On the bus, an old lady was talking to a younger girl sitting next to her.

'Excuse me,' she said in a low and halting voice. 'Are you going to be deleting your MyFace account?'

'For sure,' the girl said.

'You think I should delete it?'

'I do,' said the girl.

The lions at the entrance to the New York Public Library guarded the entrance to the building. They might have been made of stone, but their tails twitched visibly in response to the humidity. It was the face of the security guard that was impassive. Not a muscle on his face moved. It was almost as if he had never been moved by a profound thought. I had to remind myself that there were books on the other side.

A teenage girl in the checkout line fumbled with her purse. A Muslim woman adjusted her head scarf. A man dug his nose. People were doing the most ordinary things at this moment in time, when the entire world was going to change in the most profound way.

I tapped on the keyboard of the public library computer. The screen flickered on. I massaged my hands. My fingers alone were going to have a greater impact on the world of advertising than the entire body of David Ogilvy ever had. My actions would get the attention of the entire world. Journalists at CNN, *The New York Times*, the BBC, Al Jazeera, the *Daily News*, and the millions of blogs that sucked content from the teats of these portals, would do nothing else but talk about me.

I clicked on the icon for Internet Explorer. A window popped up. It asked me for a library card number. For the first time in my time in America, I experienced a negative thought towards a public institution. The New York Public Library existed so that it could serve the public good. How dare they be mistrustful towards the very public whose taxes kept them in business?

A loud drilling sound started up in the library. I turned to observe the construction worker who was so heedless of library hours. However, the sound wasn't that of a drill. It was a man. He was snoring.

He was wearing a New York Mets T-shirt. I had read enough of the *Daily News* to know that their fans were not a happy lot. The depression at the performance of his home team had spilled over to other areas of his life. His teeth were brown. Only a portion of his shirt was tucked into his trousers. His library card was on the table right next to a heavy bunch of keys. I took the card. I left the keys on the table. I am not a thief.

He continued to snore. Seven people around him altered their posture in unison. They leaned towards him and raised their eyebrows in perfect alignment. We could have been in a yoga class. Raised Eyebrows could have been a yoga pose.

A young woman complained to a security guard. The guard pushed the man on the shoulder. He stopped snoring. He opened his eyes and saw an entire row of people staring at him. He rubbed his eyes and apologized. But as soon as the harsh white light from the ceiling hit his eyes, he closed them again. He began to snore.

I complained to the guard. For the first time in my life, I used the word 'intolerable'. The guard woke up the man again. He said he would have to leave the library. The man nodded groggily. He had to be helped on to his feet by the guard. The man picked up his keys from the table before he left the library. I held on to his card.

I watched him as he was escorted into the street. A siren blared on 5th Avenue. Somebody shouted. A cab honked. I felt bad for the man. He would find it difficult to sleep out there.

I logged in to the NYPL computer. I did not want to use my laptop today. It would not do to be even remotely linked to what was about to unfold.

I logged into Roger Diamond's MyFace account. I posted a message on his wall. I copied the message and pasted it on the walls of the Coke and Skittles fan pages. These brands had been widely praised in the industry for having the courage to allow people to post comments in real-time without prior moderation. I too thought that their open and transparent attitude to social marketing was worthy of praise.

I wrote the following words on all of these pages:

This is the MyFace killer. I live among you. I do not know each of you personally. But I know every privacy loophole on MyFace as well as you know your parents or your children. Rest assured, I will get to know you. And when I do, you will die.

Please do not think that you are impervious to the fate of the other MyFace victims. They were not people that I disliked. They were not even people I knew. I just happened to find them on MyFace.

Share this message with your friends and family. And delete your account. Now.

I paused.

This was a message that would live on forever in the history books. It was important that I say something memorable like Neil Armstrong had when he set foot on the moon.

If you want to stay in the real world, stay out of MyFace.

It wasn't brilliant. But I did not have a glass of Famous Grouse by my side to goad my imagination. It would have to do.

I posted the message. I had no doubt that it would spread. In fact, it would spread faster than any virus ever had in the computer age.

There were primarily two kinds of threats that had afflicted us in the PC era, worms and viruses. Worms propagated themselves through networks. Viruses replicated and destroyed the files they touched.

ILOVEYOU was believed to have been the first threat that was both a worm and a virus. In 2000, ILOVEYOU had affected corporations like AT&T and Ford, media outlets like *The Washington Post* and ABC News, financial institutions like the International Monetary Fund and the Belgian banking authority, the department of defence and several other organizations that until then had seemed blessed by a special kind of invincibility. Within two days, the virus had caused over one billion dollars in damage.

With the growth of social networks, a new kind of threat had emerged. Like ILOVEYOU, this new threat was also a combination of a virus and a worm. However, it was more intelligent, more malicious and far more adaptable than anything that could be programmed by the mere combination of bits and bytes.

It was called a human.

Just last month, someone had posted a malicious video about the Prophet on the Internet. The human threat had been activated. It had gone on to kill over 100 people in twenty countries.

The Pakistan intelligence agency, the ISI, had recently posted a video about Indian Muslims being killed by Christians and Hindus in the north-east region of the country. In the rioting that had followed, over four hundred people had died. A further four hundred thousand had been displaced from their homes.

And now, the human threat would soon be activated on MyFace.

I logged out of the screen. I wiped the keyboard with my sleeve.

I walked out of the library. I got on to the bus on 5th Avenue and took it to the Union Square area. On 17th Street, I stared at a mannequin of a naked woman wearing the hat of a witch. I entered the store. I had seen great reviews for 'Abracadabra' on Google. One reviewer had written, 'They have everything!' I wandered the aisles for more than ten minutes, and saw that the review wasn't an exaggeration. The store was a maze of unexpected sights. Eventually, I found tufts of fake hair and a fake beard nestled between what appeared to be a cape and a thong. I was a brown-skinned man purchasing a fake beard. However, the store clerk was open-minded enough to complete the purchase without any public comment.

Jeff Garner came into my office minutes after I had sat down and rebooted my computer.

'I need you to come in the restroom,' he said.

'I don't do cocaine in the workplace,' I said.

'No, it's something else.'

He closed the restroom door.

'That detective from the NYPD was here earlier today,' he said. 'He met with some of the employees to find out whether we had ever called on that mobile CEO who was pushed under the garbage truck.'

'Had you?'

'Yes,' I had. 'They get a lot of press. His company is featured in the ad trades all the time.'

'What did the detective say?'

'He asked me if I knew the CEO.'

'And?'

'And I told him the truth. I told him that I had called on the company. But that I had actually never met the man.'

Footsteps approached us from the hallway on the other side of the door. I opened the tap and pretended to wash my hands.

'He also asked me what I was doing last evening.'

'And what did you say?'

'I told him that I was hanging out with you at Desmond's till late.'

'And what did he say?'

'He asked me till what time we were out. I said that I didn't know. However, I told him that my wife had admonished me for getting home at two last night.'

'Do you know what happened to the CEO?'

'He's still in a coma. It doesn't look like he is going to make it.'

The door to one of the bathroom stalls opened. Brett Cohen walked out.

'At the strip club, eh, boys?'

Another water tap gushed.

'One o' clock, is it? I'll remember that story too.'

I went back to my desk. I wished I had a bottle of Famous Grouse for company. It is far easier to survive a trying time when you are drinking. Each moment is slippery and slides effortlessly into the next one. However, the exact opposite is true when your mind is fixated on a particular worry.

When the mind is beset with worry, the passing of every second tests your faith in a way that the gods in the Bible could only hope to achieve. I felt that I aged significantly by the time the clock struck five.

My thoughts kept returning to Michelle. All I could think of was how she had betrayed me.

What had she seen the prior evening? Had she seen me take out the knife from the sheath? Had she seen me put the 'I found you on MyFace' sticker on the fat man's forehead? Had she seen me try to stab the fat man? Had she seen him being hit by the garbage truck?

I decided to head to Michelle's apartment in Flushing. I took out the battery from my cell phone. It was going to be one of those evenings.

Normally, I would have walked to Grand Central to catch the 7 train. However, today, speed had to be prioritized over the need to make an aesthetic commute. I needed time to flow and flow quickly. I needed it to go quicker than the B train does between 34th Street and West 4th Street. I needed it to bring me to the moment when I could begin to get answers to all that Michelle had heard and seen – and when I could kill her.

As I walked down the connecting passageway to the 7 train, a woman sang in a high-pitched voice. She was accompanied by a man playing a harp. I wondered if this were an omen of some kind. I wondered if it was not Michelle, but me, who was about to die. I wondered if people who were going to depart from this world in the near future heard a harp in the hours leading up to their death, be it in their dreams, at a subway station or during an elevator ride.

I got out at the Main Street station. I was surrounded by what seemed to be all of the one billion people of China. A lady on the pavement handed me a page written entirely in Mandarin. She was protesting for or against some issue. Something that might have been a frog or a chicken dived from the hot air into a pan of hot oil. Even the cough of the old man who waited for his food was laced with a heavy accent. Not one person on the street was involved in selling knockoff sunglasses, a laughing Buddha or an image of a happy cat.

In addition to knowing Spanish, liking jazz music and living through unhappy childhoods, Michelle and I had one more thing in common. She lived in the one Chinatown in America that made no effort to be comprehensible. Just as I lived in India's betel-juice-stained outpost in the United States.

Michelle's apartment was located two blocks west of the commotion on Main Street. From the doorstep of her building, I could see the glass façade of the Sheraton hotel and the steeple of an old church. People had sex with each other in the first building. They went to ask forgiveness from god in the other.

An old woman held the door open for me at Michelle's building. She smiled at me without really looking at me. I hoped she was blind. I didn't want any eyewitnesses speaking to the detective tomorrow.

I stood outside Michelle's apartment. The uplifting smell of five-spice powder wafted from underneath her door. Steam hissed. A spoon fell to the floor.

I could hear her voice. She was talking to someone on the telephone.

'I'll be sure to tell you,' she said.

My doubts evaporated in the stifling heat of the stairwell. Michelle had betrayed me. I touched my sacred thread and felt its reassuring weight. I knocked on the door.

Michelle's apartment was hot with steam. Her tank top clung to her chest. Sesame seeds sizzled in the oil. It was all very appealing. For a few seconds, I forgot that I wanted to kill her.

She had been a busy girl. She had been teaching both maths and Mandarin at the school. She had taken on the additional responsibility of being a police informer. I didn't know where she got the time to slice those chillies, cut those potatoes into cubes, and shred three cutting boards worth of chicken, beets and zucchinis, all the while finding time to partition her hair with a simple hairclip and look incredibly appetizing.

She released herself from the hug.

'I am so happy to see you,' she said. 'I wasn't expecting I would see you today. But I guess, all along I was hoping that I would.'

'Really?'

'Yes, really,' she said. 'I guess that's why I was cutting the beets and the zucchinis.'

If she had been as cold towards me as she had been to the chicken on the cutting board, it would have been easier for me to maintain my façade of calmness. But she was warm, like wine and like laughter.

I found her hypocrisy upsetting.

'I purchased this CD for you,' Michelle said.

She pressed the play button. Stan Getz began to play '*The Girl from Ipanema*'. As the guitar began strumming in a gentle four-by-four rhythm, my anger no longer throbbed. It merely pulsed.

I resolved not be petty. Michelle had one evening left in this world. I decided to make it the happiest evening of her life.

I put my arm around her waist. We walked to the balcony. A black bird with an orange breast hopped down the branch of a tree. Main Street, with all of its commotion, was two only blocks away. But we could hear the bird. It sang a Beatles song. I kissed Michelle.

We held each other without talking. She placed her head on my chest.

'I can hear your heart beating,' she said.

Stan Getz made his way sonorously through '*I Only Have Eyes for You*'. A clear trumpet sound kicked off '*Too Marvellous for*

Words'. The piano notes fell like pattering raindrops, as he played *'There's a Small Hotel'*.

The pressure cooker went off in the kitchen. Michelle went to turn it off with a single-minded attention. The sun had dipped in the sky. I could now see into the window of her neighbour. He was a Bangladeshi with a fat and argumentative wife. He turned on his computer. He looked intent. He was a man going to begin programming. Or watch some porn. Either way, I didn't want to see him. Just as I didn't want him to see me. I pulled down the blinds.

Michelle giggled.

She poked me in the stomach with her fingers.

'After dinner,' she said.

She stood up on her toes and kissed me on the cheek. I could not believe this was the same woman who was actively working with the police to get me arrested.

She wasn't alone. Deceit was omnipresent. It was even more pervasive than sunlight. Salespeople beamed in commercials and acted surly when you visited them in the store. Detectives acted compassionate when all they really wanted to do was see you burn in an electric chair. Parents smiled at their children in public.

Michelle threw the beets into the steamer. She looked intently at the pot. Her fingers were on her lips. I took the knife from the cutting board with the chicken. It had already been used on the chicken. Now, it would be put to use on flesh again.

I held the knife in my right hand. I walked to Michelle and pulled her closer to me. I looked into her eyes. I wanted her to look at me as she died. I raised the knife.

She was crying.

'I have a confession to make,' she said.

I put the knife down.

'But I am scared that you might break up with me after I tell you…'

'Might' was an understatement. I would break up with her. In fact, the entire world would break up with her.

'I didn't want to tell you this...but I followed you to Brooklyn last evening,' she said.

'Why?'

'Because I was suspicious.'

She sat down on the chair. I let her cry until she was ready to speak again.

'I called you on so many evenings. And you never picked up the phone. And so I thought...'

'Thought that I was...'

'I'm not crazy,' she said. 'But I can't help myself...especially... specially after what happened with that man in Taiwan...'

'I still don't want to hear about it,' I said.

'But you have to,' she said. 'He said he would marry me. I became pregnant. And then he left me. It was a huge scandal...'

My feelings towards her had undergone a profound reversal. I didn't want to kill or even fight with her. If there was to be discord in Flushing this evening, I would leave it to the Bangladeshi and his wife.

'I guess I can't fault you for being suspicious,' I said.

'It was foolish of me,' she said.

'We all do foolish things,' I said. 'I keep forgetting my cell phone. So what did you see on your scouting mission?'

'I saw you enter a bar. I observed you from a table by the stairwell. I saw that you were talking to a fat man...'

'And?'

'Was he a friend?'

'A colleague,' I said.

'I just saw you talking to him. He seemed pretty drunk.'

'And...'

'And then I left the bar when you did. You guys walked down underneath the bridge. It was getting late. So I decided to leave...'

I handed her a tissue.

'You must think I am crazy.'

'I won't lie. You are messed up. But we are all messed up. What I think is crazy is everyone trying to pretend that they don't have any quirks and fears.'

'You're not messed up,' she said.

'If you insist,' I said. 'Let me go down and buy a bottle of red wine. We can enjoy it with the dinner.'

'OK,' she said. She had stopped crying.

As I was closing the door, she called out my name.

'Arjun,' she said. 'If you see the superintendent, can you tell him that the hot water's all right in the sink? I was on the phone with him just as you entered. I said I would tell him if there was a problem.'

'I can do that,' I said.

The End

Now that I wasn't going to kill Michelle, I put my battery back in my mobile phone. It came alive with a ferocious surge of power. I had seventeen missed calls. They were all from Brett Cohen.

'Where have you been?' he asked.

'At my girlfriend's.'

'Have you been following what's happened?'

'No,' I said.

'It's the 9/11 of the Internet.'

'What happened…?'

'Tell me one thing,' he said. 'Are all the MyFace campaigns off?'

'Yes,' I said. 'I paused all of them.'

'Good man,' he said.

I covered the gap between the wine store and Michelle's apartment in leaps and bounds. I powered on her computer and went to the *New York Times* website.

With One Post, Killer Brings World's Largest Social Network to Its Knees.

So what if I hadn't gotten the world's most prestigious newspaper to pun. I had staggered them sufficiently enough into using a cliché.

The *Daily News* was the best newspaper in the world. My faith in that old bastion of quality news reporting was rock steady. However, I had to admit that I derived a deeper sense of satisfaction from reading about my accomplishments in the *New York Times*. Maybe it was the Gothic font that imbued my actions with an aura of timelessness. Maybe it was the photographs of all those opinion columnists who do such a terrific job of looking self-important. Or maybe it was just the sheer thrill of competition, of watching your article beat 'In Fight Against Obesity, Drink Sizes Matter' on the Most Emailed Articles list.

Over 250 million people had deleted their MyFace profiles in the last twenty-four hours. *The New York Times* estimated that by noon, more people would leave MyFace than the entire population of America. People had begun to jump off MyFace in Western Europe too. When Asia woke up, the sun would set on the MyFace Empire. In a surprising development, a twenty-three-year-old waitress had been found murdered at the Bar Rouge in Shanghai. A 'I found you on MyFace sticker' had been stuck to her forehead.

The CEO of MyFace appealed to people not to take drastic action. He said that MyFace took the privacy of their customers very seriously and that they were working around the clock to put even more security measures in place.

He reminded me of a boy I had read about in my childhood. A boy who had repeatedly cried wolf. And after a while, no one had believed him.

Michelle listened with wonder as I told her about MyFace.

'I didn't know it was quite that big and quite that important,' she said. 'But wait, how are these people deleting their MyFace accounts? I thought MyFace never removed your information from their servers?'

'It doesn't matter,' I said. 'Someone just went ahead and deleted MyFace.'

'Check it out,' she said. She pointed to an article in the Related News section. The article said that Scott Harpin, the CEO of the mobile startup who was hit by a garbage truck last night, was expected to come out of his coma. He was no longer in a critical condition.

'That's a relief,' Michelle said.

I would have chosen words that were quite different. But I was relieved that Scott's photo hadn't been posted on the website. Michelle had a great memory for faces.

'Oh look,' Michelle said. 'It would be fun to go there.'

She visited an article on travelling to Jeonju, a South Korean city that the *New York Times* said was full of food, history and bargains. The article said that the most useful words to use in Jeonju were Hyundai-ok odi innayo, which meant, Where is Hyundai-ok (Hyundai-ok was a small restaurant famed for its bean-sprout soup), and kamsahamnida, which meant thank you.

It was the typical *New York Times* article, a rumination meant primarily for the idle rich, of no real consequence to the daily lives of its middle-class readers.

'We should go there,' Michelle said again. 'Maybe during the Christmas break?'

I nodded my acquiescence. But I couldn't stop thinking about Scott Harpin. I saw I would have to leave America. I would have to say goodbye to its freeways, to the 24/7 hot and cold water, and to all those apartments that came with wall-to-wall carpeting.

It was a tough choice. In India, I would cease to be Tom Friedman's immigrant of unlimited potential. In India, I would be nothing more than a person who belonged to a low caste. I may not have the right to drink water from the same well as my Brahmin fellow citizens, leave alone have the god-given right to gnaw at the universal pie of opportunity. At best, I would be condemned to nibble at its remnants. In India, I would be trash.

With all prospects of upward mobility eliminated, I would walk along the streets with an apathy that would be mistaken by a passing American tourist for laziness. The only time you would see me alert and alive would be during the moments when I saw a cobra, iron or a cricket bat. Those would be the moments when I would realize that I was in the country where Mrs Clarkson cast her shadows from the white slopes of the Himalayas to the blue-green waters of the Indian Ocean. Going back to India would be the most difficult choice I would ever have to make.

But it was a choice that I would make. One always chose life over liberty. The Bible could promise you harps and singing angels. The Koran could promise you seventy-two virgins. But we will always opt for life, even if it means having to deal with a loud neighbour, a filthy neighbourhood or a cruel adoptive mother.

There were people like Patrick Henry who went around saying things like, 'Give me liberty or give me death.' But these were people who were at the end of their tether. Mr Henry had tried to become a storekeeper. He failed. He then tried to become a farmer. The crops had not cooperated. He then got married and had six children by the age of thirty-five. He found he could not support them. It was only at this stage of his life that he made the issue of liberty and death a binary choice.

I walked to the balcony and closed the door behind me. I called my travel agent in the garment district. He was an old Sikh gentleman. I trusted him. He was an honest man who could lie enough to make a four per cent margin, but never lie enough to recommend flying Air India.

'Today?' he said. 'Come over and let me see what I can do.'

His lack of curiosity at my need to travel at such short notice was most un-Indian and most commendable. This indifference must be what America inculcates in you after twenty years.

'Something's come up at work,' I told Michelle.

'Is it something to do with all this MyFace stuff?'

'Yes,' I said.

I kissed her goodbye.

'Is everything OK?' she asked. I had lingered on in my kiss for a few seconds longer than the norm.

'Yes,' I said. And even as the 7 train thudded its way into Manhattan, I was carried along by a cushion that was as soft as Michelle's kiss. I would never experience that exquisite softness again.

As I walked west towards the garment district, I looked at every sight that presented itself to me with a hungry yet attentive mind. I wanted to capture everything that presented itself. Was this the last time I would see a blue-and-white MTA bus cruise down 1st Avenue? Would I ever see those inflatable NFL dolls bobbing in the breeze outside the sports bars again? I even gazed wistfully at the trash cans that the city had placed at every intersection.

I smiled at the Nigerian men selling fake sunglasses on Broadway. Till just yesterday, I would have looked away with disdain from these people who did nothing but indulge in naked commercialism. But now, I gazed upon them with fondness. I purchased a twenty-dollar pair of Rayban sunglasses. I put the glasses on and looked at the city through part-green, part-black lenses.

The receptionist at the travel agency was watching Tom and Jerry cartoons on her computer monitor. She was laughing openly at the escapades of the impulsive cat and the clever mouse. She wasn't even bothering to hide the fact that she wasn't working. I admired her open and daring attitude. It was most American. On the other hand, I would be returning to a country, where people always had to have one window of Microsoft Excel open and on the ready.

The Sardarji greeted me with a glass of tea. I knew right away that the ticket was going to be expensive.

'Four thousand five hundred dollars,' he said.

'Isn't there anything cheaper?' I asked. It was the Indian thing to do.

He nodded his head sadly.

'Sorry, sir,' he said. 'If you want to go tomorrow…'

'It's not for me,' I said. 'It's for a friend, Harpreet Singh.'

'A Sikh…'

'In North Dakota,' I said.

'There are Sikhs in North Dakota?'

'Here is his information,' I said. I did not have the patience to have the same conversation twice in the same day.

I paid him in cash.

'Harpreet is a rich man,' I said.

He smiled. He might have been thinking of the prosperity of his fellow kin. I suspected that he was also thinking about the tax-free income he had just made.

When I left the travel agency, the sun had dipped over the Hudson. The buildings along the length of the street lit up with a fiery orange. I knew at once that this was the image of New York that I would carry back to India. I felt disappointed that it had to be such a cliché.

There were still five-and-a-half hours before my flight. I needed to buy a duffel bag and some clothing. The security personnel at the airport tend to look askance at people who travel on international flights without any baggage. I went back to the man who had sold me the Raybans.

'They don't work so well in the evening,' he said defensively.

'I don't want to return them,' I said. 'I love these glasses. I need lots of other stuff. To begin with, a duffel bag…'

'Hold on, sir.' He took out his notebook. 'What brand sir?'

'What brand would you recommend?'

He pretended to think.

'Adidas,' he said.

'Adidas it is,' I said. 'I also need five T-shirts.'

'Adidas also, sir?' he asked.

'That's good,' I said. 'That way my T-shirts and bag will match. Some underpants also.'

'Adidas also, sir?'

'They make underpants?'

'Everyone makes underpants, sir,' he said.

'Ah,' I said. 'Then I'll have some that are made by Prada.'

His eyes shone brightly like saucers full of morning tea. He was going to have a nice weekend.

'Anything else, sir?'

'Yes. A new ID. And a green card.'

'Really?'

'No,' I said. 'I was just kidding.'

The breeze blew into my face. A woman licked on an ice-cream softee. A siren blared in the distance. It appeared just like a normal New York summer day.

However, I knew there was nothing normal about it.

If this were a normal day, I would be in my apartment. I would be unscrewing the top of my bottle of Famous Grouse. The club soda would fizz. Billie Holliday would start a song. There would be the tinkling of piano notes, each one brightening up my room a little more upon its arrival. This sharp nostalgia, viewed in high definition, for things that could have been is what one must experience during death. I now understood why deportation was such a powerful punishment.

I let two cabs pass. I flagged down a taxi with a black driver. The last thing I wanted to do was speak in Hindi during the last few minutes I had left in this country. I sat back in my seat. The driver put on a CD by Fela Kuti. That's what I would have to become if I wanted to return to America. I would have to become an 'International Thief Thief'.

The tall buildings of Manhattan passed us by. Then, we went through what must have been a magic tunnel. For, on the other side, the buildings became squat, wide and without ambition. I looked over my shoulder to catch a last glimpse of the Manhattan skyline. But it had disappeared.

However, a number of billboards reminded us that we were not too far from an island of varied delights. Sprint said, 'Yes you can.' Calvin Klein said, 'Yes you should.' And the Curves Gentlemen's bar said, 'Yes you must.'

The CEO hadn't yet identified me. There were no policemen outside my building. There wasn't even a flower van. I wasn't surprised to see the shortage of policemen near the house. They had nothing on me. I was at the Volstead when Kevin Santiago died. I was in my apartment, under the NYPD's surveillance, when Alice and Simon were murdered. And I was hanging out with Jeff at Desmond's Tavern when the CEO was hit by a garbage truck. I had alibis pouring out of my ass. Of course, the CEO would soon wake up from his temporary slumber. And then, there would be more policemen on the street than there were red betel stains on the walls of Jackson Heights.

My apartment was empty. There were no uniformed men that jumped at me from dark corners. They were presumably at the hospital, notebooks in hand, waiting for the fat CEO to awaken and blurt out my description. I took out my fake Indian passport from the top shelf of my cupboard in the bedroom. The four lions that formed the pillars of the Ashoka Chakra looked at me with their stony faces from the blue cover of the passport. I was disappointed that not even one of them had taken the effort to evolve into an American bald-headed eagle.

The paint on the walls of the living room shone a bright yellow. I recalled the lamp of optimism the wall had lit inside me when I had first cast my gaze upon it. To its credit, the paint hadn't faded. It had looked on at the hurt, the anger, the little tragedies that had been played out in this apartment every evening, and had continued to shine on in a bright shade of yellow, as though confident that one day, it would descend into newer, brighter hands.

And now it would.

I moved my hands over the light-green cloth that covered the couch and the dark-brown wood of the table. Until just a few hours ago, I had thought of them as my couch and my table. But now, I realized that I had never owned them. Soon, they would belong to someone else. We go through our lives zealously guarding the things we have, even though we own them no more than we do the song of a bird.

I opened up the Ming chess set. I took out Emily's scarf. More than Coca-Cola, the Statue of Liberty, or my first sighting of the Grand Canyon, her scarf would always remind me of the immense possibilities for happiness that had once existed in America.

I walked the long hallway to my bathroom. I looked at myself in the mirror. I saw a man who had the good fortune to have lived in a casteless country. A man who looked serene in a Banana Republic relaxed-fit shirt. A man who had come to appreciate the virtues of an elaborately prepared pesto sauce. What would such a man do in a country like India?

I twisted the cap on the bottle of gum spirit. It came apart with a sticky sound. I applied a dab of the sticky substance to my chin and stuck a small clump of hair. The Buddha had said that the soul was an eternal and unchanging entity. However, as I gazed upon the hair on my face, I felt unclean, as though I had caused a freckle, a pimple or even a wart to grow upon my soul. However, with every application of the spirit, my uneasiness gave way to a sense of wonder. I marvelled at how different I looked with every passing minute. After I had twirled the turban around my head, I was unrecognizable.

However, I didn't feel energized as the customers of Abracadabra did when they wore their disguises, assumed a new identity and went to a Halloween party. These people were happy because they wanted to be somebody else. On the other hand, I felt burdened because I was being forced to be somebody else.

I left the apartment with the turban resting heavily on my head. I stopped on the third floor. I rang the doorbell. The teenager opened the door.

'Who are you?' he said.

'Te he advierto muchas veces en el pasado,' I said. 'I have really done my best to warn you in the past.'

He seemed surprised. I was about to stab him in the femoral artery. But just then a baby cried from the bedroom. I punched him with my knuckles on his nose. He fell to the ground. I went into the living room. I stabbed at the Stop button on the Sony audio system. Plastic cracked just like the bone had on his nose a moment ago. Eventually, the system disintegrated to a degree sufficient enough to be useless for the purpose of making noise. I closed my eyes and breathed in the silence.

'You play music once more,' I said. 'Or you call the police. The next time it won't be the music system.'

People who are inconsiderate of other people are normally not intelligent enough to be perceptive to subtleties. So I completed my sentence to make myself clear.

'The next time, it will be you.'

There was a cab on the corner of 73rd Street. I asked him if he wanted to go to the airport. He did.

He started the car. As I looked out of the window, I felt myself being overcome by a sense of nostalgia. It was almost as if I were looking at the world through an Instagram camera filter. I gazed at the doors of Rajbhog wistfully, even though I was going back to a country where almost every restaurant served Indian food.

I even felt nostalgic as my body was felt up during a random security check. After today, I wouldn't have to go through this most ungentlemanly public groping and fondling any more. In fact, I was going back to a land where I would not be treated with suspicion at the airports. I would have to get used to other people, namely the Muslims with their skull caps and distinct last names, having to undergo the ignominy of public suspicion.

I walked through the metal detector. The machine beeped. Everybody in the airport looked at my turban. The security officer, who was an Indian woman, asked me if I had any metallic objects on my body.

'I don't think so,' I said.

She asked me to walk through the machine again.

The machine beeped. I looked apologetically at the security officer. She refused to look me in the eye. Instead, she gazed at my turban.

'We're going to have to ask you to remove your turban, sir,' she said.

'I can't,' I said.

I really couldn't.

The turban was my Dastar. It was a symbol that represented spirituality and holiness in the larger universe. It stood for honour and self-respect within my being. If my turban was removed from my head, how on earth would I be able to retain command over my Agya Chakra, the lotus-framed guiding seat of my intuition? No self-respecting Sikh would ever consent to having his turban removed in public.

In addition, if my turban was removed, the security officer would take one look at my short hair and discern that I wasn't Sikh. She would call the police. I would be sent away to prison. Once there, I would be sent to die in the electric chair. Or even worse, I would live on as a meme that people OMGed and LOLed at on MyFace.

'I would really prefer you don't take off my turban,' I said.

'Sir, I understand,' she said. 'But we have no choice.'

'But…'

'Now, sir,' she said. 'We don't have all day.'

Two security officers materialized by her side. One of them reached for my turban. He grasped it by the sides, so that it shifted on the base.

'Hold on,' I said. 'It's not like I have a …'

I didn't have a suicide belt around my waist. However, I did have a double loop Banana Republic leather belt with a metal buckle.

'Wait!' I said.

I took off my belt. My tormentors gazed on as I stepped through the metal detector once again. This time around, the silence was complete. The Indian lady asked me to step through the full body scanner. I complied. The security guard stationed outside the scanner seemed reluctant to let me proceed to the boarding gate. But the ghost of James Madison prodded him repeatedly. He served the man a reminder about the First Amendment. The security guard had little choice in the matter but to let me pass.

I walked to the boarding area. Every man and woman waiting plane looked anxious and twitchy, as though they had all simultaneously decided to quit smoking at that very instant.

A child put a hat over her head. She pulled on it with both fingers. The mother looked at her smartphone wistfully. Only yesterday, she would have been able to post a picture of her baby on MyFace. Within a few minutes, she would be able to view the comments that followed with a warm pleasure. Now, she was compelled to continue keep paying attention to her baby.

A mother was talking to an Indian girl wearing a salwar kameez. She was speaking about the importance of getting married. After all, the girl was already twenty-five. She should have had a child by now. The girl adjusted the glasses on her face. She twisted her hair into pensive knots. She looked at her smartphone perched on the armrest of her chair. Only yesterday, it would have offered her mind a rabbit hole to dive into. Today, it looked back at her with a dark and unsympathetic countenance. She had to continue to listen to her mother.

Save for the children who ran around in random, merry patterns, every person in the boarding area wore a slightly harassed look on their faces. They looked wistful, as though they wanted to be anywhere else but here. They wished they could be in the world of MyFace.

Unspoken thought by unspoken thought, unexpressed like by unexpressed like, the tension had built up to an unsustainable degree. I felt as though we were all lentil beans stewing in a pressure cooker. It was essential that this pressure be relieved now. If it were carried over to the airplane, the cockpit would explode into thousands of pieces at thirty-three thousand feet over the ground.

A worried-looking security official seemed to sense the tension. He looked at the TV as though it might offer him a solution. I thought back to what Simon had said. He had said that the only places where one could watch CNN were at airports and on treadmills. I glanced up at the TV. And sure enough there was CNN.

My picture was on the television screen.

The news anchor's eyes flashed so brightly that they could have lit up the Empire State Building. She seemed scandalized, excited and short of breath. I thought if she didn't take care of herself, she might have an orgasm.

The anchor said that Scott Harpin, the CEO of MobiFace, a mobile advertising startup based in Brooklyn, had survived an attack by the MyFace killer. He had come out of his coma. And he had identified the killer. The NYPD was now confirming that Arjun Clarkson, vice president of media at a New York ad agency, was the MyFace killer.

The news programme went to a commercial break. A young boy ran up to me.

'Are you the MyFace killer?' the child asked.

'David!' the mother said. She raised her hand to pull at the boy.

'Don't,' I said. 'He is only a child. The MyFace killer is in New York City. He doesn't have a turban. I have a turban. Do you see the difference?'

He nodded.

'Now, tell me this. Who is going to enjoy India?'

'I am.'

'High five.'

The child raised his hand. He gave me a high five.

'Go play with your mother,' I said.

'Thank you,' the mother said. The boy put his hands in her open palms. They walked back to their seats.

I hoped she would not beat him. Or make him feel ashamed.

The greatest impressions are made upon us in the early years of our life, when we are at our most defenceless. In our youth and our adult life, we can wear our Banana Republic pin-striped outfits. We can continue to believe that we are in control of our actions for the remainder of our years.

But it is already too late.

I had played with the household laundry, which happened to include Mr Clarkson's shirt. The shirt had an image of a crocodile stitched on it. I used to love that shirt. I used to love that crocodile. The laundry also happened to include Mrs Clarkson's undergarment. Mrs Clarkson had thought that I was playing with her black bra. She thought that I was a pervert. She had yelled at me and locked me in the shed with the cobra.

One night, I had heard a noise in the dark. I had gone to Mr Clarkson's room. I had got into his bed. But he had gone for a party. Mrs Clarkson had woken up. She had slapped me.

The shame has never gone away. Even today, I can feel it pulsing within my body at all times. When I close my eyes, I can even hear it, just as clearly as though someone had plucked at a bass string and let it resonate in an empty concert hall.

'When you love this creation you see it as beautiful,' Mr Clarkson liked to quote Sri Sri Ravi Shankar. 'Love is everything.'

Neil Diamond was the first singer I had listened to. He had sung about love. 'Eternal God, Creator of All' was the first prayer I had ever recited aloud. It too was an ode to the healing powers of love.

However, love had never helped reduce the shame I carried around in my body. Michelle had tried to love me. But her every touch, every caress, every kiss only reminded me of my shame, and made it even stronger.

Perhaps, if Emily had agreed to love me, matters would have been different. Like all of us, I have been born once. In an experience that only immigrants are lucky enough to have, I had also been born for the second time.

In a new country, I had experienced the childlike emotions of incomprehension and anxiety. I had felt the eagerness to grow up fast and come of age. And in my second childhood, Emily had healed me. She had told me that it was all right to be me. She had believed there was nothing to be ashamed of.

But she too had rejected me. She had left me to cope with this world of MyFace all by myself, a world where everyone was perfect, all the time. A world in which a man couldn't tell anyone about his shame, where he couldn't even say that he didn't like dogs.

A Sikh family came into the boarding area. They approached me. I got up from my seat and moved to a place in the boarding area that was the farthest away from them. You've probably read the story of the wolf who dressed in the sheep's clothing. The moral of that story is that if you're disguised as a Sikh, you shouldn't sit next to a Sikh family. You will be found out in seconds.

I heard a swarm of activity by the security area. Five policemen entered the boarding area. The guns, keys, flashlights and other assortments jingled and jangled vividly. I looked into my duffel bag and pretended to search for something.

'Excuse me, sir,' a voice said.

A policeman was standing in front of me. He had a sour expression on his face, as though he felt resentful at having to show up on patrol duty at this advanced hour of the night. He wasn't white like Detective Crisafi. He was Korean.

'Going to India, sir?' he asked.

'That's the plan.'

'Can I see your passport?'

I fumbled in the pockets of my trousers. I hoped that he hadn't noticed how my hands had trembled when I handed him my travel documents.

He took a hard look at the photo. He then glared at my bearded face. If he had continued to stare at my countenance with such intense scrutiny for another minute, the beard on my face would unravel over a film of sweat. But he shifted his gaze to the passport. He flipped through the pages.

'So you've been to Dubai?

'I have relatives in Sharjah,' I said.

'Ah yes,' he said. 'There are so many Indians in the UAE, huh?'

'We all have to make a living,' I said.

'You've been to Korea as well,' he said.

'Yes…'

'Whereabouts did you go?'

I closed my eyes. I began to meditate. I felt a stream of air from my nose hit my upper lip. As he had always done, the Buddha would guide me.

'I went to Seoul,' I said. 'But the place I really liked most was Jeonju.'

'Really,' he said. 'That's where my parents are from.'

God wanted to mess with me today. That wasn't a problem. I was adequately prepared to take on His or Her machinations.

'Hyundai-ok odi innayo,' I said.

He smiled.

'Where is Hyundai-ok?'

'I know just where it is,' I said.

He laughed.

'Amazing bean sprout soup,' he said. 'Did you try the pork…?'

This line of questioning couldn't be allowed to continue.

'I am vegetarian,' I said.

He handed me back my passport.

'Thank you,' he said.

'Kamsahamnida,' I said.

He laughed a little more. He shook my hand. As he walked towards another passenger on the boarding gate, I reflected that what I had always said about the *New York Times* was wrong. It had saved my life today. When I went back to India, I would read all of Tom Friedman's articles again with an open mind. I would give him a second chance.

An Asian lady scanned my boarding pass with a smile. I stepped on to the jetway. I was less than a hundred feet away from freedom. I felt a cocktail of nervousness and anticipation slushing madly within my insides. For the first time in fifteen months I felt the urge to smoke a cigarette. I touched my beard. It was still in place.

A man shouted at an airport attendant in front of me.

'I can't check in my bag,' he said. 'It contains all the medicines that my mother needs.'

'Sir, we have a full flight,' the attendant said. 'And this bag is too large. Can't you please remove your medicines now and give me the bag? You'll get it at the carousel at the Bombay airport.'

'I don't care about the carousel,' he said. 'I don't want to go to the carousel. I don't want to check in the bag. There are too many medicines. I can't remove all of them now.'

'Sir, I am afraid I have to insist.'

'Don't you care if my mother dies during the flight?'

She stared at him with a vacant expression. She clearly didn't care about his mother. That made the two of us.

'Excuse me,' I said.

I walked ahead of them. I have a very low tolerance for conversations that drift into cheap sentimentality. It is why I am always a little sceptical of watching any movie that is not made by Akira Kurosawa.

A passenger shut an overhead bin. I jumped at the clicking noise. It reminded me of a handcuff. I was nervous. I even forgot to be envious of the passengers in business class. After I sat down in my seat, I looked out of the window. An airport truck carrying a pile of suitcases made its way at a leisurely pace towards the airplane. A maintenance engineer walked slowly along the tarmac. The air hostess scrawled a few words in her notebook with a rusty and scratchy nib.

The entire world seemed to be conducting its affairs stickily and slowly as though on top of a particularly viscous surface.

The man with the ailing mother came up to the row in front of me. He stashed his bag in the overhead bin. He had managed to emotionally blackmail the flight attendant into keeping his baggage. I thought that it was very Indian of him.

The passengers began to sit down on their seats. The air hostess announced that they would be passing by for a final check soon. For the first time that evening, I dared to think of freedom, of the plane that would soon soar higher than the Empire State Building and disappear among the clouds in the sky. I thanked the Wright Brothers for their imagination and their fortitude. They were true Americans. They had made my freedom possible.

An Indian lady seated next to me gasped loudly. Two armed policemen had entered the plane. They charged through the business class section. They were broad, tall and very, very angry. They rushed towards my seat.

I got up from my seat. If I was going to get arrested, I was going to get arrested with dignity. I did not want a YouTube video of a police officer pulling me up from my seat and shoving me down the aisle circulating around the Internet. I was an educated man. I deserved to be treated with dignity. I got up from my seat and ironed out the creases on my Banana Republic shirt.

The policeman glared at me.

'Sir,' he said.

'I know,' I said. 'You've caught up…'

'We're going to have to ask you to sit down.'

'But…'

'Sit down, sir,' he shouted. 'Now!'

I did as he asked. In the spirit of going above and beyond, I even fastened my seat belt. He continued to glare at me. He then turned his attention to the seat in front of me.

'You, sir,' he said. 'Please stand up and accompany me out of the plane.'

'But...'

'Sir,' he said, now speaking far more calmly than only a few moments before, 'you cannot threaten an airport attendant. I am going to have to ask you to leave the plane with me now.'

'My mother...,' he began.

I have never seen somebody getting tased before. It is a unique experience, and one that I highly recommend you partake in, should you ever get the chance.

The principal protagonist of a tasing goes through a series of heightened experiences in a very short period of time. It is all very dramatic. At first, the subject lets out a high-pitched scream. He then breaks into the first moves of the Macarena. But he does not go through with the dance. Instead, he writhes on the ground as helpless as an eel in a basket at a Chinatown grocery. He is picked up from the ground in the midst of his thrashing and turning. On his feet, he is far more amenable to the persuasions of others. A heavy drop of drool falls from his chin to the ground. But he is too overwhelmed to care at this public loss of dignity. Finally, the subject disappears from your world. He is followed by his mother and immediate family, the only people in the world who have a vested interest in seeing him alive.

The air hostess apologized for the incident. A young boy clapped. He was soon joined by the other passengers. I smiled in the dark. The plane raced towards the edge of the airport, and pointing its nose upward, took off into the sky.

I looked outside the window. The lights twinkled at me from the city below. Now they appeared to me like the stars in the heavens often had when I had observed them from below. They were far away, almost imaginary and of little consequence to my daily world. The fact that I had worried about the detective, who was now the smallest of shadows under those faraway lights, appeared to me as strange, almost ridiculous.

The Buddha had once said that just as rain was unable to break through the roof of a well-thatched house, passionate and disorderly thoughts are unable to make their way into a well-reflecting mind. My neatly ordered mind now told me what I had to do. I pressed the button to summon the flight attendant. I had a leisurely sip of The Famous Grouse.

The flight map showed the plane flying over an unknown and unnamed chunk of ice in the Arctic Ocean. The terrain below us was antediluvian and medieval, populated by dark creatures with wings and flippers. It was an ancient world made up of floating continents, one that was entirely devoid of detectives.

I drank deeply from the glass of Famous Grouse. I felt relaxed. I decided to watch a Hindi movie. It would most probably be a mockery of every enlightened thought that had awakened in the human consciousness in the post-Buddhist era. However, I felt that watching a Hindi movie on the way to India was the appropriate thing to do. It would provide me with a clue to how much the country had changed in my two years of absence.

The movie was about a wronged man who escapes from prison. He kills a corrupt lawyer, the police commissioner of Bombay and a wealthy industrialist, all the while managing to foil the efforts of the police who are incessantly on his trail. I was sufficiently enthralled.

The air hostess announced that the plane had begun its approach to New Delhi. The Indian sun shone brightly outside the window. I squinted my eyes to see if there was a cavalcade of police cars awaiting my arrival. As we taxied to the gate, I saw three policemen on the tarmac.

However, they weren't waiting for me. Instead, they were chasing a stray dog that had managed to get on to the runway from a neighbouring slum.

I joined the line for 'Indian Citizens' in the immigration area. It moved more slowly than the line for 'Foreigners'. The British had not left India. They had lived on in our minds. And we were still servile to them.

A small man in a tight-fitting grey safari suit asked me to step up to the Immigration counter. The booth he pointed to was manned by a Sikh man. I hesitated. I couldn't speak Punjabi. The officer would see through my disguise in an instant. I hadn't made an eighteen-hour flight to be arrested in India, when I could have so easily avoided the bother and got arrested at the New York airport.

I dropped my passport and landing card on to the white tiled floor.

'Sorry, sorry,' I said. I took my time in retrieving my passport and landing card off the ground.

'What are you doing?' the man in the safari suit complained.

He gestured to the lady behind me to proceed to the counter with the Sikh immigration officer. Once she had passed, I stood up with my passport in my hand. I apologized again. I called him sir. I was probably the first person who had spoken to him respectfully all day. He smiled. He asked that I stand in front of the desk manned by an officer with a Maharashtrian-sounding name.

This man clearly did not know Punjabi.

'Have a good flight, sir?' he asked in English.

'Brilliant,' I said, in English as well.

As the boy had promised, the passport beeped happily.

Outside the airport, I dodged the army of taxi drivers who made for my bag like hundreds of hungry vultures. I flagged down a rickshaw and asked that he take me to Connaught Place.

'I'm not American,' I said in Hindi. 'I'm from here. Switch on the meter.'

He turned on the meter. He did as I asked. But I felt a deep and profound sadness. If only I were American. If only he charged me five times the going rate.

I got off at Nirula's. A security guard in a blue shirt looked suspiciously at my dark skin as I approached the door. But then he took a closer look at my turban. He stared at my Banana Republic shirt that was draped stylishly over my dark skin. He let me pass.

I ordered a plate of mutton chops with hash browns. A girl in the checkout queue bumped into me.

'I'm so sorry,' she said. She looked back into her smartphone. I glanced at the large screen of her Samsung Galaxy phone. She was on MyFace. And she was commenting on a photograph. I recognized my headshot, the one that CNN had flashed in the news programme at the New York airport.

'Ghastly!' she wrote.

I touched my beard. I went to a vacant table. I began to read the *Times of India*. On page three, I saw a full-page ad quoting none other than the Benevolent One, my only faithful companion, the Buddha.

With all I am a friend, a comrade to all
To all creatures kind and merciful.

The MyFace logo was displayed prominently on the bottom right corner of the ad.

I looked up. The girl who had commented on my photo had joined a group seated at the adjacent table. She was talking to her friends.

'What a creep,' she said.

I looked at the city outside through the glass door. A light-brown dog was panting heavily in the hot afternoon sun. Heavy drops of sweat fell from its tongue and sizzled on the ground. The dog flickered in and out of my vision as I glanced at it through the tears in my eyes.

As I stepped out of the establishment, I remembered an old store I had once frequented. It was called Atlas. Atlas was located in the Hauz Khas neighbourhood, two blocks south of the Deer Park, and six blocks north of where Mrs Clarkson now lived. The owner of the store was a Muslim gentleman who took fierce pride in his craftsmanship. His family had been in the same trade for seven generations, since the heyday of the Mughal Empire.

Atlas made the best knives in all of New Delhi.

Acknowledgements

My friend Don, a Wall Street banker who was pessimistic about the long-term prospects of a certain social network we know and love, gave me the idea for this novel. I sat down to write the book – but found it difficult to line up my thoughts in a noisy apartment building. Spotify gave me access to the music of Duke Ellington, Louis Armstrong, Kenny Garrett and other happy jazz souls who shielded me from the noises made by my neighbours. Andria Litto and George Litto believed in the novel even before I did and I want to thank them for their support. The novel would have not made the journey from my Dropbox account to your bookshelf/e-reader without the incredible help offered by Nilanjana Roy. There are moments in life when even the word 'incredible' doesn't do justice to describe someone's efforts – and this is one of them. A series of empirical observations have led me to believe that Somak Ghoshal is, without a single doubt, the most efficient and astute editor in the world. The prior statement is true because I used the word empirical. And also because Somak found gaping holes in the plot through which you could have driven your SUV (or if you are the eco-conscious sort, your neighbour's SUV). I'd like to thank my parents for *actively* supporting me all those years ago when I decided to leave engineering for a career in marketing and communications. My wife Pam, who is much wiser than me, allows me to see new hues, shades and colours in people and places constantly, and makes the world new for me every day. Finally, I'd like to thank our dog, Sadie. She didn't help with correcting my grammar for the novel and refused to chip in with placing the punctuations in their proper places. But she gives us a simple and unquestioning love without pause and we've come to find that's all we really need.